His flesh was cold
as stone . . .

When she brushed her hand against Varney's face, she shivered again. Despite the efforts of the wildings, his flesh was as cold as the stone. "It's your doing I'm here, you know," she murmured. "I'd have been safer riding alone." She smiled, touched his hair, tenderness flooding her. It really wasn't his fault that some murderous bezriggid got an itch for power. "Ah, well."

She thought of the water elementals popping their clear crystal heads from the muddy river, tried to tease out their essence and turn the *feel* to earth rather than water.

For an eternity nothing happened.

Then the wildings fled to the walls and ceiling. A moment later a vast finger of stone thrust up, turned and looked at her from glittering obsidian rounds. She didn't hear words, heard no sound at all, but they were there in her head: **You call us from our sleep, belovéd. What is your desire?**

She gasped, clutched at her head as pain lanced through it, then found herself able to speak in something that wasn't exactly a language, more an intimation of emotion, a flow of image compressed into non-sound gestalts: *My lover is bespelled,* she seemed to say, *I must go seek the spieler, but I dare not leave him unprotected. Will you watch for me, keep him safe and warm?*

JO CLAYTON'S
DAW Science Fiction and Fantasy Novels:

Wildfire

Wild Magic #2

Jo Clayton

DAW BOOKS, INC.
DONALD A. WOLLHEIM, FOUNDER
375 Hudson Street, New York, NY 10014

ELIZABETH R. WOLLHEIM
SHEILA E. GILBERT
PUBLISHERS

DAW Book Collectors No. 882.

First Printing, June 1992
1 2 3 4 5 6 7 8 9

DAW TRADEMARK REGISTERED
U.S. PAT OFF AND FOREIGN COUNTRIES
—MARCA REGISTRADA,
HECHO EN U.S.A.

PRINTED IN THE U.S.A.

Blessings on Kevin Murphy,
a man of lovely, loopy wit
who gave me the idea
for the Wrystrike.

Prologue
Jal Virri in the Myk'tat Tukery

The crystal dome shimmered in the noon sun.

Wild Magic glittered as they eddied in foamy drifts about the weeping, weary girl who stood on a barren islet that was separated from the larger island by a seawater selat. The rock around her was cracked; now and then the tor rumbled and dropped pieces of itself into the selat, but she hadn't even scratched the dome.

As Faan scowled at the island hazily visible through the crystal, memories from babytime came struggling back to her, fragments with no context. A frog hopping. Ailiki leaping and dancing across dew-wet grass. Invisible hands tending her. A man towering darkly over her, comforting rather than frightening. A woman's face—not clear and every time she tried to see it better, it vanished on her.

She grew impatient with self-pity.

"Gonna gonna kick and scratch," she sang defiantly, "An't gonna catch me ee. . . ."

It wasn't the same without Ma'teesee and Dossan.

"Gods! I wish. . . ."

She dropped to a squat, pushed at the straggles of black hair sweat-pasted to her face. The ends of the longer bits were frizzled and there were charred spots on her clothing. She lifted her arm, sniffed at her sleeve. "I stink."

Ailiki rubbed against her ankles.

"More ways than one, Aili my Liki." Faan scratched behind the mahsar's ears, twisted around so she could see Desantro. The older woman was curled up on a blanket, dozing; the years she'd been a slave had taught her how to wait.

"Deso, shift it."

Desantro yawned, sat up. She glanced at the dome, ran her fingers through her tangled brown hair. "So?"

"As you see."

"Well, you tried. Now let's go find my sister."

Faan brushed impatiently at a cluster of Wild Magic hovering too close. "I . . ."

A whistle from the selat brought her to her feet.

Seawater washed about the Godalau, combing through her long white fingers, pouring over a fishtail whose scales glistened like plates of jade. Tungjii Luck stood on her shoulder waving hisser wineskin.

Heesh tossed it to Faan.

She drank, felt heat spreading through her body, burning away fatigue and despair. She passed the skin to Desantro who drank, then threw it back to the little god.

Tungjii slung the strap over hisser shoulder, curved hisser hands about hisser mouth and shouted, "You'll find the way, Honeychild, you'll gather it bit by bit as you pass along the path of discovery. Seek Desantro's kin. Look in the Sibyl's mirror, Honeychild, and follow what you see."

Chapter 1
Opening Moves in Valdamaz

1. Poison

On the morning of the vernal equinox—Parmain, the Day of Change, when the new year was born from the ashes of the old—the Augstadievon of Valdamaz was found murdered.

> > < <

Kalips tugged on the drape pull, let the morning sun into the room. She glanced uneasily at the bed curtains, unused to seeing them drawn when she came in to clean. Most days she'd find Fishface up and pottering about, amiable enough, sipping at his coffee and reading one or another of the gossip sheets that circulated through the shops on Tirdza Street or standing at a window watching the first stirrings in the courts of the Akazal.

Not this morning.

She frowned, then shrugged and went to work, sweeping, dusting, replacing towels and soap, picking up his discarded clothes, the dead silence of the rooms getting on her nerves. Not even a snore. And there was a smell. He was rotten with lovedisease and incontinent, there'd been smells before, still. . . .

It was some time before she got back to the bedroom. She hesitated in the doorway when she saw the curtains still pulled shut, then started for the bed. From the smell, she'd have to change more than the sheets. Wondering if she should fetch one of the menservants to help her with the mattress, she rounded the foot and saw the breakfast tray sitting on the bedtable, the milk curdling, the coffee and toast getting cold.

Clicking her tongue against her teeth, she eased the curtain back, then gasped and jerked it along the rail.

Hands like claws, face a blotchy blue, mouth open in a silent scream of rage and fear, the Augstadievon lay dead in his body wastes.

Fist pressed against her mouth, she ran from the room.

2. Official notice taken

The High and Holy Nestrats Turet, brother of the Augstadievon, High Priest in Savvalis, pushed through the crowd of hovering jeredarod (secretaries, minor officials) and Akazal servants, went into the Augstadievon's quarters.

The doctor beside him, he stood looking down at his brother for several minutes while the Augstadievon's chaplain swung his censer and the black-hooded Nezarits (vultures, the common folk called them, when you saw them you knew there were dead around) hovered behind them, waiting for permission to take the body and get it ready for the Visitation.

"Poison." His voice was harsh.

"Tja," the doctor said. "Cinajim, it looks like, though we won't know for sure till we feed his blood to a zurk and see if its hair falls out."

"How soon?"

"Six days, seven."

Nestrats Turet bent over the bed, tried to close his brother's eyes, but the lids wouldn't move. He straightened, looked over his shoulder at the chief Nezarit. "Take him."

3. Reaction

In the afternoon of the same day, a Pargat jered (civil servant) of mid degree made arrangements to ride out the trouble he saw coming and shared his misgivings with his wife.

> > < <

Pargamaz Patikam greeted Tariko with a touch of fingertips to her cheek, then edged her aside so the bearers could carry their loads into the house.

"What's this?"

"Hush, Taro. I'll explain later. In the meantime, let's get these things stowed."

> > < <

Pargamazev Tariko brought the tray into the parlor and set it on the table beside her husband's chair. She poured a cup of tea for him and one for herself, then settled on a hassock by his knees. "There's food enough for months there, Pak. Cloth, coal. What's wrong? Is there going to be a war or something?"

"Something. A servant found the Augstadievon dead this morning."

"Well, he was sick, wasn't he? Though we're not supposed to say what he was sick from. Nu, there'll be a mourning month, but. . . ."

"It was poison, they say."

"Oh. Do they know. . . ?"

"Who did it? No. Nestrats Turet came out of that room with fire in his eye, love. Council of the Families met, did what they had to. Named the Candidates and appointed Turet Caretaker. He'll find out if anyone can. And then . . . you remember last time, the fights and the scandals till the election was over. It'll be worse this time." Patikam shivered. "Best we keep our heads down."

4. Pargats Varney, Candidate

Blond hair loose and flying, Pargats Varney rode recklessly along Smithy Lane, the black beast under him grunting and spattering him with foam. "Hammer hammer on the Highroad," he sang into the wind. The sun shone without warmth, yellow ice in a cloudless sky. The snow was patchy as a dog with mange, the bits of dark earth growing larger as the day grew older.

When the road began the rise to Dzestradjin

Hill, he relented and let the horse slow to an easy canter. "Navarre will have my hide, treating you like this, Permakon my child," he said, and laughed at the twitch in the gelding's ears. "I don't care, you enjoyed it as much as I did, didn't you?" He scratched in the tangled mane, then swung down and trotted along beside the horse, holding him to a walk so he could cool out. "Megg's ... curse ... on ... all ... poli ... tics ... and ... politi ... cians," he chanted, timing the words to the thud of his feet on the tar that paved the Lane. "On ... idjit ... bro ... thers ... and...." He snorted and fell silent as he turned the curve of the hill and looked out over the scrubland that dropped away to the vast shadow of the Divimezh, the forest that stretched south from the river and west to the coast. It was darker and more ominous than ever with most of the leaves gone, patchy like the snow with scattered evergreens.

He shivered. The Divimezh was an image of evil as far as he was concerned. If he had the power of the god Meggzatevoc, he'd burn the hills clean. Smugglers came creeping north through those cursed trees on what they called the Greenway, bandits sheltered there, runaway churls, lice of all kinds, most of all the Forest Devils—savages slaughtering anyone who put a foot into the range they claimed.

He didn't relax until he led Permakon through the arched gateway and the wall round the compound shut out the Divimezh.

Over the clipclop of the gelding's feet he could

hear the smith's hammer. Navarre was in the forge.

He mounted and rode at a slow walk around the house, pulled the horse up and sat with his hands crossed on the pommel, watching the smith work.

The Magus Navarre. No one Varney knew had any idea when he'd been born or hatched or whatever force had ejected the man into the world. He'd been at Dzesdar Lodge for a dozen years—just appeared one day, fixed the place up, opened the forge for business.

Navarre was a square man with a pleasantly ugly face; he had long arms and a long torso and relatively short legs, but he was graceful in spite of that; there were those who swore he could walk the sharp edge of a knife blade without a waver and girls who sighed with pleasure when he danced at the Meggasvinte. He had abundant light brown hair that he wore in a single braid that hung down past his belt when he was out and moving about. It was wound about his head now, held in place with steel skewers to keep it out of his way as he worked at the anvil.

Despite the noises the gelding made, snorts, the scrape of hooves against the slate paving, he didn't look up from the axe head he was shaping.

He was chanting with the strokes of the hammer, singing some kind of magic into the metal, his deep voice dark as the iron. Probably a hone-spell to keep the edge keen.

In the shadows at the back of the forge a small figure stood beside a basket of charcoal taller than he was. Forest Devil, paying in trade, no doubt. Varney swore under his breath, Permakon sidling nervously as his knees tightened. They were always hanging about the place, infesting it like lice. He'd been caustic about it the first time and Navarre had gone cold on him, an icy anger he was careful not to provoke again. Not that Navarre would dare harm him—but he might deny his friendship and Varney didn't want that.

Pargats Varney, a son of the Seven, Candidate for Rule, sniffed his disgust at being forced to wait like a commoner in a dole line, slid from the saddle, and led the gelding around the smithy to the stable.

>><<

Navarre came in as Varney was buckling the blanket in place. "Kitya fired the salamandrit before I started work; the bathhouse is ready. Join me?"

"Shuh! tja." Varney gathered up the rags and comb he'd been using to groom the gelding, gave the beast a last pat, and left the stall.

>><<

Pargats Varney floated in the hot, herb-strewn water as Navarre lay facedown on a slatted bench while his housekeeper rubbed scented oil into his skin and curried him with an ivory comb; he was a hairy man, the light brown curl on his arms and legs nearly thick enough for fur.

Navarre lifted his head, rested his chin on his fist. "Vitra drop her foal yet?"

"Two nights ago. Filly, strong little thing, good conformation." He watched the housekeeper, frowning a little. This wasn't what he wanted to talk about, but he neither liked nor trusted that woman. If she was a woman.

Kitya was tall and thin with slanted red eyes and an eerie detachment that seemed to say what she saw around her was a dream to be tolerated but not indulged. If the shadows were right, she could be beautiful, mostly she was just strange.

He watched her as she worked on the body of the Magus, her shift damp and clinging to her, outlining the play of muscle, the graceful dance of the sinewy body. *She's got scales like a snake. I think. I'm not sure. I've never seen her in full light.* He grimaced, wiped a wet hand over his face. *And I don't want to.*

She looked at him for a moment, crimson eyes narrowed, then went back to what she was doing. Almost as if she heard what he was thinking. He felt like a boy caught with his trousers down and his hands where they oughtn't to be. *Bitch!*

"Vicanal fussing at you again?" Navarre turned over, lay with his hands clasped behind his head. "Who've you got pregnant this time?"

Varney stood up, caught the towel the housekeeper threw at him, and climbed the ladder nailed to the side of the wooden bath. He sighed, wrapped the towel about him, and sat on a bench, sucking in the steam from water dripping onto the heated stones. "Worse," he said. He scratched meditatively as he sought for the right words; one had to be careful, especially now when even the dogs on the middens would be smelling about for advantage. "Augstadievon kicked off sometime yesterday night. Council met an hour ago, named High and Holy Nestrats Turet Caretaker for the Interregnum. Which means the Families are going to be fighting over who gets the Seat come next Counting Day. Custom says Augsta Candidates are second sons, so I'm the Pargats Candidate. Which means I'm a target for poison like old Nestrats. Nu, it's true. Whispers are he was blue as moldy bread when they found him."

Navarre sat up, stretched, yawned. "I'm hungry enough to eat that Black of yours." He held out his arms and the housekeeper pushed them into the sleeves of a dark red wool robe, thick as a blanket. "Kitya has a chicken roasting and fresh bread. Join me?"

> > < <

The den was full of primitive color, blankets from the Forest Devils, pottery from the Market in Savvalis, paintings and tapestries, the firelight shifting from one to another, picking out gleams of red and gold, blue and green. Varney sank into one of the leather chairs, put his feet up, and sighed with pleasure as Kitya set a mug of mulled wine on the table beside him, then glided from the room.

Navarre stood on the hearth holding a silver

tankard with steam curling from the top. "Health," he said and drank.

"And to you, friend." Varney sipped at the wine, set the mug on the table. "That's the crux, Magus. A knife in the ribs, I can take care of that. But poison? No." He shuddered. "I need an aizar stone. What'll it cost me?"

Navarre set the tankard on the mantle, folded his arms. "Nothing. If I'm permitted to interfere that far."

"What?"

"I was warned when I settled here, Pargats Varney. If I meddle in high affairs, your god will rouse himself and squash me."

"For a puking little periapt?"

"For meddling in Family affairs. Give me a senn't, Varney. I'll make my queries and if the answer's right I'll send word when the stone's ready."

"If that's the best you can do." Varney sat up. "Vitra's a little sluggish, not coming along as well as I'd like. Veterins Maritz says not to worry, just keep her warm and comfortable, but she's my best mare and the foal shows promise."

"Ah. Tja. There's an herb the Tyrlan use after a hard birth, they call it qwal." He tugged on the bell cord. "They cover a mare's head with a blanket and under it they boil the qwal in a pot the size of a man's two fists until most of the water is gone."

The housekeeper came in, put a packet in his hand, and left. "Do it three times, no more, five hours between each boiling." He tossed the packet to Varney. "She'll sweat a lot, look dozy for a while, after that she should be fine. If not, send for me and I'll see what I can do."

5. In the Divimezh

"It is my right by Blood and Gift." The City Man set his hand on the Drum and opened his black eyes wide, willing his half uncle to submit and sing with him the Binding of Ysgarod the Mezh.

"Have you thought. . . ."

"I have thought. I WILL have it. I have begun, but I need more kuash. The Kuash of Ysgarod. Let what comes, come. Good or evil, hard or sweet. I WILL do this, Babaraum."

The old man leaned forward, set his hand beside the half-blood's. "And I will sing with you, for I know this, Ysgarod will protect the Mezh, Binding or no. IT will destroy you first, sister-son."

CABAL

Four robed figures met in a dusty vault beneath the Temple, the bones of ancient High Holies tucked into niches about them. Three men and a woman.

Two of the men were long of leg and arm, the third squatter; with the cowls pulled forward, throwing their faces into shadow, that was all that could be seen of them. The woman was slight and moved with a conviction of beauty that nothing could hide, not even thick folds of stiff black felt.

"It was deliberate," the squat man said, his voice a harsh whisper. "Not a bungle. I planned it thus. They all eye each other, haven't you seen? When the time comes, we can use the blame to eliminate he who seems most dangerous. Until then, they move with caution. No one knows where to put his trust."

One of the tall men moved uneasily. "Nestrats Turet."

"A fool. Why do you think Nestrats Lantil shunted him into the Temple? Wanted him where he couldn't spoil the old man's plots."

"There's one you'll have to square somehow. Varney's friend. The Magus."

21

"True. But not yet. He's a cool man and not a fool. I know him. Wrystrike. Tja, he'll stay out of the tangle as long as he can."

The other tall man grunted. *"And there's always Megg. Won't let the zemnik kaz us."*

The woman hissed, her head jerked as if she tossed her hair about; enough light crept under the cowl to show the clean line of jaw and neck. *"He can look and he can talk."*

The wide man chuckled grimly. *"He'll see nothing and say less. I have arranged it."*

She reached out and touched him, her hand hidden in the folds of her sleeve. *"You're certain?"*

"O tja, my dear. O tja."

Chapter 2
HONEYCHILD in Savvalis

Faan Hasmara as she was calling herself these days, Faan the twice-abandoned, settled herself on a bitt to wait until Desantro finished saying her farewells. Ailiki the mahsar jumped into her lap, kneaded her thighs a few times, then curled up against her stomach, purring energetically.

The sun hadn't cleared the rooftops yet and the wind blowing off the water had a bite to it. Brisk wind. Whitecaps out in the bay. The air up here had a different feel, a sting to it that ran like fire in the blood. She scratched behind the mahsar's ears, shivered, and drew her cloak closer about her. Ailiki grumbled at the movement, then settled back to a doze. Faan snorted. "Your coat came lagniappe," she said. "I have to pull mine on." She glanced over her shoulder at the ship, wrinkled her nose.

Come on, Desa, you know you're going to leave him, why drag it out? Lost cause . . . we're a pair, we are . . . we should forget our families and get on with the rest of our lives . . . godlost mulehead that I am, I can't, no more than her . . . my mother . . . I can't remember anything but greeny-gray eyes

and when I think Mamay, I see Reyna's face ...
that's not my fault, I was only three when Abeyhamal took me ... I NEED to know her. I suppose I do.

She put her hand on Ailiki to keep the mahsar
from sliding off her thighs as she pulled her feet
in, drew her bag around the side of the bitt farther out of the way of a line of ladesmen rushing
past, loads in their back slings that were half their
own height above their heads.

All she owned was in that bag.

Almost all. Not the money the Shadow-captain
had given her when he put her down at Kukurul—that was tucked inside her clothing, in a
pouch next to her skin. Yohaen Pok, the trader
sailing with them ... Desantro and he'd had a wild
thing going the past month ... made Faan uncomfortable thinking about it ... day before yesterday
he took her aside and told her he didn't want to
know what money she had, but whatever it was
she should keep it on her at all times. Until she
found a safe depository, he said. A respectable
innkeeper will do, he said. Ask about for one
who's got a good reputation. It's a hard world, he
said, when you don't have family, child. But it's
not all bad either. People are generally as good as
circumstances allow, he said. He patted her on the
shoulder and went off smiling, satisfied with himself. He was a good man. Desantro was a fool to
let him go, he wanted to wed her....

It wasn't much to show for sixteen years of living, what she had in that bag, a change of under-
clothes, another tunic, an old pair of sandals, the

wooden clasp Reyna had worn to hold his hair back, a book of honey poems Tai had given her on her tenth yearday, the odds and ends the water elementals had brought her—more memories than substance there, but she hauled them about anyway.

Desantro, tsah! Faan shook her head. She didn't understand it. The woman wasn't young or even pretty, but Yohaen wasn't the first to get steamed up about her, she seemed to draw them like bees to sugarwater. Anywhere they went, give her a minute and she had most of the men there gathered around her, laughing, talking . . . if her sister was anything like her. . . . *This is a busy place.* Faan looked around.

There were piles of goods everywhere . . . and ships. She counted the ones she could see from where she sat . . . seven, eight . . . fifteen in all . . . all different kinds. Two black merchanters from Phrasi with eyes painted on their bows. Lean M'darjin galleys . . . are they a long way from home! Broad sturdy coasters . . . she'd seen lots of those in the bay at Kukurul . . . a weird one, painted dark blue, red and white striped sails, a six-armed bare-breasted crab woman as figurehead. A lot of long, racy ships with a tired look as if they'd come far and hard. . . .

She stroked Ailiki's soft fur, enjoying the noise that filled the morning. Noise. That was another thing about this air . . . sounds were crisper, the voices quicker. It was hard for her to pick out the words . . . even with the unintended gift from Abeyhamal . . . gift of tongues? Whatever the god had done to her head, she picked up languages now as if she were a sponge soaking them in. Listening to Yohaen Pok teach Valdaspeak to Desantro (another of his kindnesses), she'd learned far more than he thought he was teaching. Only trouble was, she hadn't yet learned to hear as fast as these people were speaking.

A ladesman stumbled and a packet fell off his load, breaking apart on the planks of the wharf, scattering grains of pala to the wind and water.

The argument that ensued was a loud excited yammer that didn't particularly interest her; the sharp sweetish nip of the pala woke memories in her, piercing her with loss.

> *Riverman eating honey and teasing her as they sat under the gatt and listened to the feet of the ladesmen coming and going.*
>
> *Water elementals lifting their faceted faces from the brown water.*
>
> *Wild Magic fizzing about, catching the light like bubbles of crystal.*

Riverman . . . there's a river here . . . does every river have a Riverman wandering along its reaches? I never thought to ask him. . . .

Edging past the mess as the trader was demanding a refund for his lost spice and the ladesman was berating him for faulty packaging, a boy younger than she was tripped over the strap of her bag and tumbled into her lap, nearly squashing Ailiki; he grinned at her, squeezed a breast, then was up and away before she could react.

"Little rat." Desantro's voice was hoarse and her eyes were red, but she'd put a smile on her face that said no comment. "On your feet, Fa, I need some tea."

> > < <

"Tirdza Street. Tirdza means trade. Trade Street." Desantro spread the last of the jam on her toast, took a sip of the tea. "Yohaen said just about anyone we ask should know where to find ... what was his name?"

"Pargamaz Patikam." Faan wrinkled her nose. Desantro hadn't forgotten the name, she just wanted to hear someone else say it. "We need more hot water, so why not ask the waiter when he brings it?"

Desantro rubbed at her chin, straightened her shoulders. "Why not?"

> > < <

"Pargamaz?" The old man wrapped the quilted cloth about the pot and straightened. "Patikam. Nu nu, I don't know the man personally, but finding him should be easy enough. You must be strangers here."

Desantro ran her fingers through her fine brown curls. "All right, what's the trick?"

"With the maz on his name, he has to be a Pargats cousin, so he's like to be in Ash Pargat. What you do is ask the Pargat Gatekeeper, he'll tell how to find him. You got a few spare desmaks to offer, he'll send one of his sons to show you the way.

You'll be going through him anyway, all the Ashes but this'n have walls round them."

"And where do we find Ash Pargats?"

"Neka neka, Pargat. Ash Pargat. Different sound altogether." He smiled at her. "Step out on the walk and go south till you run into a wall. Gate'll be open. Ring the bell. Slegis is a lazy prat, but you can put some spring in his step if you let him hear the clink of metal."

Desantro took the hint and gave him his kod, the bite that passed with all transactions here in Valdamaz—one of the silver desmaks that he'd suggested for the Gatekeeper.

He went off more than contented and left them to the pot.

> > < <

Excited and a little sad because she was missing her friends, fitting her steps with Desantro's strides but contriving to do a dancey shuffle along the wooden walkway, whispering under her breath *Gonna gonna kick and scratch,* Faan swung along taking in the sights.

Tirdza Street was broad and busy, paved with granite setts as deep as they were wide, the age of the city apparent in the hollows worn in them. The buildings along it were mostly shops on the ground floor with living quarters above. Three or four stories high, they were built from a mix of woods cut into blocks like bricks, held together by glue not nails or such, the grain and color of the wood arranged in patterns, the outside polished until the wood had a deep rich glow. The roofs were steeply pitched, the shingles on them weathered gray, with several chimneys on each house, chimneys with fanciful caps, giggles in black iron. So many chimneys. She remembered Desantro's tales of snow and ice and shivered.

"What's wrong, Fa?"

"Winter."

Desantro sniffed. "Foolishness. We aren't going to be around that long. Besides, once you're used to it, it's a splendid time."

"I've never even seen snow."

"I thought you liked new things."

Faan moved her shoulders. "To think about. I don't know about actually freezing my . . . um . . . toes off."

Desantro snorted. "It's not even summer yet, babe."

"Hmm. They keep this place really neat. Like they polished it every day."

"Maybe they do."

Faan clicked her tongue, went back to looking around.

Most of the buildings had huge nest boxes beside one of the chimneys, with twiggy nests and long-legged white birds going and coming. Yohaen said be careful about those birds, they're called Laimail and supposed to be the city's Luck.

The shops had carved figures hanging from brackets above their doors, figures in semi round, painted with bright primal colors:

> *a man holding a hammer and knife that*
> *crossed above the round of his belly.*
> *a woman with a spindle.*
> *a robed and cowled person of indetermin-*
> *ate sex with an armload of books.*

Faan dawdled by each of the bookstores she passed, catching glimpses through the small diamond panes of piles of books and urns full of scrolls. These shops had noticeboards beside their windows with sheets of coarse paper pasted up on them, papers like those that a number of the locals were reading as they walked along. Faan wanted to see what was on those papers, but Desantro wouldn't stop; she was too impatient to reach Pargamaz Patikam and find out what happened to her sister.

> > < <

An old woman sat beside a frycart wrapping sausages in a tough, flaky dough, impaling them on wooden skewers and dipping them in hot oil until they were a crisp gold-brown. For a while she'd been doing a brisk business, then three youths wearing green tabards with a black bird appliquéd on the front emerged from a side street, trading shadow jabs and shouted dares; they crossed the street, heading for the frycart.

The old woman's customers faded fast. There was a nervous irritation in the way the boys moved and a mean edge to their voices. They were looking for trouble, ready to make their own if they couldn't find any lying around.

Desantro swore under her breath, grabbed Faan's arm, and pulled her into a recessed doorway.

"Eh-ya eh-ya, Vecsivi," the tallest of the three said. "What ye selling sa morn, Vec Zen?"

"Well, look round, Cushk." Another of the three did a step-step dance, waggling his narrow buttocks and flapping his hands. "Look look look," he warbled. "No dogs." He giggled, flung back his head so his long brown hair fluttered in the wind. "Grind 'em up wi' a pinch o pigfat."

The third caught up a handful of the skewered sausage rolls and flung them into the street. "Ash Tirdza," he shrilled and pounded the dancer on the back. "Trade trade trade, anything for sale, stinkin' zemniks doin' what comes natural. When the dogs run out, there's always cats."

"Now now, chienis," the old woman said, forcing laughter and lightness into her voice, "you know that's not so, it's good meat and pure, fresh from the Market every morning."

One of the boys snatched a handful of sausage, threw it at another, then all of them were snatching and throwing, ducking, yelling, "fresh and pure   fresh and pure   fresh and pure."

The old woman pushed to her feet, stood looking helplessly around. Storekeepers hovered in their doors, avoiding her eyes, some men in black tabards had their backs turned, deliberately looking the other way.

Three more youths came from the same side-

way, same age, fourteen, fifteen, these in red tabards with a lizard rampant.

"Look a that, Sajuk, Dinots fighting over a
bitch."

"Nay, Uts, can't y' see. Look't the nose on her.
She's their Ma, huh." They whooped and danced
from foot to foot, chanting, "Laro, Laro likes 'em
bitchy, four legs and a tongue, woof woof."

The green tabards forgot the old woman and
started their own dance. "Druz oh Druzy, foot in
mouth," they yelled back. "Block a wood got more
smarts than him."

The exchanges grew louder and raunchier until
the greens stopped playing and leapt at the reds,
fists swinging.

As they fought, the old woman tugged at her
cart and with the help of some men who'd ventured from their shops and several black tabards,
pushed it down the street till it was out of the
disturbance.

A red shoved a green, got shoved by another
green. A red snapped out his belt knife . . .

. . . and got it knocked from his hand by an arm-
length of polished wooden rod held by an older
man in a black tabard with a bronze chain about
his neck. "Foolin's foolin," he growled at them,
"but the fun stops when edge shows."

Jabbing and prodding with his club, the black
tabard separated the two groups, sent the reds
down a side way and told the greens he'd be reporting them to their Lielskadrav and if he saw
them acting up out here again, he'd have their
asses on ice for as long as he could finagle it.

When they'd cleared off, Tirdza Street went back to its usual bustle, the noise was back, louder than ever, but this time Faan took more notice of the tabarded youths lounging about and a sprinkling of the black tabards strolling along the walks, swinging their clubs by thongs looped through a hole in the handle.

"There's something going on," she said.

Desantro made a quick negating gesture. "Just ignore it," she said. "Local politics, nothing to do with us." She started walking more quickly. Faan followed, Ailiki trotting a half step in front of her.

> > < <

The Gate was a shallow arch in a wall twenty feet tall and nearly half that wide at the base with another wall running parallel to it on the far side of a wood-paved road that looked like it was used about once a century. From where she stood, Faan could see patches of scaly gray lichen and scatters of decayed leaves. The gates themselves were cumbersome things with iron studs and crossing bands; they were folded back against the walls, the hinge side facing the Ash.

The Gatehouse was built on massive beams set across this pair of walls like a dish on a table; it was a blocky structure with a Laimail nest next to the chimney, flowerboxes in the windows, and a delicate railing of wrought iron around the base. There was the sound of a woman singing; a child was visible, playing with a small toy horse, running its wheels along the beams and making horse noises.

Desantro rang the bronze bell hanging from a bracket beside a kiosk snugged against the Gate.

The shutter clacked up and a man leaned out, elbows on the ledge. "What?" he said, his voice mild, his fuzzy brows lifted. He was a small man, bald as an egg with plump rosy cheeks.

Desantro bobbed a brief polite bow. "I seek the house of one Pargamaz Patikam." Her mouth twitched into a smile that broadened into a grin as his pale blue eyes twinkled at her.

He tilted his head, waggled his brows. "Purpose?"

"I have been told my sister is his wife. She was a Vraga bride."

"Nu nu, is that so." He shifted his mouth side to side. " 'Tis complicated to explain," he said. "If you don't already know the way. You're newly come to Savvalis?"

"We arrived from the South just this morning."

"Nu nu." He winked at Desantro, tapped with his thumb on the ledge.

Desantro laid a silver desmak beside the thumb. "If you could find a guide for us?"

"Nu, I can do that." He drew back, called over his shoulder, "Lokit, get you down here." He swung back round. "My next youngest boy," he said, his pride manifest. "Young cekcek, he'll get you there, talk your ear off on the way."

> > < <

Desantro walked in stolid silence, her eyes on the ground, her face closed up. Faan glanced at her, then hurried to catch up with Lokit as he marched across the wood road; Ailiki scampered ahead of her, nosed at the road, then at the gate. Faan touched the boy's shoulder, pointed along the space between the walls. "What's this for?"

He looked up at her; his eyes went wide. "Your eyes are different colors. Why's that?"

"Don't know. The road?"

"For trouble times. When th' army hasta march. Whatcha name?"

"Faan. And you're Lokit, y' da says."

"Tja. What's it mean, Faan?"

"Just a name. The Gates aren't closed."

"Neka, han't been a mess-up in the Ashes for a long, long, lonnnng time. We turn down here, got a ways to go yet. Patikam, he's comf'table, tja. I don' know how long it's been, we han't got that far in m' hist'ry class."

"This a holiday or something?"

He grinned. "Whole week's a holiday. We get one a those every darkmoon in t' Interregnum. Lasts all the way t' solstice, Perransvinte cuts it off, that's Counting Day." His hand came up to cover his mouth, his sea-blue eyes opened wide. "We s'posed to be sad, nu." He brought his shoulder forward, tapped the black ribbon knotted about his biceps. "Augstadievon he died, so we honor 'im." His grin broke out again, impudent and full of sass.

She grinned back at him. "Sad, sad. What's that?" She flapped her hand at a long rambling building three stories high with galleries on each floor and outside stairways linking them.

"It's a Pukhus." He jabbed at himself with his thumb. "Me, when I get to be a man, that's where I go. 'Prentices, students, all that, they live there. Men move out the house and into a Pukhus 'f they not the heir, live there long as they an't married." He wrinkled his nose. "M' Da say they gonna move the Pukhussiz outside the walls, 'cause they need more room for fam'lies; tiesh tas, hope they do, it'll be grannnnd."

"What about girls?"

"Girls can't do nothing, they just stay home."

Faan snorted. "If I wanted to go, I'd go."

He tilted his head, very like his father at that moment, blinked up at her. "Nu, I expect things are diff'rent where you come from."

"Tja tja!"

"Those towers there," he waved a grubby hand, "that's Pargats House. Where the Lielskadrav lives with lots of cousins to do the work. 'M glad I don' have to be there, eh-yah. M' cousin Dojis says it's worse'n a Kyatty hell, got garidj sniffin' down y' neck all the time, have ta go to chapel 'fore dawn EVERY morning, can't have no fun at all." He did a little dance step, grinned. "M' Da say I don' have ta worry, 'm too pestery to get took."

On the other side of the street they walked down were row houses, small neat brick buildings sharing a common wall with a tiny patch of garden in front, bright with spring flowers or ceramic blobs like rocks in primary colors.

"What happened there?" She pointed at one of the houses. The shutters were closed tight with black wax seals on the cracks between them, the garden had gone to dead weeds and a tall pole was set in the hard, gray dirt, a pole with bronze disks hanging from short bronze chains along the top two feet, the disks catching the wind and clinking with dreary dull sounds.

"Nu, Pargamaz Cigser lived there till his wife died." Lokit shivered and walked faster, glancing repeatedly over his shoulder at the dreary place.

"What's all that wax and the pole mean?"

"Bad ghost there. Cigser's woman did herself. They called a ghost-layer from the Temple, but he din' have no luck either. She comes out and yells every Moondark. Cigser has took off, don' know where, well, he c'dn't stay with what that ghost said 'bout him. Pole's a Nagglet, keeps her pinned there. Just have to wait till she fades, that's what the layer said."

There were bands of children playing in the street; some stopped to stare at Desantro and Faan, others were too engrossed in their games to bother with something so uninteresting as a pair of foreign women.

The row houses broke off, the street opened into a square thick with women; some were sitting about gossiping, watching a collection of babies and toddlers, others were busy at the great stone tubs doing family laundry, still others were pulling flat loaves of bread from the communal oven at the south corner of the square.

Beyond the square the houses stood detached

with front doors painted in bright red, green, blue, orange, hot pink and gold, with masses of primroses and dahlias in tubs flanking the front steps. The farther they went, the larger the bits of land about the houses; they began seeing stake fences and waist-high hedges, a tree or two, small stone fountains. As the houses grew larger, they seemed to retreat more and more behind the veils of greenery and fencewood.

Lokit stopped before the gate of one of these larger houses. "This's it," he said. "House a Pargamaz Patikam. Yank on the pull there 'f you wanna talk to someone. Sveik, milas." With a two-finger salute and a grin, he went running off.

Almost panic in her face, Desantro stared at the metal pinecone at the end of the pullchain. She reached, stopped her hand before she touched it and stood like that for several breaths, then with a faint whimper she didn't realize she was making, she grasped the cone and pulled.

> > < <

"Dessss . . . I don't believe it . . . Des!"

"T'rik . . . I didn't believe it either . . . not till I saw you."

Laughing and crying . . . hugging each other . . . turning round and round . . . speaking together . . . breaking off . . . starting up again at the same time . . . laughing again . . . noisy and incoherent, the more than twenty years since they'd seen each other crashing on them at that moment, the sisters were excited to near hysteria.

Ailiki a warm weight on her feet, Faan leaned against the wall, arms crossed, pretending to herself she was bored by all this (her mother was supposed to be a sorcerer, a being of power, and SHE'D never tried to find her lost baby). She sighed with exaggerated weariness and inspected the entrance hall.

The austere wood paneling was a dark honey, inset squares two hands wide with linenfold carving on the raised frames; there were bronze lamps with tulip-shaped glass chimneys spaced along the walls, unlit now, the illumination provided by a slanted roof-window two stories above them. At the far end of the wide hall a staircase of darker wood curved upward, turning a corner before it reached the upper floor.

Tariko shared bones with her sister, but she must have been some years younger; she had the same abundance of light brown hair, but it was neatly disciplined into smooth bands and a large soft knot at the base of her skull. Her skin had a porcelain fineness, none of the sun dapples that danced across Desantro's face; her features were smaller, more delicate, her hands pale and narrow with long tapering fingers, her eyes were a deep violet blue. After the first moments of excitement and happiness, Faan got the feeling that the woman was hiding a strong ambivalence behind an exaggeration of the pleasure and excitement she really did feel.

Tariko drew back. "And who is this?"

Desantro coughed, rubbed at her eyes as she turned to face Faan. "Faan Hasmara," she said, her voice hoarse, "Tariko, my sister. T'rik, Faan found you for me and before that made it possible for me to travel here."

Tariko swept into a graceful bow. "Be welcome indeed, Faan Hasmara."

"You are gracious indeed, Tariko." Faan inclined her head with an equal lack of sincerity; she was increasingly sure she didn't like Desantro's sister.

"My shame that we're standing around here, come upstairs to my sitting room and we'll have some tea." She glanced at Ailiki, frowned but said nothing, then swept around and led the way up the stairs.

>><<

Tariko smiled as she bowed and handed the delicate porcelain cup to Faan; she returned to her seat behind the oval table and poured herself a cup. "Yes," she said, "I was blessed. Have you heard of the Vraga brides?"

Desantro nodded. "Someone I met on the ship mentioned them."

"Patikam's father was still alive then; it was during the Legger Interregnum ... well, never mind that, it's just that things were chancy so he wanted to make sure his favorite son was safe." She smiled into her teacup, as at some fond memory. "The way it is here, if a man wants to rise high, he marries pure; that's the sign of his ambition. An invitation to the poison cup, that's what old

Pargamaz Tisker used to say. He'd sit there ..."
Tariko nodded to the largest of the chairs in the
room. "He'd sit there and slurp his tea and look
like a stuffed owl and say over and over what a
wise old fart he was, his own words. Well, I never
complained, because it was a good thing for me.
The slaver who bought me ... that was after you
went, Desa ... he knew it was a dangerous time
here, they were changing Augstadievons, they do
that every twelve years, and a lot of families
would be at the Bridehall shopping for Vraga
brides, and he'd get an extra good price for a
pretty girl who was a certified virgin." She sighed.
"It could have been horrible, you know, but Patikam took one look at me and that was that. We
have two children, my daughter Parraye who is
fourteen and my son Zens who is nine. I've been
blessed, Desa. I'm very happy." She leaned forward. "But you, sister, what happened to you?"

Desantro set her cup down and began the long
story of her captivity and unexpected release.

As Tariko exclaimed and murmured sympathy,
wonder, clicked her tongue in exaggerated disgust, Faan settled back in her chair, Ailiki a pool
of warmth against her belly. She could smell trouble coming. Tariko was prettier and younger, but
she hadn't half the strength and warmth of her
sister—and that other thing; episodes from the
past year popped into memory and slid out again.
Tsah! chances were good that darling Patikam
would start sniffing around the honeytrap and little sister's welcome would go poof! Now that

we've found her, we really should get out of here.... Faan watched exuberance and joy play across Desantro's face, watched her continually reach out to touch her sister's arm, as if to reassure herself that it was not all a dream, that she had family again. No chance of leaving any time soon. Ah well, Sibyl said you can't live other people's lives for them.

Desantro's tale wound to its spectacular end. Tariko's eyes widened and she stared at Faan, fascinated but uncomfortable with the thought she was entertaining a sorcerer, however feeble and unformed.

Faan sat up. "Pargamazev Tariko," she said, "your courtesy has been pleasant indeed, but it is time I was finding an inn. Do you know of one you can recommend? Of moderate expense but respectable?"

Desantro was startled and not pleased by the light formality of Faan's words—as if she realized for the first time what had been apparent from the beginning; her companion and her sister did not like each other.

"But of course you must stay with us, mila Faan. There is plenty of room and you are most welcome," Tariko said smoothly.

"I am honored, Pargamazev Tariko, but I'm sure you and Desantro have family matters to discuss without outside ears; besides, I need to live closer to Ash Tirdza; there are things I must do. I'm sure you understand."

"Tja, of course, mila Faan." She got gracefully

to her feet and crossed to the door. As she tugged at the bell pull, she said, "You must return and dine with us, mila. At the beginning of the seventh daywatch. Pargamaz Patikam will be wishing to greet you."

"Tja, Pargamazev Tariko, blessings for your courtesy."

> > < <

As Faan and Dreits, the manservant who was guiding her and carrying her bag, passed through the Ashgate, Slegis slapped up the shutter and looked out. "Sveik, child. I see you found the house."

"Tja, Gatekeeper. You have a charmer for a son."

"Patcha, child. Young cekcek." He pulled his head in and vanished into the shadows inside the kiosk.

With Ailiki a small shadow trotting before them, they walked a while in silence until they reached the first shops. "What sort of inn are you looking for, mila?" Dreits' voice was soft and slow, his accent thick. This was the first time he'd spoken; till now he'd been content to walk a pace behind her. He was a tall, thin man with sunbleached blond hair and a pronounced limp that didn't seem to give him much trouble as he swung along.

"You're not from Savvalis?"

"My family work on a cattle run in the eastlands; I was a younger son and restless, so I joined the army and stayed in until I got the wound in the leg that left me lame."

"Ah."

A rumbling chuckle. "And you know nothing of that, why should you, mila. The inn?"

"Something ... hmm ... should I say inexpensive or cheap? But a place where the fleas won't be raising grandchildren on my blood and the innkeeper won't sell my room key to any rupja with an urge."

"Nu nu, what a thing. Do they actually do that?"

"It's happened a couple times as we traveled north." She held up a hand, let pale blue flamelets dance along her fingers, then banished them. "Rupjas got a shock must've put them off women for a while."

"Tsa, magic!"

"Well, I'm only a student and a beginner at that, but it's enough to discourage interference."

"So it must." He scratched behind his ear. "Nu, seems to me the Gul Bazelt would do well enough. It's small, only five rooms, but it's clean and the cook's a treasure when she's sober. t'Mazra Zotaj is a man of worth, the innkeeper, he is. A foreigner, but a man of worth."

"Sounds good to me, where is it?"

"Two streets down, one back, but you'd best drop by the Modrib first."

Faan scowled. "Modrib? I don't know the word."

"Civiel station. If you're going to stay more than

a few days, you have to register there."

She sighed, pushed her black hair off her face. "Let's get it over with, then. I'm tired. I want a bath and a nap."

> > < <

The Modrib was a larger version of the Gate-keeper's kiosk, an eight-sided tower built of wood, three stories high and aggressively plain. Ailiki dropping back to follow them, Faan went up the stairs with Dreits limping behind, stepped into a bare room with a couple of benches pushed up against side walls, a desk at the back wall near narrow stairs that coiled up to the second floor.

A middle-aged man in a black tabard was sit-ting behind the desk reading a newssheet; he looked up as she crossed the room, reached into a drawer, and set a printed page on the table. "Tja, mila?"

"I've been told I need to register with you if I plan to spend more than a few days in the city."

"Tja, mila." He dipped a wooden pen in a bottle of ink, tapped it on a thick felt slab. "Name?"

"Faan Hasmara."

"Nu nu, I have it. Homeland?"

She hesitated, then said, "Zam Fadogurum. South Continent."

"Long way from home."

"Tja."

"Age?"

"Seventeen years. Is that necessary?"

"Routine, mila. You alone?"

"No. I have a companion, an older woman."

"You're very young. She's responsible for you?"

"No. I travel with her, that's all."

"Your purpose for visiting Valdamaz?"

"My companion has come to visit her sister who is a Vraga bride. As I said, I travel with her."

"Vraga bride. Tiesh tas. What Family?"

"Pargats."

He looked past her at Dreits, nodded. "Tja. How long will you be staying?"

"I'm not sure. Not beyond summer's end. It depends on my companion and how long she extends her visit. Also what ships are in when it's time to leave and where we decide to go."

"Nu, what I'll do, I'll set you down for a month. Prialis 17, that's today, till Maijalis 17. You understand?"

"And on Maijalis 17?"

"If you wish to stay longer, come by and re-register."

"Tja."

He reached in the drawer, brought out another sheet with printing on it. He folded it in half, folded it again, then sat with his fingertips holding it down. "If it turns out that you will be staying here over winter, you must either provide proof you can support yourself or acquire the sponsorship of a citizen of Valdamaz. Savvalis is not liable for feeding or housing you. You will not be able to work while you're here, at least, not without the approval of the Caretaker and the chances of getting such approval lie between little and none. The only acceptable change of your condition is if a citizen agrees to marry you."

"That is out of the question."

"Nu, we'll see. Time is as time goes. Fee for registration is one desmak." He took the coin she dropped on the desk, pushed it into a slot in the desktop, then flicked the folded paper across to her. "Read this carefully. These are the laws of the city that you will be required to know and follow without variation."

She tucked the paper in the sack tied to her belt. "Is there anything else?"

"Only this." He pushed across the desk a small bronze tag with a line of letters and numbers stamped diagonally across one side. "This is your votaj. Carry it with you at all times, show it whenever you are questioned, it doesn't matter who does the questioning. Anyone has the right to see your votaj. Do you understand?"

"Tja, I understand."

"There's a hole in one corner; it is permitted to wear the votaj on a chain or a thong about your neck. If you lose it, no matter how, come immediately to this office. Under oath tell precisely how it was lost. You will be charged a fine, fifty desmaks, and give a replacement. Do you understand?"

"Tja, I understand." Following Dreits' instructions, as she turned to leave, she slid another desmak onto the desk, the civiel kod, then she went out.

> > < <

Ailiki leapt onto the bed and curled in a soft knot; Dreits raised his brows, set Faan's bag on the rack at the foot of the bed. "Is there anything else I can do for you, mila?"

Faan stood at the window looking down into the narrow side street. "At the moment I can think of nothing. You've been very kind."

"Then I will return at the end of the sixth day-watch and escort you back to the house of Pati-kam."

"That isn't necessary." She turned, hitched a hip on the windowsill. "I know the way now."

"Perhaps not necessary, but it is proper courtesy." When she sighed, then nodded agreement, he smiled. "Victory is sweetest when it is rendered unnecessary."

"You know the Analects of Tannakés?"

"Tja. As does any proper soldier. How come you to know them, child?"

"I had a friend who was a warrior of Tannakés."

"Had?"

"He lives, but it's a long and complicated tale."

"Until this evening, then, fare you well, mila." He bowed with awkward grace and went out, a man with Panote's inner calm and unobtrusive self-respect, whole and serene despite his shortened leg and menial service.

She sighed and slid off the sill. "You want to sleep or come with me, Aili my Liki? Bath first, then I'm going to treat myself to a wander through those bookstores I saw this morning."

Chapter 3
The Night of the Dark Moon

1. At House Patikam

Forearms braced on the table, Desantro leaned into the lamplight, the glow waking a fugitive gold in the soft loose curls clustered close to her head. "The old man's eyes opened so wide he looked like a startled bull." She widened her eyes; across from her Zens giggled and Parraye wiggled her fingers, the tips brushing across the linen mat under her plate. "And he said to Irrawa the Free-walking, 'Wana, if you won't honor your mother's bargain and wed me, I want that dress back." Everyone around was going shame shame, dirty ol' miser, but she didn't hesitate one minute. She pulled off the dress and everything else down to the skin and went marching off."

Parraye's eyes rounded. "Everything?" she whispered.

"Every single stitch." Desantro looked each one in the eye with such portentious intent they knew something more was coming; she dragged the silence out a hair longer, then smiled and went on. "Now, you should know this, it's important. The

Kawan—that's governor of the Kan, what you call a fistal here—he had a habit of riding out by himself to discover what his people were getting up to. He saw the whole thing and took Irrawa the Free-walking up on his horse and carried her back to the Kan house where he married her to his eldest son, saying a woman of such fire and integrity was a prize beyond price." She straightened, winked at Zens and Parraye. "Our mama told us that story when your mama was just a tatling running after tree lizards."

Tariko chuckled. "Tja, it's true—as the storyteller says. Des, tell them a newer truth, tell them about the time you went looking for a Whaura girl and got caught in the net snare."

Desantro wrinkled her nose. "Raki told you that, didn't he. You were in the cradle still, so it had to be him." She grinned at Parraye. "Little brothers."

Parraye giggled in a whisper, eeped as Zens poked his thumb in her ribs.

"Hmm," Desantro said. "I was just nine. It was the night after the Whaura Dance, that's when we go out and tell the trees that we thank them for their wood, it was my first Dance and out in the dark past the torches, I saw a Whaura enough like me I could've been looking in a mirror...."

The oval table was dark wood waxed and polished until the glow from the three crystal and silver lamps in a line down the middle burned deep deep in the heart of it. Faan stopped listening; she'd heard those stories before. She sat silent between Desantro and Patikam, Ailiki a warm blot on her toes, the tines of her fork moving slowly through the greens on her plate, her appetite gone as memory overwhelmed her. Suppers at the Beehouse . . . Reyna . . . her family warm in the lampglow, Jea telling acerbic tales from his nursing rounds, Dawa capping them with impromptu rhymes, Areia One-eye listening with passion and intensity . . . she was the most active, obtrusive listener Faan had met—until now . . . young Parraye had the same kind of noisy silence. She was a pretty child, with fair skin and a tendency to blush a delicate rose when her deep contralto voice embarrassed her, which was why she mostly whispered or stayed silent; it was a siren's voice in the body of a child. Odd to think of her as a child, she was fourteen and only a little over two years younger than Faan, but she seemed so unformed. Her brother Zens was nine and a scrubbed up version of Lokit, as cheeky as he dared to be with his father's fond eye on him.

When Desantro's story was finished, Tariko stood. "Parraye, Zens, study time. Des, mila Faan, if you will join us in the library, we will be pleased to share converse and wine."

> > < <

A crackling fire burned in the firehole of a tile-stove that took up a good portion of one of the sides of the octagonal room; the tiles were glazed in dark blue and green with an occasional touch of maroon, diamond shapes in harlequin patterns. Stuffed leather chairs (the leather stained maroon to match the accents in the stove) were pulled in a loose circle about the hearth, small tables beside them with crystal lamps adding to the warm glow. Outside the circle of brightness paintings and tapestries on the walls added tatters of color as the firelight touched them then shifted away.

Patikam filled long stemmed crystal glasses with a wine the color of rubies and Tariko brought them to the guests, then took her own and settled in the chair closest to the stove on the left side. Patikam sat down opposite her. He lifted his glass in an unobtrusive salute, his eyes shining in the firelight. She answered in kind and they drank the first sip together.

Faan looked down at Ailiki curled in her lap, stroked the soft gray-brown fur as she fought down a sudden, intense envy. The mahsar purred and kneaded at her thighs as if to say you do have family, what else am I? Faan scratched behind the petal ears, then tasted the wine. It was heavier than she liked, but still smooth and subtle to the tongue, almost shouting its value. She wondered briefly why the man had wasted it on her and Desantro; they were unlikely to be of any use to him. She looked up. They were still smiling at each other, still sharing that moment of intimacy, so he might have done it as a tribute to his wife. She sipped again and suppressed a sigh at her unhappy cynicism. *Keep your hair on, girl. And don't drink too much of this stuff. You're getting dizzy already.*

Patikam shifted in his chair, turning to face her.

"My sister-a-likam tells us you are a sorcerer, mila Faan."

Thwup in the gizzard. That explains the wine. Too bad, I'd rather it was the other. "Not yet, O Patikam. I barely can consider myself a student."

"Sweet modesty. It well becomes you, mila. Yet, from the tale Desantro tells. . . ."

"Ah, that. What happened was god business and I got caught in it. I was no more than a brush in the hand of a painter."

"Even so. Dreits has informed us he took you to get a votaj. Did the guard advise you about Meggzatevoc's prohibitions?"

"What?"

"Nu, listen and take care, mila. Meggzatevoc is prickly about power wielded within Valdamaz; he has forbidden any Great Magic. He'd not wait for the authorities to act, he'd squash the offender himself whether the offense were inadvertent or meant. Even little magics should be contained and constrained; it's better for all if the god is not roused."

"I see. I do wish to continue my studies. That would be allowed?"

"If you find a teacher to accept you, that teacher will constrain you, so there should be no difficulty arising from your joint activities."

She gazed at him over the rim of her glass and her perspective abruptly shifted. He was a precise pedantic man, but kind, fond of his children, even fonder of his wife, a man who disliked having to give bad news or curtail the lives of others. That was the reason for the expensive wine and the fire and all the rest. He wanted her to feel accepted and understand what he said was meant for her good. Ashamed of her suspicions, she smiled at him, lowered the glass. "Teachers. Do you know of any who'd be willing to take a temporary pupil?"

"As far as I know, there's no sorcerer of any degree in Valdamaz. There is a Magus—of course, he doesn't practice his Art here. Meggzatevoc wouldn't allow that. He works as a smith outside the walls and seldom visits the city. Ahm . . . in these troubled times, I think you'd better not venture so far. My work . . . ahm . . . it has to do with trade goods and distribution, you see. Except for the Days of Honor, I have little to do with the Powers. The best I can tell you is to inquire at the Temple. They'll know there who's available and acceptable."

"You speak of troubled times. And we saw tabarded boys fighting in Ash Tirdza, yelling things. Has it anything to do with the death of the Augstadievon? The Gatekeeper's son told me about that when I asked why he wasn't in school." She tilted the glass, watched the wine swirl, then looked up suddenly to see Patikam exchange a worried glance with Tariko. *There is something brewing here, something he doesn't want to talk about, not with outsiders. Maybe Desa can find out what's going on.*

"Nu, the Campaign is on and the Caretaker is . . . ahm . . . preoccupied. If you see more dissension, mila Faan, walk away quickly. Foreigners can be a focus for ... ahm ... spiraling madness. It's best to avoid trouble."

Desantro chuckled suddenly. "You don't know what you're asking, O Patikam. Gods and riot gather round our Faan like bees round honey. That's what her family called her, Honeychild. She's a good child, though, she'll try her best."

"Desa!"

"Pai pai, Fa, you know I don't mean it bad, but these are my kin and they need to be ready." She winked and lifted her glass to her sister, then took a gulp of the wine. "Nu, my dears, with a little luck, we'll be going on in a month or so. If the Temple seers can tell us where we can find Rakil."

Tariko frowned. "I have asked, Des. Believe me, I have."

"Vema, T'rik, of course I do, but when it's Faan doing the asking we might get a different answer. Tungjii more or less promised that."

Faan sat up, ignoring Ailiki's growl and the prick of her claws. She glared at Desantro. "Desa, that's not exactly. . . ."

Desantro shrugged. "Close enough. O Patikam, T'rik says there's to be a street festival tomorrow. Something about the Dark Moon?"

He nodded. The wine had reddened his cheeks and brought a sheen of sweat to his brow; in the heat from the stove his short curly blond hair coiled free of the oil that had slicked it down and the shimmering gold halo gave an odd innocence to his face. Happy to abandon dour warnings, he leaned forward and began describing the treats ahead.

>><<

Faan patted a yawn, lifted Ailiki down and got to her feet. "It's late; I'd best be getting back to the inn."

Patikam set his glass on the table beside his chair and looked up at her. "Neka neka, mila. I assumed you meant to stay the night. I have been thoughtless, nu. There'll be Jahta bands out doing mischief everywhere and the guards will be busy in the Family Ashes with none left for Tirdza. It isn't safe for anyone, let alone a young girl."

Faan snapped her fingers. Pale blue flamelets danced on the tips. "Let them try their mischief on me, they'll get a bigger surprise than any Jah'takash fashions."

"Neka, mila. If you hurt one of those whelps, you could stir up things you can't control, or bring such trouble on yourself we'd have no way to help you."

"I'll do no harm unless I'm forced, but I will go where I want when I want." In her determination she leaned forward in the chair; Ailiki complained and leapt down. "I have sworn that," she said. "I will be a pawn no more."

"Then let me send Dreits with you."

"Neka, two are far more obvious than one, though I appreciate the thought. Listen, I'll just slide through the shadows. Unless they bump into me, most likely no one will even notice I'm there."

He sighed. "Megg keep you, mila. If you will, you will. Do go with care and take my blessing."

2. At the Akazal—Eve of the Dark Moon

Dressed in black velvet, black silk, black bro-
cade, their jewels few (a single gleaming ruby dangling from an ear or nestling on the pale hillocks
of a woman's breasts—or an emerald or a sapphire or a single immense diamond like a drop of
hardened water), masked in gold, the masks a delicate mix of feline and female (the face of
Jah'takash), the dancers clasped hands in circles
whose forms mutated continuously as they shifted
about the floor, curling about other circles, gliding and dipping, heads turning one way, then another, breast to breast at times, at times expanded
into a true round, silent always, eyes hidden in
the shadows of the mask, male and female alike,
only the music left to take and move them.

The eight-sided ballroom was all white marble
and three stories high, with mirrors in silver
frames on each wall, mirrors that reflected the
silver lamps beside each archway with its white
velvet curtains, that reflected each other in endless repetition, repetition interrupted by the black
dancers passing by. The lamps were filled with
scented oils; they burned very bright this night,
as did the chandeliers hanging from the distant
ceiling, silver and crystal, a thousand candles each.

The sable dancers glided in circles of four, five,
as many as eight, to swaying swooping music from
a six piece orchestra—three fiddles, a drum and
two horns—tucked away in a gallery halfway up
the eastern wall. The instruments were painted

white like the hands and faces of the white clad
players.

The Corypheus stood half black and half white
on a dais beneath the gallery, masked as Jah'takash,
gold and glittering with ruby glass for eyes. His
hidden eyes sweeping across the dancers and along
the walls, he signaled with the gold and ruby wand
in his left hand to his ghostly whips, white forms
who moved about breaking up groups of nondan-
cers, sending them out to make new circles in the
intricate, elegant dance.

> > < <

Pargats Varney eased back when his circle
neared the entrance to one of the supper rooms,
pulled together the hands he was holding so he
wouldn't break the circle, then, looking hastily
about for the faceless white form of a whip, whistling under his breath for luck when he didn't see
one, he edged past the white velvet curtains shutting off the arch.

He pulled off the mask, wiped at his face.
"Jauk!"

A chuckle. "You should expect it, Varney.
Here."

He swung around, relaxed as he saw Navarre
smiling at him, took the glass, drained it. "Kyatty
Trum, don't want any of it. Assuming you mean
what I mean by 'it.' " With a grimace, he looked
hastily about, but the room was empty except for
the Magus.

"Oh?" The embodiment of skepticism, Navarre

ambled back to the table, chose a meat roll from
the finger food piled on trays and bit into it.

Varney threw himself into a chair. "Bring me
something, Varre. Favor?" He grinned. "If you
choose it, maybe I'll survive the first swallow."

"Tsa." Navarre took a plate and began loading
it. "You'd hate it if you were elbowed from the
game, my friend."

"Hmp. It's come too soon. By five years! I'm not
ready for settling down. Megg rot that poisoning
launsid."

Navarre crossed the room, set the plate on the
table by the chair. "Here's your aizar. Nibble in
peace, little man." He dropped into Varney's lap
a mottled puce and lime colored sphere on a fine
silver chain, then returned to the table for more
of the sparkling wine.

"Kyaty Trum!" Varney caught hold of the chain
and lifted the sphere. "Most hideous pauksaladaza
I've ever seen."

"Hideous but effective. You need to wear it
against your skin, you know, so tuck it away, holy
Candidate."

"Away is right." Varney drew the chain over
his head, pushed the aizar stone down inside his
black velvet tunic. "Who did they circle you
with?"

Navarre raised a brow, filled his glass and returned the jar to the ice bucket. "They were all
masked," he said.

Varney scowled. "Tact with me?"

"Say rather, within these walls."

"Trum! I suppose you're right." He gloomed at the meat roll, popped it in his mouth. "Bring that bottle over here," he said, the words muffled by the food. "Megg's sancy Tail, I can't go through this sober."

"If word gets round you're a lush, that'll sink any chances you have of the prize."

"I know, I know, do y' think I've gone soft in the head? It's m' father. He's sniffing about for a bride. For me."

"I didn't think it'd be for him."

Varney snorted. "Not with Ma and Dilsy riding him tight. Catch me marrying two Daughters. One's bad enough." He bit down into another dumpling, grimaced, and set it aside. "Concubines you don't have to listen to." He took the refilled glass from Navarre, gulped down half of it, then sat brooding at the bubbles streaming up through the straw-colored liquid. "Trouble is, wives they even get to naysay a concubine. A man has to have peace in his house."

"Look on the bright side, my friend. If your throat's cut tomorrow, you won't have to face any of that."

"You're a big help." He reached for a napkin, scrubbed at his hands. "This paint is a nuisance. Why do we have to wear it?"

"Don't."

"Hah! And get pitched out?"

"Isn't that what you want?"

"Trum! You're pricklier than an ezis tonight." He sat up. "I ..."

The velvet curtains were swept aside and half a dozen young women came in giggling and chattering. They pulled their masks off, hung them over their wrists by the cords and swirled in a cloud of black velvet round Varney; one drifted over to Navarre, took a glass from him and stood sipping at wine that matched her pale gleaming hair.

A girl with velvet violet eyes perched on the arm of Varney's chair. "Recreant, running out on us. Shame." She combed her slim fingers through his hair, tugged at a lock, laughing as he yelped, her eyes heating as he caught her wrist and pulled her hand down.

A fair freckled girl stroked her finger along his face. "Are we so dull that you run for cover? Shame oh shame. Insult of the worst kind. What forfeit shall we make you pay?"

The other three leaned over him, teasing him, touching him with their fingertips, fluttery butterfly caresses they'd learned in their deportment classes.

> > < <

"You so seldom visit us, O Magus." She was young and lovely, hair gathered in a large loose knot at the base of her skull, a style not many could wear, but it suited her understated beauty. She gazed at him over the rim of her glass from grave gray-blue eyes.

"I must plead my studies, O Dinots Kaista."

"Ah. Study. Is it so much more enthralling than I?"

"How can I answer that, O Kaista? If I say yes, then I lie and insult you. If I say no, then I insult myself."

"Quibbling, O Magus? Jah'takash forbid. Pay forfeit and dance with me."

"It is my pleasure, O Kaista." He smiled at her, then turned and called, "Varney. A challenge. Come and dance."

A shadow passed over Dinots Kaista's face, then she dipped a graceful curtsy and pulled on her mask. She'd been playing with a domesticated sort of danger and was momentarily annoyed at him for sidestepping her snare, then she laughed and clapped her hands. "Come come, Rieka, Sassie, Janina, come all of you, we shall dance."

3. Ashes after dark

Navarre slipped away from the Celebration early and walked solitary between the army barracks in Ash Dievon. In the distance he could see the shifting red glows of the Jahta balefires and hear an occasional shriek as the Bands turned violent; it wasn't a good night for anyone to be out, even him. He'd come into Savvalis against will and inclination; Family Celebrations during Campaign time were boring and dangerous, a combination he had no taste for, but the Caretaker had sent to invite him, an invitation that differed from a command only in the wording.

There'd been eyes on him all evening. Made his skin itch. He wasn't afraid, merely annoyed. He disliked being overlooked. That was a pinprick, though, to what really worried him. Why did he have to be there? No one objected when he left, having done nothing but dance about and drink their bubbly wine. He'd delivered the aizar stone, but surely that was nothing the Caretaker would bother to notice. Why? Did Turet suspect he had a hand in the Augstadievon's death? It couldn't be a strong suspicion or he'd be in the cellars of the Akazal with a spidznal locking him down and heating up the irons.

He moved into Ash Tirdza and walked south along the wide street, heading for the inn where he'd booked a room, the noise of the Bands growing louder and more explicit though he hadn't run into any of them yet. Megg forfend he did! Many of the prowlers would be Family cousins and younger sons. Bad business if he had to hurt one of them. He pulled his cloak closer about his body, moved deeper into the thick shadows beside the buildings and hurried along the street, impatient to reach the inn where he could settle over a mug of hot cider and try to sort out the events of the night.

From a side street ahead he heard yells, curses, then the patter of running feet. Swearing under his breath he stepped into a doorway and pulled the cowl forward to hide the pallor of his face.

Long hair streaming, a shadowy insubstantial form ran toward him, the stink of magic strong on it. It? No, a girl with a cover of no-see-me pulled in tatters about her. A stranger, but his kind if not his kin.

He stepped out, caught her.

She fought him, surprising him with her strength. It was like trying to hold an angry python.

"Quiet." It was a whispered shout, enhanced. She went still. He wasn't the only one who could smell magic. "I'm a friend. I won't hurt you."

She snorted. "For sure you won't." Small blue flames danced along her arms, then were gone. "Or you're ash." A rather wobbly chuckle. "As in wood, not district."

"Stay behind me." He relaxed his grip, stepped into the street, sweeping back the cowl as he did so. The purpleshirts chasing the girl swerved, stopped.

One of them set his hands on his hips and glared at Navarre—Pargats Derigs, an unpleasant brat, one of Varney's cousins. "Not your business, O Magus. She's blessed to Jah'takash."

"Play your tricks on street drabs, Derigs. This one isn't your meat."

"Who says?"

"I do. You want to call me on it, take it up with the Civielarod in the morning. Fool with me and you won't see morning."

The tall blond youth stared at Navarre for several moments, then he shrugged and walked away. His satellites trailed after him, vanishing with him down a side street.

Navarre turned to the girl. "Kyatawat's five hundred hells, girl, what are you doing out alone after dark, especially this night?"

"Getting back to my room. Not looking for clients, if that's what you think."

"Didn't anyone warn you about the Dark Moon?"

"What's that to you?"

"What it is to any man with honor in him. Tell me."

"I was warned." She had a stubborn set to her face, a degree of wariness but no fear; her eyes were odd—even in the moonlight he could see they were different colors. "I chose to come away." Her mouth twisted. "I won't be led about by the nose. And I don't need your protection. So you can go wherever it is you were heading."

"No doubt you can," he said. "But if you'd singed one of those whelps, the least you'd earn yourself is a public scourging."

"I know," she said. "It's why I was running." She wrinkled her face in a comic grimace, clicked her tongue. "So you're right. And so I dip you this curtsy . . ." She held out phantom skirts and bent her knees. "And say patcha, O Magus."

"Imp. Where are you staying?"

"The Gul Bazelt on Jurra Way."

"I know it. Come along."

She walked beside him, now and then looking up at him. "I heard trouble ahead when I was coming along Tirdza Street, so I turned off into one of the side ways thinking I was going to go round it. And then ran right into that lot. They came sweeping round a corner and we bumped before I knew they were there. Wrecked the no-see. Potzheads."

"Them?"

"Nu. . . ."

He laughed. "What's your name, girl?"

"Faan Hasmara."

"I'm Navarre."

"I know."

"Nu, Sorcerie, are you coming to stay or just visiting?"

"Visiting. My friend and I, we just got here this morning. Her sister was a Vraga bride."

They turned into a winding side way. "I see," he said. "How far along in your studies are you? Have you found a Master?"

"You know I haven't or I wouldn't be running loose like this. How far? Baby steps." She glanced at him again. "I'm looking for a teacher. While I'm here. Not as an apprentice."

"There aren't many who'd take a student without bond."

"Ts! I've an aversion to bonds."

"I'll think on it and send word in a day or so." He stopped in front of the Inn. "Take a bit of well-meant advice this time, young Faan. Stay inside after dark. Especially during the Dark Moon."

She laid her hand briefly on his arm. "Unless there's reason not to, I will."

> > < <

In her room Faan kicked off her sandals and stretched out the bed. Ailiki leapt up and snuggled against her. "Well, Aili my Liki, what a night!" She chuckled, felt the mahsar's answering rumble against her ribs. "And what a man!"

CABAL

The woman pulled her robe close about her and turned slowly, her body eloquent of scorn as she looked over the catacombs. "Why do you insist on meeting in places like this?"

"It's my sense of what's fitting," the wide man said.

She heard the acrid humor in his voice, made an angular gesture with her muffled arm. "You! You mock us. Be careful, half-blood."

"It is the jester's right, dama. The dance on the edge of oblivion."

"Be thankful the others aren't here. They're misers when it comes to recognizing rights."

"As we both know. Or why would you be meeting me now?"

She moved her hidden hand in a sharp flat gesture, cutting off the argument. "That conceded, why am I here?"

"You have access to the Caretaker."

"To his bed."

"All men talk. Sooner or later."

"Babble."

69

"I trust your cleverness, dama."

"Ts!" She folded her arms across her breasts, her hands sliding into the opposite sleeves. *"He's sniffing after the Magus. He's set a Temple Diviner on him, a water skryer, an old woman. She's blocked from the smithy but anytime he leaves, she'll be feeling about after him."*

"There now. Was that difficult?"

"Ts! I hope this meeting yields more than that."

"A conspiracy is only as strong as the weakest link."

"O wisdom O platitude. Are you talking about me?"

"I'm not such a fool. No names, but you know who I mean. One is weak and needs careful herding, tja?"

Her cowl bobbed in the shadows as she nodded agreement.

"And one is clever, though not so clever as he thinks. And treacherous."

Again she nodded.

"We need them both—until the thing is done. You're a woman and I am . . . what I was born. Direct rule is out of the question. We can maneuver the one, the other will betray us with the same deftness as he betrayed Nestrats as soon as he has what he wants, tja?"

"Tja."

"I know what you're thinking, lovely one. Why do you need me?"

"I'm sure you'll tell me."

"We are indissolubly linked, dama. Destroy me and you ruin yourself."

"Blackmail or murder?"

"Neka neka, neither one. I have a . . . I won't say friend . . . an acquaintance who is bound to me. One who has certain abilities and a Demiurge to back him. If I fall. . . ."

"I die?"

"Certainly not. My mind is not so limited. If I fall— by whatever means, dama—you will wake the day after an old wrinkled woman with dropsy."

"Ahhhhhh."

"And don't think you can discover my acquaintance or counter the spell. The spinner is hidden, lovely one, the spell is spun already and only waits the trigger."

"You frighten me."

He chuckled. "No."

She shrugged, the felten folds brushing heavily together. "Nu, then. Is that all?"

"For the moment."

"The next meeting, make it a place without vermin."

"I'll think about it. Atvas, dama."

"Atvas, spider."

Chapter 4
The Day of the Dark Moon

The city was full of clamor and clashing cymbals when Faan woke on her second day in Savvalis. She yawned and stretched, filled with an inchoate sense of well-being, which she enjoyed for a moment without bothering where it came from, then her mind drifted back to the night before and the Magus. *Navarre.* She drew her hands up her body, cupped them over her breasts—then sighed and sat up. He was obviously unimpressed by her; when she said she needed a teacher, he turned it off with a gentle obduracy, an adult talking to a child.

"Tiesh tas, Aili my Liki," she said to the mahsar who was sunning herself on the window ledge. "I'll figure out some way to make him want me. Maybe I could ask Desantro how she does it. . . ." She frowned. Somehow that was a distasteful idea. "Are you hungry, my Liki? Let me wash and get dressed, then we'll go down and see what they've got in the eating parlor."

> > < <

Dreits was sitting on a bench in the lobby. He got to his feet when he saw her coming down the stairs.

"Virs Patikam and Sva Tariko sent me to discover if you got here safely," he told Faan when she stopped before him. "They wish you to know they respect your independence, but were worried about you."

"It is kind of them," she said with an equal formality, "but as you see, I'm fine." She rested her hand on his arm. "Come. Join me in the parlor for breakfast."

"It is not proper, mila. I'm a servant."

"Nu, that's absurd, Dreits. You're a citizen and I'm only a visitor, not even a trader, so you're most certainly ranked higher than me. Besides, I like to talk when I eat. Makes the food taste better."

He chuckled, shook his head, but followed her into the parlor and sat in the chair she pointed out.

"I have already eaten, mila."

"Then have a cup of tea, nu?"

> > < <

Faan sighed with pleasure, slipped her last piece of buttered bun to Ailiki, then let Dreits refill her tea mug. "The Celebration has started already?"

"With the dawn," he said. "This is nothing here, you should see the Family Ashes. And Ash Megg. Which reminds me. Before she slept, Sva Tariko consulted the Book of Omen for this day and determined that Sunhigh is the most propitious time to give a question to the Diviners. She asks you to meet her and the mila Desantro at the South Entrance to the Temple shortly before then. I'm to show you where, if you permit, mila."

> > < <

Ailiki running ahead of them, they followed a laughing shouting line of holy dancers with their drums and flutes and ribbons through the Gate into Ash Dievon. A short distance into the Ash, Dreits led Faan aside from the more traveled routes and they walked along a wide graveled path as much alone as if they were in a wilderness.

"Those tall buildings over there, behind the oaks," he said, "they're the army barracks, where they train the cadets and house the Augstadievon's army; you've seen some of the cadets, I hear, those youths with the tabards. The parade grounds are behind the buildings, you can't see them from here. The rest of the Ash is playground and parkland with ornamental waters and miscellaneous gongoozles."

"Huh?"

"Like that." He waved at a sculpture standing on a low plinth, a twisting, soaring fabulation of black iron and fieldstone.

"I love it," she said. "It's laughter made visible." She giggled as the little mahsar reached the top of the tall structure in a series of scrambling leaps, then launched herself for the ground, unfurling skin flaps between her wrists and ankles. She landed beside Faan, the flaps vanished, and she went lallopping off.

"Tja," he said. "This is one of the better ones. Some of the others are merely foolish and some are leaden attempts at whimsy that don't come off. The birds like them and children climb them, so I suppose they aren't wholly worthless."

"Leaden attempts at whimsy? I think you're an unusual servant, O Dreits. For an ex-soldier."

"Spedj-ne spedj-ja." He limped along in silence for several minutes, then he said, "I went as a soldier because there was nothing else I could do. I was the sixth of seven sons and my family couldn't afford to keep me on the cattle run. We weren't in favor with the local Kadrav so there wasn't a hope I could get preference to the Temple school. Then I was wounded in a border raid—I don't mean we were raiding, it was a dozen Tyrlan, horsemen from Eyaktyr they are—and when I was healed, I was lame, so the army didn't want me any more. I didn't feel like starving, so I took what work I could find. Virs Patikam is a kind man. I accompany Sva Tariko when she goes out, run her errands, take care of his library, buy books for him, tutor young Zens in arms and in return he gives me free time to study and four days a month to myself."

The winding, deserted path was graveled and shady, the noises of the Celebration were muted by distance and the trees around them, the sounds of water falling faded in and out as they passed several of the many fountains of the parkland.

Flowers perfumed the breeze and the sun was warm. Ailiki ambling beside her, brushing up against her now and then, soft fur like a kiss against her ankle, Faan slowed to a stroll. She liked Dreits and the day was lovely.

"I ran into the Magus last night," she said.

"Nu?"

"Mm. There was a bit of fuss with a Jahta band. He chased them off. You needn't mention that unless you feel you have to. I could have handled them." She grinned. "Fire in the face can discourage the most amorous and these were just boys."

"Bad boys."

"The Magus named the leader. Derigs, he said. A tall blond with a pocked face."

"Tsaaah! There are some born for hanging and that's one for sure. Tungjii kissed you, mila, bringing Navarre to drive him off."

Faan snorted, used the toe of her sandal to send a bit of gravel bouncing along ahead of them.

"It's the truth, mila. Derigs has a contempt for women. Fire or not, he'd have kept at you until you had to kill him, which I don't doubt you could do quite easily. Bad business, mila. Very bad."

"That's what the Magus said."

"Nu nu, you've got other work in the Temple this day, child. Burn some incense to Tungjii Luck. It's not good to neglect himmer when heesh looks your way."

"Tja tja, Papa!" She giggled, then glanced sideways at him. "Tell me about Navarre."

"What do you want to know?"

"Oh, all the gossip you have, the whispers that

everyone knows, the common folk I mean, ones like you and me."

"Common? You? Not a chance, mila."

"Common in the sense that they who run things mean it. I might have Talent, but by birth I'm a foundling. And you're sidestepping, old soldier, slip-slipping away. Tell me about Navarre."

He put out his hand and stopped her. "Why?"

"Shall we say the pitter-patter of a maiden heart? He's very much a man."

"Neka."

"Not a man?"

"Who's being evasive now?"

"Tiesh tas." She sighed, turned serious. "I need a teacher."

Dreits frowned at her. "Neka. I don't think so, mila. That would be a bad idea."

"Truly, old soldier, I do NEED a teacher. The Talent grows in me and unless I understand how to control it ... do you see?"

He looked round, limped off the path toward one of the fountains. "Come," he said, "let's sit a minute. We've plenty of time before you need to be at the Temple."

They sat on the rim of the fountain's basin with the water splashing down behind them, the sun warm on them, the light breeze blowing occasional fine sprays across their shoulders. Ailiki curled up on Faan's feet and dozed.

"Ask yourself," he said. "Why would a man of Power come to a place where such Power is forbid?"

Faan laced her fingers together, twisted her mouth.

"Labi labba, mila. He could be tired of being bothered, he could simply want to study a while and satisfy his needs by working with his hands. But he's been here twelve years now and shows never a sign of leaving."

"So?"

"You know better than I how Talent calls to a person. Ask yourself this, then. Would you let your gift lie fallow for over a decade?"

"My name is Faan, O Dreits. My friends call me Fa. Tell me."

"There's something wrong with his Talent. There was a sailor come in on a ship from some far place, the name changes every time the story's told and I've heard it a dozen times, they say he saw Navarre riding down Tirdza Street with Pargats Varney and said to another walking with him that Varney'd better watch it or the Wrystrike'd land him in ordure hot and steaming."

"Wrystrike?"

"It's a long tale and confused, but the gist is that when the Magus was young, he made an enemy and this enemy cursed him most cleverly. He can't control what happens when he works the Great Magics. The little are like finger exercises to him, he doesn't have to think what he's doing, it comes out right, he can put an edge on a knife that will slice a thought in half, his axes never rust or grow dull, his arrow points seem to smell out their targets, he puts hardness and lightness in his horseshoes so that a beast he's shod can race the wind.

His use to the Families and the army makes him welcome here, more so than most foreigners. And the Families know better than to ask for what he's unwilling to give. Meggzatevoc sees to that. So you can see, O Faan, he can't teach what you need to learn."

"If the stories are true."

"With that proviso, of course."

"Patcha, Dreits." She laughed and stretched. "Ahhhhh! I do feel better. He turned chilly as ice-breath when I talked of teaching. It wasn't me, it was him, it was him him him." Ailiki grumbled, got onto her four feet and stretched her body as Faan had, then sat up on her haunches and waited.

"Tja. The word is he's a cool man but a fair one."

She jumped to her feet, too exuberant to sit still any longer. "Come on, old soldier, show me the Temple, we'll both go pat Tungjii's belly and wish for Luck."

> > < <

They passed through the broad arch into the outer South Court of the Temple, two more in a congested crowd of Celebrants, crossing from the noise on the outside into an unbelievable cacophony inside the walls. Ailiki kept close to Faan, staying between her and Dreits so she wouldn't get stepped on.

There were bright pavilions of canvas backed up against the walls, striped in purple, gold and green, the colors of Jah'takash; in them were palm scanners and crystal skryers, yarrow casters and entrail readers, spell spinners and prayer writers—with long lines of people leading up to each, dressed in holiday clothes and holiday moods, courting couples holding hands and ambitious jereds seeking charms to help them rise in the civil service, shopkeepers and anyone else with an anxiety about the future, even some desperate gamblers.

There were ecstatic dancers who whirled in never ending spirals about and about the court, the Celebrants avoiding them with amiable unconcern, jugglers and fire eaters, acrobats and animal trainers working their beasts for the rain of coin from those who stood in the lines.

A minstrel sat cross-legged on the Singing Stone, his lute in his lap and his cap on the Alms ledge, playing whatever songs the onlookers were willing to pay for, making up rhymes when his repertoire failed.

Incense sellers sat at tables near the steps with their cylindrical vases of joss sticks, their perfumed candles guaranteed all wax, their baskets of phials with scented chrisms inside, their cruses of lamp oils.

Faan bought a phial of sandalwood essence to rub on Tungjii's belly and Dreits bought two sandalwood joss sticks. His face wrinkled in a grin as he limped up the steps with her. "To celebrate a new friend, O Fa," he said. "Should you feel the same, name me Ditton."

Ailiki trotting beside her, Faan danced backward up the broad stairs leading into the Temple, waving her hands and chanting, "Hail, O Ditton, friend of Fa." Her words were lost in the noise so only he heard them and her dance no stranger than the skipping of an ecstatic. No one noticed them and after a moment, this oppressed her though she didn't understand why. She quieted and waited for him to reach her.

The South Entrance to the God Chamber had wide shallow steps, fifteen of them, leading to a shadowed portico with immense columns supporting an entablature with a frieze of figures so ancient and weatherworn that all she could tell about them was that they seemed to be human forms. There were three double doors into the God Chamber, dark and gleaming with depressed squares a foot on a side like an oblong checkerboard, the lines between the squares raised like the walls about the Ashes; they stood open, thick as a man's body and heavy as stone.

She shivered as she passed into the twilight that filled the vast space beneath an immense dome, a twilight pierced by sunbeams slicing down from narrow irregular openings in the drum that supported the dome, hazy with drifts of smoke from the burning incense. The chamber was full of echoes, feet and coughing, the chants of a line of minor priests following a censer swung in wide arcs, the murmured prayers of seekers, nervous giggles from the scatter of children. It had a potent, holy feel, as if the gods had breathed in here and left the taint of their power behind.

The statues stared at her; in the flicker of the

votive lights set round their feet, their faces seemed to move, to frown, smile, sneer, muse.

Despite her entanglement with the gods of Zam Fadogurum, she'd never before been inside any Temple, let alone one so ancient and numinous as this one. She was antagonist to the Iron Father so had no reason to visit his House, and the Honey Mother's cathedrals were Groves of Sequba trees. When she was little, Panote the Doorkeeper told her all the tales and named them for her so she'd know them: the god paramount Perran-a-Perran; the god of bad jokes, surprises, shocks and frustration Jah'takash (the one honored this day); Tungjii Luck male and female and more ancient than all the others; the god of love and death Amortis; the god of the sea the Godalau; the god of fire and volcanos Slya Fireheart; the god of forests and mountains Geidranay; the god of childbirth and women's things Isayana; the god of storms and storm dragons the Gadajine; and last of all he of whom no one would speak more than his name, the Chained God Unchained.

They were all here, staring down at her from their great stone eyes. Even the little gods were here, clustered like mice on a stone table between two columns; she knew two of them—Sessa who finds lost things and Sulit who hoards secrets, the rest were strange, one or two very strange indeed.

"This way, Fa. Tungjii's always tucked away." Dreits limped toward the figure of the Godalau, reared high on her fishy tail. "As if heesh were a reproach to the others. As heesh might be, O Sorcerie; heesh has never been respectable." He chuckled. "Not in the sense that they who rule mean it, though you and I, I think, know better."

Tungjii's statue was small and ancient, carved from some dark and tight-grained wood, its breasts, belly and phallus smoother than glass from generations of rubs. It was crudely carved but caught a lot of hisser twinkle and more than a touch of cross-eyed whimsy.

Ailiki snorted, went to crouch in a corner of the alcove with her paws across her nose as Faan peeled away the wax from the mouth of the phial, poured a few drops in the palm of her hand. "Tungjii Luck," she crooned as she rubbed the oil into the wood, polishing the pudgy little god's belly and breasts, then hisser bald head and the wildly waving fringe of hair above hisser ears. "Kiss the Godalau for me and praise her saucy tail."

Beside her, Dreits lit his joss sticks from a candle flickering in a low round pot and thrust them into the sand basin between the little god's feet, then he handed Faan a wipe from the pile of white rags on the low table beside the pedestal.

A bell rang three times, the sound muffled by the weight of stone around them. Faan looked up. "Third watch?"

"Tja."

She rubbed the oil off her hands, dropped the rag in the basket behind the pedestal. Arm in arm, they bowed to Tungjii, then strolled through the God Chamber and out onto the portico, Ailiki darting ahead of them.

Dreits glanced at the sun. "There's a whole watch left. Fa, I'm a man of much curiosity and you are a fascination. Would you talk to me, tell me your history?" He pointed to the mahsar sitting on the bottom step, waiting for them. "And how you acquired that odd little creature."

"It's not all that interesting, but if you don't mind wasting an hour or two ... will you get in trouble being away this long? I don't want to lose you your place."

He shook his head and took her hand, leading her down the steps. "Virs Patikam made you my work this morning. And history of all kinds is my delight, strange events in stranger places. Nu nu, what's tedium to you is honeysong to my ears."

"Honey. Odd you should say that. Labi labba, it was like this. ..."

> > < <

Faan shifted on her boulder, brought her foot up, rested it on her knee. "And so here we are, Desantro and me, without a clue where we're bound." She waved a hand, a gesture meaning nothing except perhaps that she'd said all she could. Ailiki looked up from the flowers she was eating, then went back to chewing petals.

Dreits smoothed his hand over his hair, smiled at her. They sat in a pile of worn boulders with a stream curling past, one of the gongoozles in the parkland, another quiet place, the sounds of revelry coming muted to them. "It's sad I am to be saying it, young Fa, but you've no judgment when it comes to a tale. Not interesting? Tsa, child.

You've drunk Tungjii's magic wine and danced with gods."

Her mouth twisted into a brief smile. "Easier to tell it than to live it. Besides, it's finished. What we're after now is finding Desa's brother."

Dreits frowned at the grass where his feet rested, absently rubbing at the vertical line between his brows. "Books can tell secrets better than men some times," he said finally. "If you know how to look."

"Nu, Ditton, slavers don't write books or even care what names the meat they vend claims for itself."

"That's not what I mean. This is Meggzatevoc's Land, but the Kyatawat Powers sometimes slip through and seize a bit of it for themselves. I read in the Scholar Kaitek's *History of Oddities* that one of them, the Powers I mean, lives in a pool here in Ash Dievon. Its name is Qelqellalit and it answers questions according to its fancy, only once a person, so it's wise to think well what you ask it. And don't trust the answer too much; there'll be some truth in it, but more ambiguity."

"And you found that pool?"

"Tja."

"And you asked your question?"

"Tja."

"And the answer was helpful?"

"I'm still studying the implications of what I saw. There is enough unknown to last the rest of my life, so tja, Sorcerie, it was a very satisfactory answer." He got to his feet. "Do you wish to try the pool?"

"Why not?"

He turned, head up as if he were scenting the wind, then summoned her with a wave of his hand and started limping into the groves planted beside the boulders.

Pure white plum blossoms blew about them, peach trees bent over them with pale pink petals fluttering, new green leaves like scimitars mingling their acrid odors with the sweetness of the blooms. Almonds and cherries, persimmon and pomegranate and others whose names she didn't know had set their blooms and made a fugitive glory for them.

Ailiki keeping close to her for once, she followed Dreits, bemused by the laughter she felt in him, laughter at himself, at her, at everything serious and grim in the world. As if he'd found an inner peace after great turmoil. She'd met only one other with that kind of surety, Panote the Doorkeep, the Servant of Tannakés of Felhidd.

They crossed a path and moved into the darker world of fir and pine, cedar and redwood, into whispers and strong acrid odors; the ground was brown and springy with discarded needles, dotted with cones.

At last they reached the heart of the conifers, pushed through a wall of young firs to find a small round pool shaded by an immense deodar, dark water smooth as glass.

She waded through the resistant air and knelt beside the pool, Ailiki pressing close against her leg; she braced her hands on her thighs and leaned over it until she could see her face reflected. All the way here, she'd thought about her question, had finally chosen one she decided encompassed all the others. "How do I release my mother?" she murmured to the pool.

The water stirred, ripples spread out and out from the center, erasing her image; overhead the deodar whispered with the peculiar sibilance of conifers and its perfume fell in waves about her, pungent green essence. She felt again the numinous awe that had surprised her in the God Chamber ... something was happening, something. ...

The water cleared. In the pool she saw herself standing beside Navarre on the tor by Jal Virri, in his hand a blue jewel with a star at its heart, a jewel the size of his fist.

The ripples came again, spreading and spreading across the water, erasing the image and when the water settled, even her own reflection was gone.

Dreits' hand closed about her shoulder. She sighed and got to her feet, followed him back through the miniature forest and onto a graveled path, the mahsar, subdued, at her heels.

"Navarre," she said. "Did you see?"

"Neka, Fa."

"Navarre and a jewel. Tungjii said I'd find the help I need en passant in the hunt for Desantro's kin. Navarre comes with the sister. I suppose I'll find the jewel when I locate the brother. If the vision is true."

"There's truth of a kind, but Qelqellalit can also show what you want to see. So be careful, Fa."

"It's Navarre you're talking about." Ailiki

tugged at Faan's trousers, lifted a small black hand. Faan sighed, picked her up, and cuddled her in her arms.

Dreits glanced at the sky, grimaced. "Time runs oddly in there; we'd best hurry or you'll be late."

"But. . . ." She looked up. The sun was almost at zenith. What had seemed a few moments under the deodar must have been nearly an hour. "Let's go."

> > < <

Dreits bowed and limped back down the steps, leaving Faan to the sisters waiting for her.

"Atvai, atvai, Sva Tariko, I'm late, I know. Don't blame Dreits, he did his best." Faan set Ailiki down, spread her hands in mimed apology.

Tariko drew her hand back and forth in a cutting-off gesture. "Neka, mila, it's we who are early. I didn't want to miss you."

Behind her, Desantro winked at Faan, pressed her palms together, and rolled her eyes up.

Tariko jabbed her elbow backward, sniffed as she heard her sister grunt. "The Virs Patikam made an appointment for us this morning, so we'll be having a private reading." She turned, started across the portico. Over her shoulder, she said, "We go down a hall behind the Table of the Little Gods. It's the room where I went before to ask about Desantro and Rakil." Her voice dropped as she stepped into the charged twilight of the God Chamber. "It was a long time ago, just before Parraye was born."

>><<

The Divinatory was an eight-sided room, its walls faced with bronze squares a handspan on a side. Polished to a mirror gloss, they reflected in a golden haze everything else in the room including the other walls and the lamps on them, flames repeating endlessly, image upon image in infinite regression.

In the center of this room the Diviner sat at an eight-sided table, three stools aranged in a line across from her. She was an old woman, her face shadowed by the cowl of a black cloak that hid her form except for the delicate white hands that rested lightly on each side of a crystal bowl filled with water. Her hands showed her age, but they were beautiful despite that, long and slim with tapering fingers and almond shaped nails, the skin white and very soft, a web of fine wrinkles woven across the surface.

The acolyte lined Faan and the sisters in a row just inside the door, then went out.

"Who will speak?" The Diviner's voice was deep; it might almost have been a man speaking if her gender were not so obvious despite the cloak.

"I." Desantro took a step forward, stood with her hands folded at her waist.

"Whose answer is it?"

"Ours. We have the same need." She hesitated, looked around at Faan, then faced the Diviner once more. "Though perhaps different reasons behind the need."

"Two of you are sisters, that is writ in your faces. Who is this other?"

Ailiki clinging close to her, Faan took a step forward to stand beside Desantro. "My name is Faan Hasmara and I seek serendipity."

"And the beast? Never mind. I see. Come here, girl. Bring the stool on the end and sit here." She touched the table to the right of the bowl. When Faan had done this, she said, "Take my hand."

The room grew quiet and the stillness stretched on and on; when Faan started to speak, the Diviner's other hand came up, warning her to silence.

"Your lifeline is a tangle of knots beyond my strength, Sorcerie, but I feel that you've spoken truth. Neka. I must ask you to be still while I seek or you will drown me in your passions and burn away my vision. Hold yourself bound, Faan Hasmara. For my sake and your own." She turned to Desantro. "Speak the question."

Desantro closed her hands into fists. "We must know how to find our brother Rakil who was taken as slave with my sister and myself."

"That question was asked before, but circumstances have changed; perhaps this time ... seat yourselves, O sisters, and I will seek."

When they were settled on the stools, the Diviner drew in a long breath, let it out slowly, repeated this over and over until she was swaying steadily, her head bent over the bowl.

The water shimmered, like liquid diamond it shimmered. For an instant Faan saw from the side the image of Navarre holding the great sapphire with the star at its heart. It faded at once and she knew with certainty the Diviner had seen nothing.

The old woman began a mumbled chant that went on and on though no word of it was intelligible.

The water in the bowl rose in an eerie horripilation and crooked lines of silvery light ran through it.

The chant stopped, replaced by a repulsive lip-smacking and gargling, then even those noises terminated. The air in the room seemed to go rigid. Faan could hear herself breathe, a harsh, rasping sound, echoed by the sisters just enough off cadence to be irritating.

The Diviner's head drooped lower and lower until the edge of her cowl touched the bowl; her whole body twitched, she went rigid for a moment, then braced her hands flat on the table and pushed herself upright. After a moment she cleared her throat and spoke. "There is more than there was when you asked the first time, Pargamazev Sva Tarikam. Your brother Rakil lives and is well. He was a youth, is now a man. Sometime after Winter's End and before next Midsummer's Eve, two of you will greet him and take his hand. Where he is, I cannot tell. There is that which prevents me from seeing, I felt it before, it's stronger now. There are forces at work here far beyond my powers to unravel." She coughed, lifted the bowl, drank the water.

> > < <

As Tariko was passing the fee to the young acolyte, Faan looked back through the open door.

The Diviner was holding the bowl, her cowled head bent over it; after a moment she flung it away as if she could no longer bear the touch of it; Faan heard the crash as it hit the bronze wall and shattered.

Desantro laid her arm along Faan's shoulders, hugged her. "Labi labba, Fa. All we could do is try."

"And we know he is alive, at least there's that."

Desantro wrinkled her nose. "Tja. The rest of it. . . . " She shook her head. "I never much fooled with promises, they had a way of fading on me."

Still subdued and keeping close to Faan, Ailiki trotted with them as they followed Tariko through the God Chamber and down into the busy court, pushed through the crowd and plunged into Ash Dievon on the wide March Way that led directly to Ash Tirdza and Tirdza Street.

Masked, with ribbons in purple, green, and gold fluttering from their arms and legs, Jahta bands danced along the way, chinking tambourines, thrusting them into the faces of people heading for the Temple, chanting, "Pay the Lady, pay the Lady, pay for pleasure, stint for pain, pay the Lady, pay the Lady."

Mostly they got copper nidjes and interrupted their chant to squeal, "Nidj skittul, nidj skittul." Penny Miser, the words meant, mocking the grudging gift.

Flower makers twisted their circles of colored

paper into blooms and strung them in garlands, selling them to the questors and their children.

"There's a Celebration each Dark Moon," Tariko shouted to the others, raising her voice so she could be heard above the clamor.

The blind were everywhere—men, women, and children seated in groups on both sides of the road with begging bowls by their knees—singing wordless songs like the bird flocks they resembled in their bright robes. Coins were dropping with bright tinks in those bowls as the Celebrants moved past them.

"But each one's different some ways. This time its the Labdar of the Blind collecting, the next, it'll be the Labdar of Orphans, then the Labdar of the Lame, then the Labdar of old soldiers without family, each month something different." Tariko crossed to the side of the way and dropped a silver drusk into a bowl beside the knee of a sleepy child. When she got back to them, she said, "You must put something in at least one bowl. It's to avert Her notice, the Mischiefmaker, I mean."

> > < <

When they turned into Tirdza Street, Tariko walked ahead while Desantro stopped Faan and said, "We're meeting Yohaen Pok for tea, then he's going to show us his silks. Want to come, Fa?"

Faan was tempted; the beauty of the day, the holiday mood of the locals, and even the traders crowding here on Tirdza Street called her to play and forget for the moment, but she had things to think about, things to do. Filled with a sudden impatience at herself and everything around her, she shook her head. "Keep this to yourself, Desa, but I saw something in the water the Diviner missed."

"What?" Desantro caught hold of her shoulders. "Did it tell you. . . ."

"It wasn't like that." She touched Desantro's wrist and the woman dropped her arms, sighed.

"I was hoping," she said.

"I know. I don't want to talk about it, Desa. Not here. But it has to mean something, I'm going to try to find out what."

Desantro touched her cheek. "You're a good child, Fa. Come see me tomorrow, then. We can have some tea and talk. You're right, this isn't the place or the time."

> > < <

Faan stretched out on the bed, Ailiki a warm weight on her stomach. She reached down, scratched behind the mahsar's ears, smiled when she felt the vibrating purr. "Aili my Liki, I think we should get busy. You feel like a ride? They must rent horses or something somewhere in this Ash. Traders wouldn't bring their own, not on ships. Unless they were selling them, of course. According to what I've heard, the next country south is horse country, so that's not likely. Wonder how much it costs. Tsa! My Liki, my funds are melting like ice in the sun and I haven't a clue how to get more. No training, no backing, nothing. I'd worry if I didn't feel so lazy and comfortable. Nu, li'l friend, you're no help. You should be pricking me with your claws, making me get up and go to work." She sighed and sat up, laughing at the mahsar's grumble. "First a mirror, then a ride. I think."

Faan stood and looked around the room; it had a worn comfort to it, a long oval of braided rag rug beside a woodframe bed, a table, crisp white curtains at the window, a chair, a basin and ewer on the washstand. It was clean and dusted; when she checked she found her sheets had been changed. Dreits had done well for her. She smiled, shook her head. Well enough for living, but for practicing her Art? "Tiesh tas, Aili my Liki, it'll have to do. This isn't something I can play with out under a tree somewhere."

She dug through her bag, found the pearl the water elemental had given her, lowered herself and sat cross-legged, the pearl on the rug in front of her. Ailiki jumped from the bed and pressed up against her, warmth and vigor at hand if she needed it. She smiled, rubbed the mahsar's head, then focused on the pearl.

As she sank into the trance she needed to evoke the Mirror of Farseeing, she felt forces gathering around her and within. Frightened by the turbulence but stubborn, she brought forth the mirror between her hands and forced herself to visualize the great sapphire with the star at its heart. *Where!* she demanded, *where does this lie?*

Image of stones and water, small gold fishes

swimming past, sense of strong currents welling
up from the earth.

*Tiesh tas, so it's in a pool fed by a spring. Where
is this spring?*

Image of a lock. She'd seen that time after time
when she tried to compel the mirror to show her
Desantro's brother. Forces, the Diviner said,
forces at work here far beyond my powers to unravel. *Beyond me too, obviously.*

Labi labba, tell me this. She brought to mind
Navarre as she'd seen him in the torchlight the
night before. *Where?*

Image of a man in a leather apron, musclar arms
bare, sweat pasting his hair in wispy curls to his
neck, hammering out a lancehead; a small dark
man crouched in the shadows beside a basket of
charcoal.

*That's what I thought. So, how do I get there
from here?*

A map appeared in the mirror, a skeleton out-
line of the city with a pulsing dot toward the south
end of Ash Tirdza where the inn was. As she
watched, the dot extended itself into a line, following Tirdza Street to the Gate, through the Gate
into Ash Pargat, along Pargat Street until it
reached the outer wall; it hesitated there, apparently as an indication she might have difficulties
getting out of the city, then it went gliding swiftly
along the Mezh Highroad for about the width of
a finger, turned off the road and slid another fin-
gerwidth west to touch an outlined circle.

"Nu, I have it," she said aloud. She let the mirror fade and sighed with relief as the intrusion

faded with it. Ailiki stretched and yawned, went stalking off to plant herself beside the door.

"In a minute, Aili my Liki. If I'm going to ride, I'd better have my boots."

> > < <

Faan pulled herself awkwardly into the saddle, wriggled around trying to find a way to be comfortable; the mule's back felt wider than a table. The ostler had his fingers hooked through a bridle strap; he was watching her, a worried look on his lined and bony face.

She got her feet turned out and her knees settled. "You said he had a mild temper."

"Isna him I'm fussed about."

"I have ridden before, though 'twas a while back."

"Shouldda gone for a divric and a driver."

"My business is my own." That'd been her first choice, but it simply cost too much—though she wasn't about to tell him that. She sighed, leaned forward, and scratched along the mule's close-clipped mane. "That's a good mule." His ears twitched and he snorted, she hoped with pleasure. "Ahhh tja. What's his name?"

"Kiedro." The ostler stepped back as she lifted the reins from round the horn. "It's your bones, mila."

"Spedj-ne spedj-ja. I should be back before sundown. If I'm not, don't fuss yourself; it just means my business is taking longer than I expected. Hand me up Ailiki, the little beast there. She could jump up easily enough, but I don't want to spook Kiedro."

When Ailiki was settled, she tossed the hostler his saddlekod and dug her heels into the mule's flank.

> > < <

Riding more confidently as she passed out of Ash Tirdza, Faan risked a wave to Slegis the Pargat Gatekeeper and smiled with pleasure as the movement didn't throw her balance out.

Pargat Street was clotted with holiday makers, men dancing with men, women with women, groups talking at high volume so they'd be heard over the beat of the drums and tambourines, the sounds of flutes, horns, and other instruments. There were many more children than at the Temple or on Tirdza Street, children clustered about acrobats and fire eaters, prestidigitators and Jahta Fools.

The mule plodded placidly along, undisturbed even when a masked Jahta Fool raised a curly horn and blew a blast in his ear, a piece of malice that Faan ignored because she couldn't do anything about it; besides, a nearby black tabard (whom she knew now was called a civiel) laid rough hands on the Fool and marched him off.

There no more incidents; she let the mule handle the crowd which thinned as she got near the Outer Wall. The paved area around the Mezh Gate was deserted except for the civiels playing stones-and-bones in a three-sided hutch. The great double gate was standing open, but the way was blocked by a weighted bar.

They ignored her long enough to make sure she understood her place in the ladder of life, then one of them pushed his chair back and came out to stand frowning up at her, a clipboard in his hand and a red pointed pencil.

"Foreign?" he said.

"Tja."

He set down an x on a line by some printing she couldn't read. "Votaj?"

She slipped the thong over her neck and dropped the bronze square into his hand.

He wrote down the line of letters and numbers on it, then tossed it back. "How long you gonna be gone?"

"If nothing unexpected happens, I should be back by sundown," she said as she replaced the votaj. "I'm just going for a ride. It's a pleasant day and I haven't seen more of your land than these city streets."

He scratched at his cheek with the blunt end of the pencil. "You're sorta young to be riding round alone like this. It's dangerous out there."

She shrugged. "Nu, I won't be going far."

"I think I'd better have you sign this, mila. It's a waiver; once you pass this Gate you're on your own."

She shrugged and took the clipboard; after a minute's thought while she translated the sounds of her name into the local symbols, she wrote *Faan Hasmara has been warned and understands her responsibilities.*

When she passed it down, he glanced at it, nodded. "As long as you know," he said. He looked at her, then out along the Augstadievon's Highroad, then down at his clipboard. Eyes still on the form, he said, "Keep to the Highroad, mila. The straudjarod usually stay clear of that. And whatever you do, don't go anywhere near the Mezh. That's the forest. There're Devils in there who pay no mind to law or courtesy." He didn't wait for an answer, but marched over to the weight at the end of the bar, pushed down on it, and stood waiting for her to ride out.

> > < <

Hundreds of small houses clustered near the Wall, built on both sides of the road, growing outward ring by ring; like the Edge she'd grown up in, these were the fringe people, the shutouts who had no chance of a house in an Ash, foreigners, mixed bloods whose fathers refused to claim them, the disowned and discarded. At first she couldn't tell what the little low buildings were made of, but finally she decided it had to be chunks of sod; the walls had a furry look, green from the new grass that was let grow but clipped short; it was as if Spring itself were painting the houses. There were small, trim kitchen gardens by each house, and more often than not, flowering vines trained round the doors; the walkways were unpaved, but beaten hard, swept clean, with painted pebbles laid in lines along the edges. It seemed to her these Northern people were born neat and had more neatness hammered into them until it was like air they breathed.

The children had not yet reached such a high gloss; there were hundreds of them running in the dirt ways, playing on the roofs of the soddies, shouting, half-naked, dirty as children always get. Even so they didn't disturb the pebbles or trample the gardens. Some of them stopped their playing to stare at her, but they stayed in the shadow of the houses, shy as wild things.

> > < <

Beyond the soddies the grass began, grass as high as the mule Kiedro's shoulders, stretching in a silvery green to the eastern horizon.

The land to the west was completely different, as if the Highroad itself generated the change. She rode past small fields watered from communal wells, worked by men and older children; she assumed they came from the soddies. They didn't look up when she rode past, no holiday for these workers—unless they had their carnival last night.

Beyond the farms the Westland turned dry and barren, there was a tangle of scrub, a few tattered trees, and a lot of dead weeds. And she was the only living thing under the sun except for three raptors flying in long spirals so high overhead they were little more than black angles scrawled on the crystalline blue. She should have felt lonely and frightened; she'd never been so cut off before from other people. Instead, she was quietly happy, at one with earth and sky. The mule Kiedro plodded placidly along, head bobbing, ears twitching. Ailiki dozed, a warm spot against her stomach. *Odd,* she thought, *I don't need people; I wonder if it's because of my Talent, if my mother felt this, too?*

That took some of the warmth from the day, so she stopped thinking and simply let her senses flow.

> > < <

The mood lasted until she saw the turnoff and the walled smithy high on its hill, dark against the sky. "Nu, my Liki, there it is."

Hoofbeats sounded behind her.

She clutched at the mule's bobbed mane, looked over her shoulder.

Dark green cloak like wings behind him, hair gilded by the sun, a man rode a great black beast as if a demon chased him; he galloped past her, foam spattering her, turned the stallion into the Smithy Lane, slowing a little as he hit the steeper part of the rise.

"Labi labba, O mule, aren't you glad I'm not that fool?" She sighed. "He just about kills any welcome we might expect, my Liki. Nadets! Nu nu, we might as well try. Can't hurt, huh?"

Chapter 5
Winnowing the Candidates

1. The Councilroom in the Akazal

Though it wasn't constructed with comfort in mind, being hard, angular, and heavily carved, Pargats Varney lounged in one of the Candidate chairs set on the dais beside the Caretaker's Sedilis. He yawned, made a gesture at covering his mouth; he was annoyed and bored. Three of the Caretaker's sardzin had rousted him from his bed before noon and barely waited for him to dress before hustling him here. The sardzin were a nasty combination of bodyguard and secret police; even members of the Seven Families jumped when they said jump.

A few moments after he settled himself, the Council of the Lielskadravs came trickling in, Nestrats Pasak (nephew to the Caretaker, though that hadn't saved him from being routed out of bed like the rest of them), Ledus Cikston, Kreisits Kasero, Vocats Jelum, Dinots Arpouz, Tupelis Crensat—and coming in last, fuming all the way, face turning purple with suppressed rage when he saw his son, Varney's father, Pargats Vicanal. They took their seats around the table in the great carved chairs of the Grand Council, their jered secretaries on stools beside them.

The heirs came in with them, dropping into the sedils reserved for them behind the low rail that separated visitors from the officials. Varney grimaced as he saw his brother amble through the door, looking amiable and elsewhere. That was a pose Velams liked to put on; it'd stopped fooling Varney before he'd hit puberty. Velams got what he wanted when he wanted it. He made it seem like things just happened that way, but Varney'd seen the strings up close, had felt them jerking him about. These days, as soon as he decided what it was Velams wanted, he got out of the way fast.

The other Candidates dribbled in with the heirs, most of them looking as cranky as he felt. He knew all of them, though none were friends.

Ledus Druz was a splendid male, handsome as a god, intelligent only in narrow spots, with a great mane of gold hair and a trim tight beard; he was an army man, capable and liked by his men, but blunt and disastrously outspoken. If his scowl was any measure of his intentions, this meeting was going to turn into a rout.

Kreisits Begarz was also an officer in the army, but he'd never bothered to join the men he nominally commanded, sending instead a younger half brother—for which Varney had heard his men giving fervent thanks when he'd run across them the few times they were called to Savvalis.

Dinots Laro was a historian, a cold man with few friends. He was tall and thin, with blue shadows under his eyes and a mouth that continually drooped open as if there were something wrong with the muscles round it. His breath was sour and his fingers stained with ink; there were stories about him on his off hours, unpleasant stories that Varney preferred to ignore.

Tupelis Steidz was the last one in; his hands were shaking and his face a ruin. If he'd gotten any sleep last night, it hadn't done much for him. He was a gambler like his father, his debts reported to be awesome; as Tupelis Crensat's second son, he was a Candidate, but no one with a brain in his head would vote for him.

There was a buzz of talk, the scrapes and whispers of nervous shiftings, but no one ventured to complain aloud at the summons.

Varney leaned forward and glanced down the line of Candidates. One of the chairs was still empty. Was that why the Caretaker wasn't here either, was he waiting for the last man to show up?

It was Vocats Apsis who was missing. He was a quiet man, intelligent and amiable, interested in magic not so much as a form of power but as a system of logic. He was Vocats Jelum's third son, not his second, his place in the list a result of his mother's ambition. Jelum had lost his first two wives; one drowned herself in the river Dzelskri, the other had succumbed to a mysterious and incurable illness. Vocatssev Tupelis Lysann, Apsis' mother, was Jelum's third wife and she was as clever as she was ambitious, with a smothering consuming love for her only son. Jelum was an ancient monster who'd ground down his elder sons into pale nonentities; he got on better with his bastards—he had thirteen living at last count, aged three to fifty. Since he couldn't prefer them over his legitimate sons, he'd let Lysann talk him into favoring Apsis.

The double doors into the Council Chamber crashed open and Caretaker Nestrats Turet came stalking in, behind him half a dozen sardzin grouped around a rolling table, its wheels rumbling and squeaking as they pushed it across the parquet floor.

Varney leaned forward as Nestrats Turet strode toward the dais; he put his hand to his face, rubbing his forefinger along his cheekbone, concealing his expression without making a point of it; the old vulture was as observant as he was obsessed—the scowl on his face and the flaring of his nostrils meant something else had happened to stir him up.

The Caretaker stopped beside the steps to the dais, crooked his finger at the sardzin. When the table was brought up to him, he set his hand on the pall covering it, jerked the black cloth from the body. "As you see," he said, his harsh voice overriding the gasps and oaths from the Lielskadravs, "the poisoner has been busy, though he's changed his weapon."

Vocats Apsis lay on the table, his head crushed in above his ear. Varney flared his nostrils with distaste; Apsis deserved better even in death.

Turet folded his arms across his chest, ran hot

blue eyes over everyone in the room before he spoke. "I brought this corpse here as a warning. And a promise. Watch your backs, O Candidates." He smiled, a small tight twitch of the lips. "Or rather, as a warning to all but one of you. Someone has been clever, or has a clever friend. I have had the Diviners read the death of Apsis. There was a cloud; they saw him enter it; when it faded, his head was smashed in. I will discover you, O murderer, in the end I will have you. And I will hang you with my own hands because you killed my brother." He swung round and stalked out, the sardzin following, leaving Apsis' body uncovered on the improvised bier.

Old Jelum pushed back his chair and walked around the table to his son. He stared down at the body for a long minute, then shrugged. "Fool," he said. "I suppose it'll have to be Oirs after all."

> > < <

The Council broke up in a flurry of shouting and crossed accusations.

Velams sauntered over to Varney as he headed for the doors. "You're reckless enough to worry me, Vay." He put his hand on his brother's arm as he walked beside him. "It would be ... pleasant ... having an Augstadievon in the Family. A corpse, no."

Varney looked hastily around; they were alone in the hall for the moment. "Won't be by poison, the Magus gave me an aizar stone."

Velams smiled, but his eyes still had a guarded look. "Nu, brother, we've just seen that our busy little slepka doesn't constrain himself to one means. Watch your back and sleep alone."

Varney blinked, startled. "A woman?"

"A tool, Vay. You heard the old vulture. Slepka has a friend with a slippery magic, by which I mean he gets round Megg, and he's picking off the likeliest first which points to you, Druz, or Begarz as his next target." His hand tightened on Varney's arm. "Believe it or not, I'm fond of you, brother. I would be most annoyed if you got yourself killed."

2. The Smithy

Pargats Varney slid off his steaming mount. "Navarre, we've got to talk."

Hammer tap-tapping with a powerful delicacy, the Magus continued putting the finishing touches on a leaf-shaped blade, a lance point for the Forest Devil squatting in the shadows. He thrust the point into the fire again, pumped the bellows with his foot. Without turning, he said, "Take care of your horse, virs. We'll talk when I've finished this, not before."

Varney glared at the broad back. *Again,* he thought, *again he makes me wait on one of them.* He pushed his anger down and led Permakon to the stable. He needed the Magus too much to let Navarre's mannerisms drive him away.

He was as sweaty as Permakon, so he pulled off

his cloak and his shirt, tossed them over the edge of the stall and began rubbing down the stallion with a handful of soft rags and a brush, enjoying the play of his muscles and the smell of horse that was all around him, horse and wood, earth and clean straw, uncomplicated things that were what they were with no betrayal in them. "Eh eh, throw up the mask," he sang in a pleasant tenor; he had a good voice and he knew it, he liked to hear himself sing.

Eh eh, throw up the mask
Moaning is for misery
My love's as fair as morn
Eh eh, she's kind to me

He paused to catch his breath, heard the scrape of hooves and a small gasp, and looked up.

A girl stood in the stable door. She was slender with skin like dark cream, flawless and glowing from the wind, hair falling past her shoulders in a black silk waterfall—and her eyes were a wonder, one emerald, the other sapphire.

He preened as he saw those strange eyes widen and grow dark; it had happened before, one of the gifts the gods had given him, girls seeing him and tumbling into love with him. It was a magic thing, this melting stir in the loins, but it never lasted; one had to catch it on the wing, enjoy it till it faded, and bid it farewell without regret.

Over her shoulder he saw the long, lugubrious face of a mule, the twitchy ears, mumbling lips, and remembered the rider he'd passed on the

Mezh Road. He'd barely noted her. How strange. "Sveik," he said, "mila fair."

"You're not Navarre." Her voice was deeper than that of most of the women he know; it sounded older than she looked.

"Neka, that I'm not. I'm Varney. Pargats Varney. A friend of his."

"Ah." She grasped the mule's bridle and brought him into the stable. "Where should I put Kiedro?"

"The mule? Any of the empty stalls should be all right. Does Navarre expect you?"

"I don't think so. Could you help me with this? I don't know much about saddles and such."

He patted Permakon on the hindquarters and went to help the girl strip the gear off the mule and fetch grain for him. As he worked, he said, "You've come to ask him a question? Or to have him forge something for you?"

A small beast had followed the mule in and was nosing about the stable. It trotted back to her and sat on her feet as her face went blank, then bland, the smile that remained a gesture only. "That's for the Magus," she said. "Patcha for your help, virs."

It made him like her more that she didn't try to please him, despite her blushes and her charged awareness of him; she wasn't just a pretty girl, there was character in her. "Atvai, atvai, you're right, I'm wrong. Wait for me. I'll take you to him when I've got my shirt on."

She gazed at him gravely, then looked down at the beast by her feet. "Well, Aili my Liki," she said, "shall I?"

The beast got to its feet and went trotting out, its longer hind legs giving it a comic gait.

"I'll wait outside," she said. When she reached the doorway, she looked over her shoulder. "My name is Faan. Faan Hasmara."

> > < <

Navarre banked the coals in the firepot, stripped off his leather apron, and wiped his hands on the rag Kitya set out for him each day. He grimaced as he thought of Varney waiting for him with some new urgency and cursed under his breath his own inability to exist without the complications of acquaintance. He'd enjoyed the insulated delicate contact with the Families his friendship with Varney brought him, where nothing was asked of him but his presence, where pretty daughters flirted harmlessly with him and the food was good. *Pay the piper, Magus; you've danced and dined, now you have to work off the debt. Tsa! It's beginning to look very much like I'll have to be moving on.* He leaned against the corner post, scratched his back against it like a black bear, and like the bear his temper was soured by the pressure of need.

He pulled the skewers from his braid and let it fall, shook himself, and started for the stable.

When he rounded the corner he stopped, compressed his mouth. It was the girl from last night, the little Sorcerie, come, no doubt, to tease him

into teaching her. He hadn't read her as being like
that, but it was perhaps too long since he'd dealt
with a woman of power. Not that she was a
woman yet. Probably still virgin. Virgins bored
him. Ignorance bored him.

Varney came from the stable, whistling as he
fastened his shirt. "Magus," he said and his eyes
slid to the girl; they had a heavy lidded, stallion
look Navarre had seen there before. Varney
grinned at him, almost prancing.

The girl turned pink and looked uncomfortable.
He watched her a moment, felt a touch of sadness
as he saw what had happened. Another victim to
Varney's blue eyes. He lost some of his irritation
at her.

"The two of you go up to the house. Kitya will
take care of you; she's getting tea ready. You know
the way, Varney."

> > < <

Clean and pleasantly tired, wearing a close-
fitting robe of fine black wool, Navarre stepped
into his sitting room and stopped just inside the
door.

Varney and Faan were seated by the fire, the
tea table between them. Her face flushed, her eyes
shining, the girl held her cup in both hands, using
it like a soldier's shield between her and Varney.
He was leaning toward her, teasing her with his
eyes and his smile.

She's really quite lovely, Navarre thought, *and*

*shy as a wild thing under that precarious compo-
sure.* His mouth twitched. She'd forgotten him fast
the moment she saw Varney. Good thing he wasn't
interested in her. His self-conceit would have
taken a kick where it hurt.

Neither of them noticed him until he crossed
the room and reached for the teapot; his mouth
twitched again when he saw the start that almost
dumped Faan's tea in her lap. He took his cup to
his chair, lowered himself into it. "You wanted to
talk to me, Varney?"

Faan set the cup down and got to her feet. "If
you could tell me where to wait?"

Varney laughed. "Neka neka, Faan Hasmara.
This will be public gossip soon enough." He
shifted in his chair to face Navarre. "The poisoner
was busy last night. Vocats Apsis had his head
smashed. Civiels picked him up, dead as a rock."

"Nu nu, it was Dark Moon. Jahta bands get
above themselves now and then. How do you
know it's not just something that happened?"

"Old vulture Turet, he put the Temple Diviners
on it. If it was Jahta, the head-banger would be in
a cell waiting to hang. Neka, Magus. The killer
blew smoke and walked. What I wanted to ask,
will you look and see if you can pick up something the Diviners missed?"

Navarre sipped his tea and frowned at the fire.
He was being pushed to the edge of what was
possible for him and he didn't like it. "I'll think
about it," he said. He turned to Faan, his irritation
stirred up again. "I told you I'd send you the

names you wanted. When I say I'll do something, I do it."

"Neka, that's not it, that's not why I came."

Before she could say any more, Varney got to his feet. "My turn," he said. "I'll go talk with Kitya."

She smiled, her bicolored eyes gleaming. "And my turn to say don't be silly. There's none of this particularly secret." She turned serious. "When my companion, her name's Desantro, when she was still quite young, Hennerman raiders killed her family except for her, a brother and a sister, sold the three of them as slaves. Events that brought Desantro and me together, um ... things worked out so she was set free with, um, compensation, and we've been looking since for her brother and her sister." She wove her fingers together, stared down at them. "Tungjii promised I'd get what I want, which doesn't come into this, by helping Desantro."

Varney leaned forward, startled. "Tungjii?"

She lifted her head, her face gone soft and yearning, her eyes shining at him. For a moment she said nothing, then she nodded. "It was in the Myk'tat Tukery. The Godalau came swimming past with Tungjii riding her shoulder. Heesh tossed me hisser wineskin and I drank and the day turned golden. And heesh said to me, 'You'll find help, Honeychild, as you pass along the path of discovery.' "

Navarre cleared his throat. She swung round to face him, eyes wide, the bones in her face more visible as the skin tightened over them. "How did you find the sister?" he said. "Was it Tungjii told you?"

Her tongue flicked across her lower lip. "Neka. A Mirror. It wouldn't show me the brother, only the sister."

"Why?"

"I don't know. It might be some god messing me about again. I don't want to talk about that."

"I see. Why me?"

"Do you know Qelqellalit's Pool?"

"I've heard of it. How did you come across that? It seems rather obscure information for someone who's been here only a day or two?"

"That's not important. I asked my question and the answer was you."

"What?"

"Nu, it was a little more than you, of course. I was told that the pool is not exactly reliable, all in all, that it tells the truth with a twist. So I don't know if it's you or the jewel that's important."

"Jewel?" He scratched at his jaw, irritated again. She was dribbling out information in between glances at Varney, her attention obviously not on what she was saying. "You've had some training, Faan. Give me the data clearly and concisely and let me do the interpretation."

Her eyes narrowed and her lips thinned as she bit back an angry answer.

Good, he thought, *get her mind out of her crotch.*

In a few crisp words she told him what she'd

seen in the pool, then later in the Diviner's bowl.

"A sapphire with a star in its heart," he said. "Big as a man's fist. Massulit. It has to be." He set his cup down. "What else did you do?"

Her bicolored eyes had a bite to them; her mouth widened briefly into an involuntary smile. He would swear she was enjoying herself more sparring with him than blushing at Varney. "I went back to my room," she said, "and cast a mirror. The Jewel is in a pond somewhere, a pond with goldfish and fed by a spring. I asked where the pond was, but it wouldn't tell me. I tried once again to find out where Rakil was, that's the brother, but it wouldn't tell me that either. I got nervous and dissolved the mirror. I decided you might know something about it. It seems you do. So what is it and where is it?"

"Massulit," he murmured, stroked his forefinger along his jaw. "I would have thought you'd studied the Talismans by now."

"Never mind what I have or haven't studied."

He smiled at her. "It's a stone of power, one of the Great Talismans. Some years ago, before I came here, I heard rumors that they were moving. They do that, you know. They lay dormant for years, even centuries, then they get restless. I have no idea where Massulit is now. But I don't think you need bother hunting it, Massulit seems to be reaching for you. You'll find it when it feels the time is right." He frowned. "You said you got nervous. Tell me about that."

Her eyes slipped around to Varney, then she

shook herself and sat gazing down at her hands. "It was like a boiling, inside and out. My face was getting hot."

"Tja." He tapped his fingers on the chair arm. Ignorance, it always came down to that. "You were tempting disaster when you cast the mirror, Sorcerie. Do you understand how close you came to death?"

"I was warned about trying any Great Magic, but I don't know any. A mirror is only a little thing, it's one of the first things I learned."

"How old were you?"

She rubbed thumb against thumb, frowning as she considered the question. "I was eight ... nearly nine ... when I started lessons with the Sibyl, I cast my first mirror when I was ... eleven, tja, eleven. It was a hot day about a week before Midsummer's Eve. I watched Reyna going about his rounds. . . ." Her face was somber, her eyelids lowered; it wasn't a happy memory. She cleared her throat, looked up, eyes narrowed. "Why?"

"It isn't usual to teach that to one so young."

"The circumstances were far from usual. I don't want to talk about that time."

"This isn't merely curiosity, Faan."

She gazed at him gravely, nodded. "Labi labba, I accept that. Ask. I'll answer as I choose."

He laughed, he couldn't help it. She wasn't giving an inch more than she had to. "Tell me your pedigree, who was your father, your mother?"

"I was stolen from my mother when I was three. My father I know absolutely nothing about, nei-

ther name nor face." Her hands were twisted together now, the knuckles white. "For a long time
the Sibyl was forbidden to tell me anything, but
the day I left her, she said this, your mother's
name is Kori Piyolss; she is apprenticed to the
Sorceror Settsimaksimin."

"You went to find her?"

"I don't think you need to know that."

"Tja, that was mere curiosity." He got to his
feet. "Come here."

She stood and came toward him with the awkward grace of her youth. He took her right hand
in his left, set his right hand on her brow and
closed his eyes. "Nu nu," he murmured, "the Talent grows in you, it burns my hand. This is a bad
place for you, Sorcerie. I tell you it would be better if you left. I swear to you, I will do what I can
to locate Massulit and I will send to you all I discover." She moved under his hand, not trying to
break free of him, more a negation of what he was
telling her. "Neka, child, listen to me. You are in
danger if you stay in Meggzatevoc's Land. What's
developing in you will be a challenge to the god
and he deals very suddenly and thoroughly with
challenges." He took his hand down, stepped back
from her. "And I can't protect you. Do you understand." She looked away from him, the blood hot
in her cheeks. "I see you do. You seem adept at
collecting obscure information." He twisted his
mouth into a wry grimace. "Listen to me, Faan.
Ride north and wait for your friend in Kyatawat.
Not far in, Kyatawat has its own dangers. As long

as you're past the border and out of Meggzatevoc's Land, that's all you need."

She shifted uneasily. "Nu nu, I hear you, Magus. There's a problem, though. I have almost no
money, I couldn't possibly afford transport or a
guide. Not to mention supplies."

"How old are you?"

"What has that to do with anything?" Once
again she was unable to keep herself from glancing at Varney who was lounging in his chair, listening with visible fascination to these exchanges;
she seemed desperately distracted by her awareness of him, only intermittently able to concentrate on what Navarre was saying.

"Just tell me."

She shrugged. "Seventeen."

"When did your lessons stop?"

"I didn't say they did."

"When?"

"When I was fifteen."

"I assume someone took care of you when you
were growing up."

"I don't want to talk about that," she said flatly;
her odd eyes darkened, then dropped away from
his.

Ordinarily he'd have given up by now, let her
go her way; what happened to her would happen
and so be it. He didn't want her, he didn't like
her, but there something about her that reached
past his defenses and demanded he take care of
her. He didn't like that either, but he gave in to
it because he had to. "Labi labba, child. As a pro-

fessional courtesy, I'll lend you enough to keep
you comfortable and provide a divric and a driver
to take you to Kyatawat. Sit down, please." He
waited until she was back in the chair, sitting
stiffly on the edge of the seat, her hands knotted
together. She was a proud creature, that was obvious; she resented having to take from him, a
stranger. She was also intelligent, so she didn't
refuse. "You have to return to the city. I'll
send. . . ."

"Never mind that, Navarre." Varney sat up. "I'll
ride back with you, Faan." He gave her a wide
shining smile, his eyes half closed and gleaming.
"You shouldn't be on the road alone this close to
night."

For a moment Navarre found himself forgotten
as the two of them gazed at each other; he cleared
his throat. Faan blushed and turned back to him.
"You'll want time to talk to your companion," he
said, tactfully ignoring the silent exchange between her and Varney. "And time to get ready to
travel. I'll arrange for the divric and driver to ar-
rive at sunhigh; that should get you across the
northern border shortly after sundown. If you
have questions about anything, we can talk by
mirror once you're in Kyatawat. Is there anything
more you'll need?"

"Neka, you've been very generous." She got to
her feet. "Patcha, Magus." Her mouth curled into
a tight smile. "It would be nice to have a calm
and uncomplicated life like ordinary people."

Navarre chuckled. "You'd be very bored, child.
Very bored."

He watched her leave, wondering what it was about her that was so compelling it could reach past barriers he'd spent years erecting between himself and the importunate world.

In the doorway, Varney turned, lifted a brow. "I'll see you tomorrow, Navarre. Late tomorrow."

3. On the Highroad

Varney leaned over to Faan as they rode through the gate. "The north border's not all that far from Savvalis, would you mind a visitor, mila fair?"

She laughed breathlessly, shook her head. "My pleasure, virs."

"Mine," he said and laughed with her.

After that, they rode without speaking until they reached the flat with its scraggly bushes and clumps of dead grass, then he brought his mount closer, touched her arm. "Are you really so adamant about your history, Faan Hasmara?"

She tilted her head and looked at him from the corner of her eye; it was such innocent and unpracticed flirtation that he was enchanted. "Why?" she said.

"Because you interest me. Why else?"

"It's just a lot of people doing terrible things to each other. I. . . ." Her eyes widened, she raised a hand, then went limp and slid off the mule.

Varney started as he felt a sharp prick in his cheek; he ignored it and reached for her—and a weighted rope coiled round his neck. He was off-balance and it only took a single tug to send him

tumbling to the ground; he caught a glimpse of
dark faces hanging over him, then there was another more solid pain in his head and he dropped
into darkness trying to curse the Forest Devils
who'd taken him and killed her. Poison dart ...
the aizar stone ... damn their souls to Kyatawat's
five-hundredth hell!

Chapter 6
Honey in the Hole

Varney surfaced with a groan. It was night, chill and quiet, though somewhere nearby there was a fire that gave enough light to show him part of a tree trunk a few paces off. His head throbbed and his body ached as if he'd been whipped. He tried to lift his hand. He couldn't. Ropes around his wrists, his ankles. Trum! Forest Devils ... someone got to them ... poisoner ... blesséd day I got that stone ... Faan ... Kyatty trum!

A root was digging painfully into his back. Branches from some spindly bushes hung over him. They were between him and the fire. He wriggled around, lifted his head as he bumped into something soft.

Faan was lying on her back with her hands folded across her ribs; her thumbs were tied together with a fine black thread which looked like her hair; her feet were bare, her big toes were tied together also, the same fine thread, or hair, or whatever it was. At first he thought she was dead, the bindings some sort of Forest Devil magic meant to confine her ghost, then he saw the slow lift of her shirt. She was breathing. It was supposed to be poison the Devils put on their darts. Fatal in a breath. Nu nu, she certainly was special. Even got to Navarre, had him throwing money around when he hadn't a hope of tupping her. Or maybe the wish. Old man, old. . . . He peered into the shadow under the trees. The little beast was gone, what happened to it? For that matter, what *was* it? Witches were supposed to have familiars, demons that ran about in beast form . . . she wasn't a witch . . . at least Navarre hadn't called her witch . . . he called her "sorcerie" . . . whatever that meant. He rolled away from the girl, wriggled around until he could see past the bush.

There was open space beyond, where a tree had fallen and rotted away; the moon was up, directly above the clearing, a sliver still, but wider than he expected. Trum! Two days gone. At least that.

A small stream cut across the grass and scrub, circling round a boulder like a giant cowpat, a bulging, flattened mass of light colored stone with a slight dip on top. Two Forest Devils squatted in the sway, a meager fire between them, an old man and a boy holding a drum on his knees. They weren't talking or doing anything, just waiting.

He was only tied at wrists and ankles; if he could get his hands loose. . . . He glanced at Faan again, dismissed her with a shrug. She boasted she could take care of herself, looked like she'd have to. He flexed his wrists, testing the ropes, but the Devils knew their knots, no joy there; he began contorting himself as quietly as he could to bring his arms around to the front so he could get at the bindings with his teeth.

Each time he put pressure on them, the coils of rope tightened until they were biting painfully into his flesh—and there was something wrong with his elbows; he couldn't move them out from his body.

"Well?"

The word was whispered, but carried clearly to him. He stopped struggling and stretched his neck so he could see around a bush.

There was a shadow under the trees on the far side of the clearing, a stubby figure, short, but at least a head too tall to be a Devil.

"Why did you call me here? Did he get away?"

The voice was hoarse, impatient. Varney scowled; there was something ... he strained to hear better, but he couldn't dredge up more than a vague feeling he'd met that whisper before. . . .

The old man grunted. "Neka. The darts refused to kill. They live."

"They?"

"There was a girl with him."

"There would be. I don't understand. The poison didn't work?"

"They are protected. The girl sleeps but will not die, the man didn't even notice the dart, we had to use the throw rope on him."

"Why didn't you cut their throats and leave them where they fell?"

"They are protected."

"You keep saying that. What does it mean?"

"You know."

"What are you going to to with them? You swore. . . ."

"You lied."

"Neka. I didn't know, I still don't. Where are they? I'll see about this protection business."

"Only if you swear to take them away from the trees before you touch them."

"I'm not prepared. There are too many eyes out there to go raw. If you don't like the knife, what about a noose?" The whisper was hoarser, more impatient. Varney strained. If only that creature would lose its temper and speak a hair louder. . . .

"Neka. It will not be. We will hold them, but we will not kill them for you or allow you to kill them while they are with us."

"Why?"

The ancient just squatted on the boulder, gazing into the fire, saying nothing.

"But you will hold them?"

The ancient looked up, cleared his throat, spat. "We will do that. For two Dark Moons. If you do not claim them before then, we will take them to the edge of the trees and release them."

"Varney has his moments. Take very good care he doesn't escape you."

"They cannot. Ysgarod has spoken. They will not leave the trees."

The shadow stood for a moment as if pondering further arguments, then it faded with as little noise as a patch of mist.

Varney went back to struggling with his arms, stubbornly trying to force his bound wrists past his buttocks.

The old man squatted without moving until the moon sliver dipped down behind the trees, then he put out his hand.

The boy reached over his shoulder, took a shepherd's flute from the case strapped to his back, laid the flute across the old man's palm.

Sweating and grinding his teeth, Varney stretched his cramped limbs and listened with apprehension to the windy tune the Devil coaxed from the flute. It meant something, he was sure of that. Calling for help? They couldn't mean to leave him and Faan laid out here like trussed chickens. He glanced at her from the corner of his eye and gasped.

Pale red tongues of fire licked over her. She burned without being consumed.

He turned his head and stared. The fire was gone, she was a length of darkness only slightly more solid than the shadows around her. He looked away, caught her from the corner of his eye again. She was bathed in flames. Weird.

Forest Devils materialized around him, carrying poles linked by woven rope. Ignoring his struggles, mute as stones, they rolled him onto the rope web, belly down, his face pressed into the mesh. Then four of them picked up the poles and trotted off with him.

They moved with a surprising speed, weaving through the Mezh as if they had owls' eyes, silent as owls on the hunt. The slant of the litter told him they were taking him higher in the mountains, deeper into the Divimezh. He shuddered.

He'd loathed this place all his life, now he was plunged in the middle of it, will-he, nill-he.

They trotted on and on, tireless and silent, until the sky was pink with the afterglow of sunrise, then they moved from under the trees onto a patch of black stone where even moss had a hard time growing. They dropped his litter beside the mouth of a hole in the stone, jarring his head and scraping the skin off his nose.

"Trum! Listen, you lopps, you're asking for trouble, treating me like this." He humped his body, wriggled around until he was sitting up, glared at them. "M' father's a man with a short temper. You think he can't find out who's got me? Think again. He'll burn this flea patch down round your ears."

Two of them jerked his arms out from his sides while a third passed a rope around his chest. He yelled and tried to muscle himself away from them, but one of them got him with a hard kick in the kidneys and while he was bent over from the pain of it, they yanked him from the litter and dragged him over the lip of the hole.

It was a long way down and he acquired another collection of bruises as he bounced off the irregularities in the sides of the hole, then stumbled and fell as he hit the littered bottom. The rope began sliding away. He tried to wind it around himself, make them pull him up or abandon it, but the drum started rattling, the rope stung him like an adder and he couldn't move.

A moment later they lowered Faan, taking more care with her—which irritated him, who was she but some foundling bastard, a foreigner without any ties here. He still couldn't move. Her feet were in his face, then she was lying over him, limp as an overcooked klimis.

The Devils threw down blankets, lowered a basket loaded with bread and cooked tubers, if his nose was any judge, then a dripping wooden bucket. Apparently they weren't being left to starve or die of thirst.

He heard a scraping, grunts, then the light was gone. They'd put the lid on the hole.

"Uts. Nadsic jauks!"

The dark dissolved the paralysis that had kept him immobile. He wrestled Faan off him and scrabbled around, trying to find a shard of stone with an edge on it so he could work on his bonds.

> > < <

Faan woke as Varney was trying to dribble water in her mouth, getting most of it down her neck and in her hair. She sputtered, pushed his hand away. "Trying to drown me?"

"Kyatty trum, you're finally awake."

"Nu, I am." She pushed up, groaning as her muscles protested and bruises made themselves known. "What happened? Where are we?"

"Down a hole."

"I see that. Nu, maybe not see, considering. The rest of it?"

He made an odd little sound, like a cross between a snort and a hiccup, but didn't say anything for a while, then only asked, "You hungry?"

"What's the problem, Varney?"

"You know." His voice had an edge to it; he was trying to sound insouciant and amused and not quite making it. "You heard what I told Navarre."

She wiped at her face, discovered that she was thirsty. "Nu, it's dark. I can't see a thing. I'd like a drink now, please."

"Hold out your hand."

She felt a slick knobby thing pressed into her palm; her fingers were pushed around it, closed inside his.

"It's a gourd," he said. "With the top cut out."

The water had an astringent taste and it was none too fresh, but it felt like nectar to her parched throat. She emptied the gourd in a couple of gulps; he took it away, and a moment later was pushing it back in her hand, refilled, the water sloshing over her wrist.

She drank, sighed, wiped her mouth. "Is there a soak or something? Where's the water coming from? Do we need to take care how much we use?"

"No problem. The Devils change buckets every sundown. When they bring food. They're due in about an hour."

"Every sundown? How long have we been here?"

"Five days."

"Huh?"

"Five days in this hole, seven or eight since we were taken. You've been unconscious the whole

time. I've got some water down you, but no food.
How do you feel?"

"Scared. Mad." She sipped from the gourd, lowered it to rest on her thighs. "Seriously, Varney,
what happened?"

"Forest Devils ambushed us. Darts put you out
but didn't kill you. Didn't bother me at all because I'm protected against poison, Navarre did
that. They got me with a throw rope, then
knocked me on the head. Carted us both into the
Divimezh too scared to kill us since the darts
didn't." He related all he'd heard and seen in the
clearing. "Nu nu, here we are." He grunted. "And
here we're going to stay, unless you can do something, Sorcerie."

"Don't call me that." She drained the gourd and
he took it from her, startling her. "How do you
do that?"

This time he didn't pretend to misunderstand
her. "You don't know?" he said.

"Obviously, else why ask."

"Nu, that's even weirder than I thought. When
I don't look directly at you, I can see you and
everything around you in the light of ... um ...
you look like you're sitting in the middle of a fire.
A pale red sort of fire. Very decorative."

"Tsa!" She shifted around, then caught a whiff
of herself. "Lauaus, what a stink. We've got to get
out of here."

"Hmp."

She could hear him moving about, cloth scraping on stone, shards rattling; impatiently, she

crafted a willo and flicked it into the air over her head.

The hole slanted steeply to the right, then from what she could see seemed to head upward. The walls were black with pinhead bits that sparked as they caught the shifting, bluish light of the willo, then faded as they sank back in shadow. Varney was over by a basket; he turned, startled, as the willo lit up the cramped space; he was holding a flat loaf in his right hand, a blob of something in his left. He blinked, his eyes watering in the sudden brightness. His face was smeared with dust, its lines blurred by a gold stubble like wheat after the reaper had passed. She hated to think what she must look like.

He set the loaf down, put the root or whatever it was on top of it. "You must be hungry, you haven't eaten for a week. It's bread and tuber, monotonous, but it keeps one alive."

She wrinkled her nose. "Since you mention it, tja, I'm starving. But wait a bit. I want to clean up first. Nu nu, I don't see how you could stand it."

His face reddened—the flush had a purple tinge in the willo's unflattering light. "It's not all you. It's been five days, after all."

She nodded, started to explain what she intended to do, then shut her mouth and quenched the willo; bad enough she could do what he couldn't, she didn't have to rub his nose in it—as the thought occurred to her she had to stifle a giggle. He wouldn't like that, he'd think she was laughing at him. He'd looked like a little puppy over there, eager to please and uncertain of his welcome. Uncertain! She was irritated with him, annoyed, but having him this close turned her bones to water. *Down girl, you've got work to do. Concentrate. Remember what the Sibyl said. Besides, the way you smell right now, even a dung beetle would trot off.*

Concentrate.

You burned the paint off you and Ma'teesee and Dossan when you were only twelve. Paint's harder to get rid of than filth.

Concentrate.

It hurts. Oh, Ners, it burns. I won't be stopped. I won't!

There. That's the way. Sear it clean, stone and flesh. My flesh, his . . . nayo! don't lose it, Fa. Concentrate. That's the way. That's it.

Ahhhh.

Her shirt and trousers were hot but clean. The danger roiling around her retreated as she let the casting fade.

She crouched a moment, head on knees, then pulled herself together and crafted the willo again. "Nu nu, that's better, isn't it. Neka, Varney, wait there, let me come to you, I want to see if my legs will move, I feel like I've got cramps in every muscle."

She could see him watching her, hand stroking his suddenly shaven jaw. He shrugged. She rolled onto her knees, grunted with pain as her weight came down on a sharp-edged bit of stone, then she crawled out of the niche where she'd lain.

As soon as there was room to stand, she got to

her feet, stretched extravagantly. "Ahhhh! that feels good."

He turned his head away, glanced at her from the corner of an eye—and she remembered what he'd said about the fire. "It's gone," he said. "Looks like you scared it away."

She put her hand on his shoulder, the touch burning through her, she felt herself blushing, lowered herself to her knees beside him and dropped the hand to her thigh; she wanted to brush against him, but she didn't; she was afraid to, she didn't know what she might do after that. "You said something about food?"

> > < <

The drumming started about about an hour later; there must have been half a dozen drummers up there; the sound throbbed through the stone.

Faan looked startled. She blinked. Her body seemed to melt as she collapsed to the floor of the hole, her eyes shut, her breathing slowed way down.

Varney stared, startled, then cursed the Forest Devils as he understood what had happened to the girl. They were afraid of her, so they knocked her out before they took the top off the hole.

The rope snaked down to him, weighted as usual by an oval stone with a hole in one end. He'd been through this too many times before to bother throwing a snit; there was nothing he could do, not if he wanted food and water. He tied the rope to the bail on the bucket and they pulled it up, lowered it in a breath or two, filled with water. He sent the food basket up the same way, got it back, then heard the scrape of stone against stone as they shoved the cap on and shut out the ghostly gray light that had crept down to him for the few moments the hole was open.

He drank some of the fresh water, glanced at Faan, wrinkled his nose as he saw her bathed in fire. "Nu nu, girl, what an oddity you are. A lovely one, too." He settled himself beside her, now and then touching her hair, stroking his finger down her cheek, waiting for her to wake.

> > < <

Faan came floating from dream into a delicious semiawareness; Varney's hands were touching her lightly, possessively, fingertips gliding over her lips, along the curve of her ears, drifting downward to press with feather delicacy on her breasts, tickling her stomach. She murmured something incoherent, turned to him. . . .

> > < <

When Faan woke again, Varney was curled around her, snoring, his head heavy on her breasts, his arm on her stomach. She was sore and sticky—and filled with an anger she hadn't expected. Breathing hard, she wriggled from under him; he mumbled and sighed and sank back into a heavy sleep.

The thing that was always watching her stirred ominously as she flashed herself clean, but she snarled at it, startled it into retreating. When she was done, she crafted a willo and went stomping about the hole, inspecting the walls, trying to decide how to attack the problem of getting out. She didn't intend to spend another hour down here, come what came. Let Meggwhatever do his worst.

The willo spiraled up and up, suddenly blinked out. The blackness was stifling, as if a blanket had been thrown over her; she gasped and started panting, shrank back and crossed her arms over her head, struggling with the sense that the whole mountain was about to come down on her.

Tiny voices whispered at her.

Lovee, chickee, don't be sad. Not so bad, it's not so bad. See o see, big bad dark it's Meggee's bark, he don't bite, never quite. Lovee chickee, you know we-ee.

Wildings?

See o see, you do know we-ee.

Can you answer questions?

We-ee litt-lee, honee chickee, what we mayee, we will sayee.

What killed the willo?

Shaaamaan snuffee all thee try-ee, up top magic stop.

How can I get out of here?

Trickee, chickee. Hard, pard. Think and slink. Go fro, adjourn, return.

The voices faded and from the corner of her eye she caught a glimpse of translucent fire forms blowing away, flowing into stone. She sighed, her urgency gone and with it, much of her anger. She crafted another willo, set it to hanging in the air above the water bucket and settled herself beside Varney.

She eased a strand of his hair out of his eyes; it was so fine and fair it belonged on the head of a small girl, not a grown man who'd just proved himself competently male. She frowned. It wasn't right, what he'd done. He'd stolen her courting time from her. Taken it as his due.

The lock of hair curled round her finger, tickling her. Her throat went dry and her nipples hardened till they hurt. *O Tai, O Wise One, I wish you were here. Reyna, you know about this, you could tell me what to do, why didn't you ever talk to me, explain this . . . I don't even like him, but he makes me . . . Mamay. . . .*

She stared into the dark, captured by memory.

It was night. She'd gone to the Sibyl's Cave to snatch a moment's peace when neither god nor mortal would be pulling at her, trying to make her into their idea of what she should be. She was tired, tired and sad.

Reyna came from his assignation with Juvalgrim, moving with assurance through the secret entrails of the mountain, and found her sprawled in the Sybil's stone chair. He took her hand and led her down the perilous path to the Sacred Way; for a moment they were just happy, mother/father and daughter once more, so happy she spoke almost at random, talking to hear him answer her, grave and sweet.

Near the last flight of stairs on the Sacred Way Faan touched Reyna's arm. "You love

*him, don't you. What's it like, being in love
with someone?"*

*Reyna was startled; in the moonlight, Faan
could see the twitch of his mouth and that
quick toss of his head that sent his hair swinging, things he did when he was embarrassed
about something but was trying not to show
it. "In love," he said slowly. "Nayo, that's not
it, Fa. That's pretty pink pleasures, sweat and
sweet agony. I had that a few times when I
found my first clients." He went down the
stairs thinking about it, his hands clasped behind him under the cloak; it was almost a
dance, his body balancing easily. "Nayo. This
is different. Love? I don't know. There's
friendship and fondness, oh diyo, and passion. It's not bad, you know. Friendship and
fondness and passion."*

"Does he love you?"

*"It's hard to say with Juvalgrim. He's a secret
man. He needs me. That's enough, I think."*

"Need." She shivered. "I hate that word."

Her mouth twisted in a sad smile. *Pretty pink
pleasures. Not so pretty and not so pink, O Mamay. Pleasure, I don't even know if there's any
pleasure in it, I've never felt so. . . . No friendship,
precious little fondness. Need. Gods! There's need.
Mamay, Mamay, how do I get out of this?*

She leaned over Varney and listened to him
breathe; every seventh exhalation was a tiny whistling snore that made her heart flutter. She could

smell him, a vigorous male smell that she couldn't have described but drank in like incense. She adored the way his neck was set into his shoulders; his arms were smooth and firm, the muscles sleek under a skin like ivory where the sun had never touched him. When she set her hand on his shoulder, she could feel the life in him strong as a river in flood.

The Wildings came rushing back.

Honey chickee, listen we-ee, slide to side, play the mole, 'nother hole.

Mole? They shimmered in a red-gold maelstrom half inside the stone across the hole from where she was sitting, buzzing with excitement and puckish glee.

Honey chickee, we plus thee make us free. Swap rock break block.

Swap rock . . . ah! You mean change it to air.

Transformations . . . she'd just started on them when Abeyhamal Bee Mother snatched her from the Sibyl's lessons. She reached down, found a shard broken from the walls, tasted it, held it, and felt into it. If it wasn't the same, it was a close cousin to the stone in the Sibyl's cave. *Transformations, tja, why didn't I think of that. What an idiot!*

She put out her hands and called the Wildings into her, warm and tickling, familiar and eerie. Around her she could feel the warning heat, the pressure that demanded she let go, desist. She ignored it. Let Varney sleep, leave him out of it. What she wouldn't say even to herself was that she knew he couldn't endure the sight of her power, that he'd feel diminished and do something else to make himself dominant again.

The stone melted into air, layer by layer, as she dug out a long oval in the wall of the hole.

In five minutes she saw a sudden darkness and knew she'd broken through into another hole.

CABAL

"To the new Candidate." A gloved hand lifted a crystal glass filled with ruby wine. "So fortuitously raised to that honor."

"To the new Candidate."

Two more hands lifted their glasses to salute the fourth conspirator, Vocats Oirs, named by implication.

The glasses disappeared beneath the cowls, reappeared empty, then the four sat in a circle in the meagerly furnished room, an attic in one of the Ash Tirdza inns.

Oirs drank his own wine, set the glass down with a click on the scarred and stained table they were gathered around. "All very well," he said, "but what about Turet? Won't he be suspicious? Haven't I profited by that mulkidger fool's death?" He twisted round to face the second tall man. "You don't have to worry, Laz, because when it's your brother's turn, he'll only be wounded, you'll be the hero for saving him.

Kreisits Lazdey caught hold of Oirs' arm, twisted it. "No names. You know the drill, fool. No names."

"Let go of me, lopp. Labi labba, I forgot." He

141

rubbed at his wrist. "What does it matter anyway,
he . . ." he nodded at the wide man, "he says he
has these meetings blanked so those nadsic Diviners can't read anything no matter what they try. And
if it weren't so, we'd've been lining up for the hangman long before this."

The woman sat silent, her gloved hands crossed,
the tip of her chin showing ivory in the light of the
single candle set in the center of the table.

The wide man laughed easily. "Nu, friends, go
lightly. It's true there's no danger from any Reader,
but habits are hard to break, so let's not get them
started. No names, my friends, it's simply a matter
of prudence." He reached across the table for the
wine bottle. His arms were unusually long for his
height; it was as if all the extra bone in him went into
them, not into his legs. He poured an inch of wine
in his glass, shoved the bottle toward Oirs. "Your
father will think better of you coming home with wine
on your breath and perfume in your hair, you know
it. So drink and relax. We've more to celebrate then
either of you know."

The woman leaned forward. "Already?"

"Of course. As soon as Turet called that meeting,
I knew what would happen and I was right. Varney
went running for Navarre, wanted the Magus to hold
his fair white hand."

"Varney?"

"You got Varney?"

"Varney's dead?"

"I have him, tja, and he's not dead. Remember,
we planned to rid ourselves of at least one of the
contenders by laying the guilt on him. I'd thought of

Tupelis Steidz for this, since he wouldn't have a chance otherwise, but too many people know how feeble he is. With Varney it'd be different. Believable. When he's found dead in damning circumstances, then Turet will be satisfied and we'll be safe.''

Oirs fidgeted with his glass; when he spoke, the usual whine was back in his voice. ''If he doesn't get away.''

''He won't.''

''But if he does?''

''It won't change anything. He doesn't know who took him. We simply collect him again and play the game out.''

Oirs sat silent a moment, his shoulders hunched over, then he said, ''If you're sure. . . .''

''Quite sure.''

He got to his feet. ''Nu, I. . . .'' He let it drop and went out.

Kreisits Lazdey pushed back his chair. ''I've duty in an hour.'' He chuckled. ''Begarz almost likes me these days, I'm a simple soldierman, you see, faithful and another vote.'' In the doorway, he turned. ''Our friend who left. I smell ambition. Remind him, will you, that none of us can afford to take the name as well as the game.''

> > < <

The woman pushed back her hood, plucked a handkerchief from her sleeve and patted at the perspiration on her face. She was delicately boned, coldly beautiful, her fine hair so blonde it was almost white. "He's right, you know."

"Tja. But we still need Oirs."

She nodded. "For one thing, to keep my esteemed cousin conscious of his limitations. Brown eyes speak to a stain on the line. His mother's line, of course. He hates her for that, Laz does."

"May I remind you, he's not all that fond of you, lovely Nenova."

She waved that away. "I confess to a weakness, my friend."

"Hmm?"

"Varney. When he dies, make it quick, will you?"

"You, too?"

"He was a mere child and I was married to that buffoon, you know. It was a pleasant interlude. He appreciates women, Varney does. We like that."

"Nu, I'll see to it."

"I pay my debts."

"Before the fact?"

"Why not? The innkeeper here is incomparably discreet. As you know."

"Tja, dama, that he is. It would be best if you arranged the details, since I am what I am."

"You think too much about that."

"And you don't?"

"I find it . . . interesting. I'll come for you when things are prepared."

Chapter 7
Magus on the Move

Navarre stood in the archway, arms folded, brows drawn together as he watched Faan and Varney ride away. They were in no hurry; Varney was lounging in the saddle, murmuring something to the girl who had her shoulders hunched, her head tilted to one side. Navarre heard her smothered laughter, her deep voice answering, shook his head and went back into the house.

Kitya was waiting inside the door, her eyes slitted. "Your supper's ready," she said, her voice purring as it did when she was too angry to shout. "You should eat it while it's hot."

"Nu, bring it to the workroom."

She caught hold of his arm, her long fingers closing with such strength he grunted with pain. "Let it alone."

"Be quiet. You don't know what you're talking about." He broke free. "Do what you want. You know where I'll be."

His workroom was the top floor in the squat tower he'd built into the east corner of the house, with narrow ventilation slits but no windows. Heavy black felt drapes hung from a ceiling track about a hand's breadth away from the walls; the floor was paved with black tiles fitted so closely that the lines between them were almost invisible. There was a tall cabinet against the north wall and an ebony table in the center of the room, a glass and silver lamp burning on a silver disk in the center of the table. The hexagonal top had silver lines inlaid in the ebony, a hexa inscribed across a penta and a scatter of glyphs, words in a language alien to this part of the word.

Navarre went to the cabinet, got out a silver mirror and a burnishing cloth, took them back to the table. He sat polishing the mirror face and brooding on the forces that were driving him into acts he would much rather have avoided.

His continuance here was based on containing his use of the Art within carefully defined and very narrow limits. Meggzatevoc had hovered about him, watching him for the first three years, making Himself known whenever Navarre approached those limits; as time passed, that presence receded, leaving Navarre at peace.

Now . . . ah, now it was different. He was going to push at those limits, deliberately, if cautiously. He had to know why he found himself involved with this child in affairs that were none of his business, that, if he were fully in command of himself, he would ignore. Had to know. Ignorance was dangerous.

There was a knock on the door.

"Come," he said and set the mirror aside.

Kitya pushed past the drape, a tray with short legs at the four corners held against her stomach.

She set it beside the door and left without speaking.

He glanced at the food, shrugged and went back to polishing the mirror.

The moment came when he was ready.

He touched the tips of his fingers together, then massaged his temples as he fought for will and focus.

Blurred at first, slowly clearing, sharpening, Faan's image appeared in the mirror, sitting as she had in his parlor with hands straining together, her grave bicolored gaze intent on him.

He teased out the tangle of timelines woven about her, noting the nodes, then began reading the *lines*, pushing back and back until he felt the tingle that told him here was the answer he needed. Deep within the mirror tiny, sharp images moved and spoke:

The mahsar popped out of the air beside Faan who was a black-haired, odd-eyed baby of three; the beast hissed at the Bee-eyed Woman. (Navarre grunted as he recognized her as a local god, improbably out of her homeland; he didn't know her, but he could remedy that later if necessary.)

"Good," she said. "I was waiting for you."

She hummed and the mahsar curled up with her back against Faan, deep asleep.

Faan yawned; her eyes drooped shut and she slept.

The Bee-eyed Woman hummed another note.

A honey shimmer trembled about the child.

"Be lovéd," the Bee-eyed Woman crooned over her. "Let he who finds you cherish you to death and beyond. Let them who dwell with you cherish you. Be lovéd, Honeychild."

The Bee-eyed Woman hummed.

A block of crystal hardened around Faan and Ailiki the mahsar.

The Bee-eyed Woman hummed a double note, spread her arms.

A dome of crystal formed about the island, stopping everything inside.

He read the lines that coiled about the baby, then those about the island as the Bee-eyed Woman's boat went gliding off. With Meggzatevoc's eyes searing him, the god's anger rising, he drained every fraction of information he could coax from the silvery timelines, though much of it was meaningless at the moment since he hadn't the matrix of the child's history to set it in.

Carefully he disentangled himself from the timelines and drew his consciousness toward the present.

Something else was observing him.

Cool, measuring, immense ... no intimation as to WHO watched, only the stink of power, power so vast he had no sense of edges.

Not Meggzatevoc nor one of the Kyatawat Powers, not a local god at all.

One of the Great Gods.

He surfaced, wiped the sweat from his brow.

A Great God.

Which meant he might as well get used to the idea of being linked with the girl. Massulit seeking her, a Great God using her. *Be lovéd, Honeychild.* He snorted and pushed the chair back. "No wonder I turned into her sweet dada." As he stood, he lurched, suddenly dizzy, the energy he'd expended in the timesearch recoiling on him. "Wrystrike," he muttered. "I hate. . . ."

Uneasy and filled with a scratchy resentment, he stumbled to the tray, lowered himself to the floor and sat cross-legged, eating food gone cold, drinking lukewarm tea. He didn't want to be tangled in this affair, gods used you with no regard for your desires or your well-being, but he had no choice.

No choice. That was what galled him most. *Be lovéd, Honeychild.*

He looked at the meat congealing on the plate, grimaced as his stomach knotted, relaxed, knotted again. Another bite and he'd be heaving the whole mess up. The room was suddenly stifling, the walls closing in on him. He needed open air and the solid reality of tools for the hand, not the mind.

He got heavily to his feet, went down the squared spiral stair and out through the kitchen to the smithy, where he sat on the anvil and contemplated his options.

> > < <

A bray startled him from a depressed evaluation of his immediate future. "Skumung tha! What now?"

He slid off the anvil and went round the house to the court. Just inside the arch Faan's hired mule was moving restlessly about, his head held high and to one side to keep the reins from underfoot, his hooves clattering on the flags. Faan's beast was sitting on the mule's shoulders, her small black hands twisted in the cropped mane. She stared at Navarre and made urgent sounds, almost-speech that he didn't need to understand. The launsid behind this had struck again, hitting at Varney and getting the girl with him.

He scowled at the mule and the mahsar. "Which doesn't make sense. If she's killed, it negates everything I read. If I read true. I accept it as true. Therefore, she's alive. And if she's alive. . . ." He raised his hand as the mahsar chittered at him again. "Quiet. Wait." He caught hold of the reins and led the mule into the stable, got him settled with grain and water, then hurried down the hill, the mahsar at his heels.

> > < <

Reading the *lines* as he walked, he followed Faan and Varney down the lane, not bothering with the words or the sexual tension intensifying between them, concerned only with their physical well-being. Where the slope of Djestradjin Hill flattened and there was cover on both sides of the road, thorny brush and clumps of tall grass, the traces crumpled suddenly into confusion wrung with pain. He looked down at the mahsar. "This is it?" He was startled when the beast nodded vigorously, then he shrugged; it wasn't usual for those with Faan's Talent to have a familiar, though the little creature wasn't exactly a familiar, but he was coming to expect peculiar idiosyncracies from this odd-eyed child. "You'd best get some room between you and me." he told the beast. "I don't know what will happen. It could be nasty. No doubt you're aware of my problem, since your companion certainly is. Shoo! Go!"

The mahsar sat on her haunches and grinned at him. "Ne ne," she squeaked at him.

"On your head, then. Your ghost will have to explain to the little Sorcerie." With a nervous laugh, he wiped his hands down his sides and started his probe.

Smithy Lane was paved with tar and gravel, the tar so marked with the crescent bite of horseshoes that it was hard to read anything into the signs he saw with his everyday eyes. Certainly there was nothing to show whether Varney had managed to put up a fight. Or the girl.

No blood—that would have shone like phosphor to his magesight. So, most likely no fight.

His palms were sweaty again and more runnels of sweat were creeping down through his hair, sliding down his neck.

The stink of magic was so strong it was nearly choking him; it slid over the brush and the road in an oily yellow fog. "Smoked," he murmured. As with Apsis' death, a mirror would show him nothing, he was sure of that.

He had to get past the block, slide along the timelines and come out before the ambush. If it weren't for the Wrystrike and Megg, he could twist Time's tail and change the outcome. He didn't dare. Varney and Faan were alive now. Probably alive. The curse might kill them if he interfered. Or him—and he had no wish to invite death. Despite his frustrations he found life amusing and full of savor.

He shook his arms, moved his shoulders. "Skyon Dren! Ahhh hahhh ahh. . . ."

The air had gone damp and chill, the earth under his bare feet felt alive, as if he stood on a great restless beast that was on the edge of waking.

Grim and determined, he sought focus and intensity, breathing slowly, ignoring the rumbles in the earth, the hostile hiss of the wind. He could feel the curse gathering force, the grumbling boil of Megg's anger, but as he moved with increasing ease along the glowing silver *lines* of Time, encapsulated so he wouldn't intrude, effectively insubstantial, he also felt the high glory of doing what he was born to do, what he'd put aside for so many dull years. Dull. On-na wha! Dull. Say it, man of fear. He shouted silent laughter, stretched his back and strode forward on Faan's *line* to the moment of the attack.

Faan and Varney came riding along, talking. (He didn't listen to what they said, it didn't matter and it would have disturbed his concentration).

Small dark figures rose from the grass with blowpipes longer than they were (he saw the darts blowing flat and hard, sinking deep in the flesh of Faan and Varney, he knew those darts, that poison, Varney had his stone, and if his reading was right, Faan had other protection, nonetheless, he stiffened and nearly lost focus as he saw the lethal thorns strike them.)

He saw Faan's face go blank, saw her slide from the mule, saw Varney pulled from his mount by the throwrope, saw him clubbed unconscious.

He saw the mezhmerrai come gliding from their ambush, saw their agitation as they inspected their victims, twitched the thorns free and inspected them, saw them throw Varney and Faan on the back of the black stallion and lead him off. The mule they left behind. In his capsule Navarre smiled; they didn't approve of mules, considered them perversions of nature. He spared a moment of sadness for the stallion; the mezhmerrai found horseflesh a great delicacy they had all too seldom. There'd be feasting in the Forest this night.

He shook himself loose from his fascination, disciplined the urge to do more than look and began the rush back, running ahead of a growing heat.

As he broke out into present time, he was flung up the hill by a blast of power.

He fell. Landed hard.

Fire leapt skyward on every side.

The mahsar was beside him, suddenly, pressing

into him, with no intervening between states of there and not there.

Coolness flowed round him.

The Wrystrike went further awry and left him safe in the circle of the mahsar's will.

He got to his feet. "Patcha, I . . ." His knee buckled and threatened to give way; his leg was suddenly a river of pain. "Myah!"

He looked down. The whole side of his robe was burned away; the skin that was visible was raw red and smeared with ash—but his bones were intact. "For which I thank you, O mahsar." He could feel the bruises fruiting in his flesh and yearned for a hot bath with leaves of pipar and kaltuvy steeping in it.

He flexed his leg, winced at the pain. "Nu, mahsar, it's walk or spend the night here. Are you hungry? You're welcome to take whatever you find tasty." He began limping slowly up the hill, his leg getting stronger as he moved.

> > < <

A plump baby of a man stood in the arch waiting for him, hair the color of moonlight, eyes the clear green-brown of a mountain tarn, flickering with shadow like the dapple of blowing leaves. Huge eyes. Owl eyes. Meggzatevoc.

Navarre halted; the first few seconds he was tense with fear, then he relaxed. This was Meggzatevoc's Speakingform; he wouldn't have bothered if he'd meant to smear Navarre across the landscape for breaking his tabu. He bowed, for courtesy's sake, then straightened his back and gazed at the god, conceding nothing.

The Speakingform blinked slowly. "Don't do that again," IT said. ITS voice wasn't exactly a sound, more a vibration in the bone that left Navarre weak and sick. "You won't like what happens," the voice went on. An unseen hand reached inside Navarre and twisted; the pain was indescribable. He fell to his knees, hunched over, groaning. "Worse than that. A lot worse." The Speakingform stared at him as IT sank into the earth like water draining away. In seconds IT was gone.

He crouched where he was, gasping, swimming in an agony he'd never suffered before in his long life.

A softness brushed his burned leg. Small fingers clutched at his arm. Coolness spread through him. Strength came trickling back and he could breathe again, straighten up. He unfolded a hand that trembled like an old man in palsy, touched his fingertips to the mahsar's head. "Patcha, friend," he said, coughed and spat.

After a moment more, he got to his feet and went inside.

> > < <

"Look at you." Kitya slapped the dishes onto the tray with a controlled violence that threatened to shatter them. "One day! One towyok visit from that tepeyinyin and you lose half your skin! Forget her. Stay out of this."

He snatched his cup before she got it, gulped down the rest of the tepid coffee. "Can't," he said.

"Karoo!" She stomped across the kitchen to the sink beside the stove and began unloading the tray. "Can't brand you for what you don't do."

He laughed. She turned to glare at him, her dark red eyes like lava boiling. "Neka, neka, Kat. Your people may be given to reason, but this lot follow their preconceptions and don't let facts disturb them."

She began scooping hot water from the reservoir in the stove, pouring it over the dishes in the tub, muttering as she worked, none of it loud enough for him to make out the words.

"Varney talks a lot," he said.

She snorted.

"Half the House will know he came to see me. That's enough to damn me when he doesn't return." He leaned back in the chair, enjoying the warmth in his middle, the remembered taste of his breakfast. "You should worry about that, Kat. Women and slaves, the only testimony the judges will take from them is what's given under torture."

"Sreeks, the lot of them!"

"I don't know that one."

"Animals. No culture, no sense." She whipped back, snatched the cup from him and took it to the tub. "Send me home."

"Tiesh tas, I said and I'll do. I'll arrange passage after I leave the House."

"Neka. Don't. I didn't mean it."

"Hmm. It would be better if you did."

"You said how it would be and so it has been. I have no complaints. There has been pleasure and a full belly. I am Moug'aikkin. We know how to work and we know how to serve." She pulled a pot from the soapy water and began scrubbing it, looking at it rather than at him. "We know how to be true if these sreeks don't."

"I should be back by nightfall if nothing intervenes. Raise the callflag for Kaundar. If he comes, that means this business is limited to a single cilt; if he doesn't, it's the Mezh I'll have to deal with. Ysgarod."

She twisted her head around, looking over her shoulder at him. "And if it's his cilt?"

"It won't be. They hate the Valda too much; no amount of gold or trade would tempt them; any of his lot would cut the throat of the messenger before he got a word out." He stood, wincing as his bruises protested and the burned skin began burning again.

"Why didn't you let me do a heal on you, V'ret?" She'd calmed down; reason always worked with her. After a while. The Moug'aikkin were poor in goods because they lived in a barren land, but in other ways they were rich indeed; more than once he'd regretted the need to leave them.

"Evidence, Kat. I want to have bruises to show when I talk to Pargats Vicanal, he has the intelligence of a kahnaloo. . . ." He smiled fondly at her as he saw the mischief return to her eyes. "And the disposition of a rutting bull." He crossed to

her, rubbed his hand down her face. "Behave
yourself, midza-mikan."

> > < <

The hostler frowned. "What happened to the
girl? She didn't fall off, did she?"

Navarre laughed. "No. She found other transport. How much?"

He paid the man, added a double kod, remem-
bering Faan's worried face as she talked about
limited funds; it felt good to be generous in her
name. "Got room for my horse?"

"Virs Zotaj gen'rally wants to keep stalls for
clients." He looked at the coins in his hand,
shrugged. "Not my business if you a client or
nothing. Bring 'im back along here."

> > < <

The street outside Pargats House was swarming with people going in and out of the broad
gate; it was the first business day after the Dark
Moon and that generally brought a vigorous chaos
to the Family Ashes. Civiels outside the walls labored to bring some kind of order in the street,
while the court was sprinkled with guards in blue
tabards with appliquéd horse forms rearing; they
sauntered about, keeping a stern eye on the more
orderly traffic of traders with their samples, captains reporting from Pargats ships currently in
port, messengers from the Rancoladz, the huge
country estate, and less identifiable individuals

who worked for the House or meant to establish connections with it.

He threaded through the mob outside, nodded to Teiklids the captain of the Pargats Guard as he passed through the gate; Teiklids had seen him often enough with Varney when the Guard escorted the House daughters to and from Celebrations.

The Grand Court was a small village in itself, with high narrow apartments pasted against the north and south walls like cells in a honeycomb. Pargats cousins lived here, holding important positions within the complex business life of the Family—the House Steward who took care of provisioning, repairs, and ran the servants; the Rancoladz Steward who set policy for the Kadrav and his men who did the actual work on the Country Estate; the Ship Steward who did the same for the Captains on the ships the Family owned; the head buyers; the Librarian; the Family Varredo (who was mostly forgotten, except when the Lielskadrav wanted a bit of truthreading or spying done)—and, of course, their families and their servants. The business offices were here, pasted against the street wall on both sides of the main gate.

There were other courts—the servants' court around back, the guards' court, the stables and all that entailed.

The House itself had three nodes.

In the center were the public rooms where receptions were held and the entertaining was done.

The north wing belonged to the Lielskadrav,

his wives, his concubines, his children. Separate, but reached only through this wing, there was a smaller set of suites built around a garden with fountains and flowery walks. Here the unmarried daughters lived, once they left the schoolrooms, here they stayed if they never married, here family widows could return if they wanted to.

The south wing belonged to the Heir, generally though not necessarily the Lielskadrav's eldest son. And his wives, his concubines, his children. The sons of the house who were still unmarried lived in suites attached to this wing. This was where Navarre dined with Varney before they went to whatever Celebration they were favoring that night.

He wound his way through the bedlam in the Court, heading for the House Steward's office. He wasn't looking forward to the wheedling he'd have to do to get Pargamaz Chelassey to arrange for him to see the Lielskadrav. Chelassey had made himself into a copy of Vicanal, aping his hostility to foreigners. Of course, he also wormed around to please the Heir and Varney, so he'd eventually arrange the meeting.

Navarre exchanged greetings with the guard at the door, stepped inside, settled himself on a bench to wait for Chelassey to notice him.

> > < <

Pargamaz Chelassey bowed and backed from the room.

The Lielskadrav scowled at Navarre. "What's this about?"

"First, though, sit down, Navarre. Drink tea with us." Pargats Velams closed his hand on his father's shoulder; the old man sputtered but subsided into his chair, waved Navarre to another, then sat glowering at him from beneath the hedge of his wild white brows. Velams moved behind his father and stood with his hands resting on the chair's back.

"I thank you for your courtesy, O Virs." Navarre took the cup from the maidservant, sipped at it, set it down. "I am come on a matter for our ears only," he said.

When the room was cleared, he leaned forward, hands on his knees, spoke slowly and carefully. "Shortly after the passing of the Augstadievon, Pargats Varney asked me to craft for him an aizar stone. With Meggzatevoc's leave, I did so and delivered it to him the night of the Dark Moon. Yesterday he came to see me to ask if I might be able to look more deeply into the death of Vocats Apsis than the Temple Diviners had. Because he was my friend and a target of this murderer, I agreed to investigate as soon as I could clear the matter with the god. He left shortly before sundown, riding alongside another visitor, a young woman who has nothing to do with this, except that she had come to consult me on matters of the Art and was with him when he was taken."

Velams caught his father by the shoulders and used his weight to hold the old man down. "Neka!"

he shouted, his tenor voice cutting through his father's roar. "Hear the man out. Then we'll know where we are. Magus, the time for circumlocution is past. Short and sharp. Tell us." His fingers dug into his father's muscles, but his face was calm, his voice steady.

"The girl was riding a mule. It came to the smithy after the attack. I traced it back. I used my Art and read the occurrence. Don't bother trying that with a Diviner, the act was smoked. The attackers were the mezhmerrai. You call them Forest Devils. They used poison darts, but Varney wore the aizar stone and the darts had no effect; they roped him, pulled him down and knocked him unconscious, then they threw him and the girl on the back of Varney's black, went off with them. They were both alive, the chances are good they'll stay that way."

Velams walked rapidly to a cabinet, poured a glass of ogabrenj and brought it to his father. "He's alive. At least there's that."

Vicanal snorted, glared at Navarre. "If you believe that zemnik."

"He has no reason for lying; indeed, he has proved himself a true man by coming to tell us this when there was no need for it."

"Come to save his nadsic skin," the old man growled, but it was a feeble effort and he knew it. "Nu! Magus. How do you know they won't just strangle him once they get him under those nadsic trees?"

"The mezhmerrai have certain superstitions;

they won't kill where their darts fail them. Since Varney went in alive, he'll stay alive."

"Nu, then, where is he?"

"I've no idea. The Divimezh has strange eddies in it; no sort of farseeing works there, either my kind or that of the Temple Diviners."

Velams wiped his hand across his mouth, his eyes shrewder than he was wont to show them. "You're going into the Mezh after him."

Navarre blinked. In his rambling chats, Varney had said more than he realized about his elder brother; he respected Velams immensely, loved him, was jealous of him, never understood him, was sometimes afraid of him—in all, presenting the picture of a formidable man. "Tja," he said. "He's my friend." He stood. "I came to tell you what happened because I might not be able to do so later. I don't know how long it'll take to find him and free him, but if we don't appear by the next Dark Moon, you'd better think of us as dead. In the meantime, I suggest you get busy discovering who's behind these attacks and see if you can persuade him—or them—to retrieve your son. A two-sided approach will be more effective."

"Forest Devils," the old man grumbled, "they don't. . . ."

Velams snorted. "They don't leave the trees without a reason, you know that, Father." He turned to Navarre. "Is there anything you need that we can provide?"

"As I said, find the plotters and cancel their orders."

Velams bent, rang the bell on the tea tray. When the maidservant came in, he sent her for a guard to take Navarre back through the halls. "Be sure we will do what we can," he said.

Chapter 8
Danger in the Divimezh

"Varney, wake up." Faan shook his shoulder again, almost sobbing in her wearness and urgency.

He snored.

This time she found nothing appealing about it. She slapped his face, pinched his ear. Nothing worked. He was limp and unresponsive, completely out. She swore, the curses of the Edge rolling off her tongue as she pulled him up and got her shoulder under his arm.

Half lifting, half dragging him, she staggered across the hole and into the opening in the wall.

Wheeling in an agitated sphere, a kind of wilding willo, thirteen wildings floated ahead of her, guiding her.

With the rest of the Wild Magic swirling about her, clucking at her, scolding her for going too slow, chiding her for burdening herself with that inert lump of meat, she struggled to haul Varney along the rough blowhole, going away from that noisome hole that smothered her until she felt like dying.

Her feet burned, sweat dripped into her eyes,

her breath came in harsh gasps, but she kept going and kept going, following the red flutter of the guiding sphere through the confusion of intersecting holes, Varney on her back, his arms over her shoulders, his head pressed against hers, his feet dragging over the stone behind her.

> > < <

A long time later she heard water dripping, felt a coolness blow against her face and Varney sneezed in her ear. He didn't wake, but the noise jumped her from her daze. "A little more," she croaked. "Move your feet, Fa."

A moment later the wilding sphere blew back into her face, stopping her a step before she'd have stumbled into a deep pool collected in a dip in the blowhole, fed by a trickle that wandered down one of the walls.

Shrugging Varney off her shoulders, she lay on her stomach beside the pool, scooping up water with her hand, drinking until the worst of the burning was gone.

She pushed herself up.

The wildings had settled on every bump in the stone, wedged themselves in every crack; their wavering pale glows lit up what was a black bubble in the rock, turning desolation into an odd sort of beauty. She understood for the first time what Varney had meant when he said the little fires were decorative.

"Which reminds me. . . ." she said aloud. She

crawled over to kneel beside Varney and saw that his feet were bleeding where they'd dragged over the punishing stone; she tore the end off her shirt tail, dipped it in the water and washed them off, clucked nervously as more blood welled up. She sloshed the cloth in the water again, wrung it out and slapped his face with it, slapped again and again with no result.

Hands twisting the rag, pulling it apart, she sat on her heels and glared at the wild magic. *What is this? What is it? Tell me.*

We-ee tryee, honee chickee, we-ee sayee leave he be.

What does that mean?

Up top Shaamaaan stop.

Can't you fix it?

We-ee littlee, honee chickee, hack the crack, slip and slide, go and glide, make a fuss, end of us, Shaaa-maan snuff, enough enough?

In other words, you can't help. To wake Varney, I have to catch the Shaman and make him do it. Is that what you mean?

You see you see, follow we.

The wildings swirled off the walls and surged toward the hole that opened on the far side of the pool.

Wait. Wait! I can't leave him like this. She touched his face. *He's starting to freeze, and what if something comes along and eats him . . . rats. . . .*

The fluttering flamelets came back, hovered uncertainly, swirling around, touching each other as if they consulted over a problem they hadn't thought out.

Then they swooped down on Varney, burned
around and through him, warming him a few degrees—as they said, they were little creatures
without much power. A handful pinched off from
the rest and rose to flutter in front of her. *Honee
chickee, earthsnakes wake for your sake, callee
crawlee, come watch Varney.*

She gazed at them, confused, not understand-
ing, then she remembered a story Panote had told
her of a time when she was a child and earth elementals had come to protect her. *You were frightened, he said, and you called them, huge gray
serpents slithering down the wynd behind you. It
made a mess for a while, every idiot in the Edge
wanted a blessing from you and here you were a
baby hardly three years old.* She held her hands
palm out and pushed them away from her, as if
she pushed away all she didn't want to hear.
"More god business. Nayo! I won't! Nayo nayo."

The wildings swirled agitatedly.

What'd she say, won't she play, what what?

She took a deep breath, lowered her hands. *Isn't
there any other way?*

There was no answer. The Wild Magic darted
around in aimless, agitated arcs. She had the feeling they were ready to go off and leave her if she
didn't do something soon. She shivered; without
them to guide her she could wander down here
in this stone sponge until she dropped dead.
"Tiesh tas, get going, Fa, you've got no choice. As
usual."

She shifted from the squat until she sat cross-
legged, wincing as the chill struck up through her.

When she brushed her hand against Varney's face, she shivered again. Despite the efforts of the wildings, his flesh was as cold as the stone. "It's your doing I'm here, you know," she murmured. "I'd have been safer riding alone." She smiled, touched his hair, tenderness flooding her. It really wasn't his fault that some murderous bezriggid got an itch for power. "Ah, well."

Because she couldn't remember the event Panote recounted or the elementals who'd hovered over the baby Faan as she ran in panic down a wynd, she thought of the water elementals popping their clear crystal heads from the muddy river just to look at her, tried to tease out their essence and turn the *feel* to earth rather than water.

For an eternity nothing happened.

Then the wildings fled to the walls and ceiling. A moment later a vast finger of stone thrust up, turned and looked at her from glittering obsidian rounds. She didn't hear words, heard no sound at all, but they were there in her head: **You call us from our sleep, belovéd. What is your desire?**

She gasped, clutched at her head as pain lanced through it, then found herself able to speak in something that wasn't exactly a language, more an intimation of emotion, a flow of image compressed into non-sound gestalts: *My lover is bespelled*, she seemed to say, *I must go seek the spieler, but I dare not leave him unprotected. Will you watch for me, keep him safe and warm?*

The earth serpent's head turned and bent down,

snuffled at Varney, then more of the elemental's body oozed up from the stone, coiling in a kind of bed beneath him and the head shifted again to lie protectively on his chest. **Go, belovéd, we will watch for you.**

The wildings flowed off the walls and darted for the hole on the far side of the bubble. Hastily Faan rounded the pool and followed them into the dark.

She trotted along for several minutes, enjoying the freedom she felt without Varney dragging on her, feeling guilty every other minute when she thought of him back there, spelled into a coma and oozing blood. She stubbed her toe, swore, slowed to a walk, limping a little. *Why'd the elemental call me belovéd?*

The wildings swirled uneasily. *We-ee littlee, honee chickee, heyday, canna say. Seal conceal why cry.*

Tsa! I wish you would talk straight. Do you mean you know why, but something or someone keeps you from answering me?

See it so, way it go.

With a shrug of their collective shoulders, the wild magic flowed on.

> > < <

The moon's fattening crescent was low in the west when she pushed through thorny bushes and stepped into the open. *How long till the sun comes up?*

Soon's the moon go below.

Thanks. She pushed hair out of her eyes, ran her fingers through the tangled mass, tore another strip off her shirt, and tied her hair at her neck in a neat tail. *Labi labba, take me to your shaman.*

> > < <

Huge and knotted, the trees brooded; she had a feeling they were breathing, moving, not impelled by the wind but by the storming life within them, by their hostility to intruders—to her. As she followed the wilding willo, noises gathered around her, things moving in the scanty underbrush, rustling in the weeds, peering at her from the branches over her head, more and more of them.

"It's a jeggin parade," she muttered under her breath. "How am I supposed to jump him with this audience?"

Frail ghostly figures slid from the trees and stood watching her, each one growing denser as she drew nearer to it, fading again as she left it behind, as if they took solidity from her until they were wild-eyed girls staring hate at her, lifting hands in threat as she moved past them, then ghosts again still hating her. She began wondering if she were rushing into disaster, running downhill so fast she couldn't stop until she crashed.

It was true. She couldn't stop. The Mezh was aroused, the shaman would be feeling it already. She should have stayed inside the hole, sent the wildings to explore. And waited for daylight. Too late now. *You think I'd learn,* she told herself.

The earth shifted under her feet, strands of briar whipped out, tangled about her legs, ripped at her ankles, small stones rolled into her path and bruised her bare feet when she stepped on them, bird droppings splatted down at her, landing in her hair, on her shoulders, her arms, her nose.

Cursing and miserable, she flashed herself clean again and again; the flamelets that were baby fire-demons flickered along her arms, but she suppressed them when they grew too feisty. She'd gotten her belly full of destruction when she danced women into maenads for the Honey Mother and sent them raging against their men.

A bushy little beast trotted into her path, crouched, lifted its tail and sprayed her with a stench so awful she dropped to her knees, her arms pressed against her mouth, her eyes burning, her stomach knotting. She fought for control, the fire-demons leaping on her arms, burning blue in the vapor, burning away the stink. Drinking it in, growing stronger as they swallowed stench and hate.

She flashed away the last of the vapor, lifted her head and raged at the forest. "I nearly lost it, fools! Listen to me, I don't want to hurt anyone, but there are things that defend me; if they get loose, there's going to be a lot of hurt."

She felt they understood her, had the sense the Gathering drew back from her. The path was clear and the wildings were more relaxed; they stopped whirling about her and reassembled themselves into the guiding willo.

The rustles trailed along, the eyes were still on her, the hot breath of hate came out of the trees at her, but the worst harassment stopped and the watches stayed back. After a few moments she sighed with relief and dropped into an easy jog.

> > < <

The village was a collection of dome-shaped houses scattered along both sides of a small stream. In glades around it, there were dozens of garden plots with tubers and pod plants growing vigorously. It was not dawn yet, but the cilt that lived here were out, even the children, standing around in clumps, talking and staring uneasily at the darkness under the trees.

Faan walked slowly into the open, the wilding willo hanging over her head, blue fires rising like wings from her shoulders. She passed between clumps of mezhmerrai and walked into the center of the neat little footbridge arching over the stream; it was made with casual skill, held together with hand-carved pegs and grass ropes wound round and round the parts.

"I will speak with he who spelled my friend."

A group of older men came warily toward the bridge, stopped when they were still several yards from it. "Go away," one of them said, stumbling over the words as if he barely knew what they meant. "Perlop, sihrlahin. Bu'hut'ta'kam sini."

Pain stabbed inward from her temples; she swayed, blinded by sweat, then she was under-

standing what they said, Abeyhamal's Gift oper-
ating again, taking no note of her wishes or her
well-being. "Go away, witch," the man had said,
"we don't want you here." Nu, that was just too
bad. They were going to have to put up with her.

She rubbed the back of her hand across her eyes
and searched for words in this new language that
was flooding into her head, said finally, "Bring
me the shaman who spelled my friend and me. I
only want to talk, I don't want to hurt anyone."

They stared at her, arms folded on their painted
chests, nostrils flaring, stubbornly resistant to her
plea.

"Listen to me, please. I'll burn the village if I
have to. I don't want to do damage to anything or
anyone. Don't make me do it. Please?"

Between two of the houses, a youth whirled a
sling and loosed a stone at her.

The fire-demon on her left shoulder flared
hugely, arced to meet the stone, licked it up, and
continued the arc to devour the slinger. It happened too fast for Faan to stop.

She forgot everything else as she struggled to
pull the demon back as it fought to continue its
rampage. Sweating, teeth biting into her lip, distracted by the need to keep the second demon
from loosing its bonds, she finally subdued it, then
stood swaying and gulping in huge mouthfuls of
air. When she could speak again, she gasped,
"Please."

Muttering and angry, the people of the cilt began closing in on her.

"Wait." Followed by a silent boy with a drum dangling from one hand, an old man came from one of the houses. He silenced the rising mutter from the cilt with a lift of his hand, passed through the cluster of elders and stopped before the bridge. "What do you want?"

"Varney unspelled."

"Then?"

"Nothing. We leave."

He stared at her, his little black eyes sunk in wrinkle nests, his mouth pursed. He nodded, started to speak.

"Not here. I don't want him waking in the dark, alone. We'll go to where he is, then you wake him."

He scowled at her, jerked around as one of the elders set a hand on his arm and whispered urgently in his ear.

"Tid!" He pulled free. "Leave this to me. Singli," he said to the boy who stood close behind them. "Go in the rumm, do the bruntun till I get back."

The boy's lips trembled a moment, his eyes were huge and frightened, but he bowed his head and trudged off.

The shaman felt at the pouches on his belt, then set his hands on his meager hips. "Motj?"

"What I say, I do," she told him. "Once he's awake, you're free to leave. If you don't bother me again, I won't bother you."

"There is one dead."

"Not by my will, but by his act. He attacked

me, provoked my defenders who are not beings of great patience. I stopped the fire as soon as I could."

"Ia, that was seen." He shook himself and took a tentative step toward the bridge. "Lead and I follow."

She swung round and marched off, the people of the cilt backing away from her, glowering at her, muttering things she didn't want to hear.

The shaman followed.

Behind them a drum sounded inside one of the houses, a boy's voice was raised in a wailing chant.

> > < <

Lighted by the wilding fires, the elemental lifted its head, focused its obsidian eyes on the shaman who stumbled, then righted himself and marched grimly around the pool.

You have soothed my heart, O belovéd, she told the great dark serpent, sliding easily this time into the strange communication she'd found before. *Is there aught that I can do for you?*

To serve is sufficient, belovéd. The serpent bowed its head, then melted back into the stone.

Ignoring all this, the shaman squatted beside Varney, took a bundle of sticks from his pouch, used flint and steel to kindle a small flame. He dropped dried leaves into the fire, crouched over them, snuffling in huge drafts of the spicy smoke.

When he was deep enough in trance, he swayed

from side to side, his thighs spread, his hands fumbling over Varney's face. He muttered and groaned, plucked a single hair from Varney's head, then bellowed hoarsely and fell back. After a moment, he blinked and got to his feet. " 'Tis done," he said. "Wake him if you want. He only sleeps now."

She didn't want to trust him, but it was politic to show she did, so she nodded. "T'kasi, shir." She waited until he circled the pool and walked into the darkness beyond, then she dropped beside Varney, pinched his ear.

"Huh?"

"How are you, Var? You've slept forever." She glanced along his body, saw with wonder and relief that his torn feet had healed themselves; if the serpent had done that, she owed it more than she'd acknowledged. *Service is all,* it said. Blesséd be it.

He sat up, rubbed at his eyes, a gesture that renewed the flow of tenderness and need in her weary body. "I don't remember. . . ."

"You must have been asleep on your feet. I widened a crack and we crawled out through it. There's water here, not much else. While you slept, I went ahead a ways, found an opening to the outside not too far from here."

"Make one of those lights, will you? This weird red stuff gets on my nerves."

"Nu, I will." She crafted a willo, set it floating above the pool. "That better?"

"Much."

> > < <

When they pushed through the thorny bushes and came into the open, the sun had risen above the trees, shadows running long ahead of it. Varney stretched until his bones creaked, fetched a long shout, wheeled, and caught her in his arms. He danced her round and round until they were both dizzy and fell laughing to the grass.

He kissed her, jumped to his feet. "Let's get out of here, Sorcerie. I hate these nadsic trees."

She sighed and got to her feet. "Have you any idea where we are?"

"Not a crumb. Doesn't matter, all we have to do is go downhill and east, we'll come to the edge sooner or later." He started off even before he finished, striding downslope, his shadow jerking behind him.

Faan followed more slowly. Her whole body ached and her head was stuffed and heavy as if she were coming down with a bad cold. Maybe she was, she'd worn herself to a nub without food or rest. He didn't know about any of that and he wasn't going to if she had any say.

The going was rough and Varney slowed before long, began to pick his way along the mountain-side, trying to hold the line, but once they were away from the lava fields, the trees shut out the sun and at times it was even difficult to know whether they were going uphill or down.

The daylight Divimezh was less intimidating, but there were daylight dangers as well and Var-

ney remembered them suddenly. Despite her protests, he tore a limb from a tree, stripped off the
small branches, and made himself a staff.

The darkness under the trees grew thicker after
that, the rustles about them louder and angrier.

After an hour or two, Varney drew his hand
across his mouth, combed his fingers through his
hair. "Trum! You think there'd be water around."

Faan limped closer; she was scratched and
stone-bruised, so weary she could barely stay on
her feet. She leaned against a tree, eyes half
closed, watching him as he turned, scowling, trying to decide where to go next. "Do you want me
to find water?"

He turned his frown on her. "Why didn't you
say so? Do it."

She closed her eyes, felt the wildings' flittery
touches against her skin. *Will you? For me?*

Honee chickee, follow we.

Go slow, I'm not up to more than a crawl.

*Slow we go, forget that zit, miseree more than
three.*

Never mind him, I'm as thirsty as he is. She
pushed away from the tree. "Listen, Var. I'm tired,
so be patient, will you? I don't know how far it is,
but there is water."

> > < <

She stretched out, plunged her face into the
stream, let the icy water wash across her burning
skin until she had to breathe, then she gulped
down as much as she could swallow. When she

sat up, Varney was watching her.

"I'm hungry," he said. "You?"

"Tja. Of course. Do you know what we can eat? This place is strange to me, I wouldn't know what would kill me if I bit into it. Besides, it's only Spring. There won't be berries or things like that, will there?"

"Easy enough. Find us a Devil village. They'll have food, you burn them out, we take it from them."

Mouth dropping open, she stared at him, then closed her eyes, seeing again the face of the stone-throwing boy being burned to ash. "You can't mean that," she said finally.

"You can do it. I know you can."

"Neka." She pressed her hand against her mouth, swallowed repeatedly, unable to get the vision—and the smell—out of her mind.

"What's the fuss? They're savages, not even human, and they nearly killed us. It's only fair that they feed us. Whether they want to or not." He came closer to her, cupped his hand around her neck and stood rubbing his fingers up and down the curve of her nape, gently, delicately, persisting until she was breathing in quick little pants and barely able to think. "You can do it, little Sorcerie. Keep us alive."

She pulled away from him. "Neka," she said breathlessly. "If we have to go hungry a few days, it won't kill us."

"Stubborn little mulicher," he said, a peevish note in his voice.

He's spoiled, she thought, *a bratty boy. Gods, I wish he didn't make me....* "It was one of the first lessons I had to learn," she said. "The Sibyl pounded it into me. First and last, do no harm to the innocent. Ill done rebounds on the doer, in proportion to the deed."

"Innocent!"

"What about children left hungry, houses you want me to burn? I won't do it. I can't."

"And if we starve, won't you be harming us?"

"Tsa! We're not babies. How long can it take to get out of this place anyway? I remember what you said, five days in the hole, six or seven from the taking. It's an easy subtraction, five from seven. Two days, Varney. Four at most since we don't know the best ways."

He shrugged, walked away. Over his shoulder, he said, "We'll follow the stream. At least we'll have water when we want it."

She stumbled after him, raging at his thoughtlessness. He was punishing her for standing against him. And for stopping his revenge. Tja, that was it, it wasn't starving he was worried about, he wanted to punish the mezhmerrai for laying hands on him, returning him to a stony womb, helpless as an infant. His broad well-muscled shoulders showed through the rents in his shirt, his blond hair fluttered in the sweet caressing breeze of this lovely spring morning. He was such a beautiful man. Why oh why did he have to act like that?

The wildings clustered around her, muttering

their worry among themselves, whispering their
anxieties in her ears. When she paid no attention
to them, they fidgeted about, then landed on her,
touching her everywhere, sliding into her, leaching away the poisons of fatigue, filling her with
their tiny bits of strength, fluttering languidly
away when they'd given her all they could.

The Mezh seemed ordinary this morning, the
trees simply trees, standing sturdy and huge in
the sunlight. There was a web of birdsong and
the rasp of insects, a hushed padpad and scratching of small-lives who ran about just beyond view
in the weeds and shadows and debris on the rum-
pled brown forest floor. But there were other
things that ran along the great limbs that crossed
and meshed over her head, things that watched
her, watched Varney. Eyes on them all the time.
Sense of something waiting. For night? She didn't
know. Too stubborn to halt for a rest, Varney
slogged along beside the stream, pushing impatiently through whippy brakes and stinging brush,
leaving her to make what progress she could
though she hadn't half his size or strength.

On and on they went, through the unchanging
Mezh, the sun glinting on the stream, the sky a
crystalline blue without a sign of a cloud.

Faan's legs ached, she was sticky, sweat trick-
led into her eyes, insect bites were a puny nuisance that mounted with their numbers into a
consuming irritation. There was a floating sensa-
tion in her head that came from lack of food, a
dizziness that brought her more bruises and

scrapes when her feet came down wrong and branches she missed slapped her in the face.

It was a long nightmare, that day's march. She was beginning to realize just how sheltered her life had been; despite all the horrors she'd seen, the death and pain had belonged to others, not to her. Sympathy, tsa, it was all very well, but to understand pain you had to feel it in your own bones, with your own skin.

A stone rolled under her foot and she crashed hard on her buttocks, her head flipped back and cracked against another stone. Gods, it hurt. She got cautiously to her feet and went on, there was nothing else she could do, what was the point of lying there, groaning, no one would come take care of her.

> > < <

She blinked. She was lying flat, the wildings fluttering nervously above her. It must have been only seconds since she went down because she could still hear Varney tramping along downstream. "What.... I fainted. I remember doing that once before. It lasted longer." She rolled on her side, then onto her knees and eased herself onto her feet, her hands pressed against her thighs to add support to her aching back, then she started on.

If she held herself very carefully upright, her back didn't hurt. sometimes, though, she stumbled and pain flashed through her. But it was gone fast, a grunt and a freeze, and it was over. She chuckled suddenly, a feverish noise though she didn't notice that. The power to destroy the Mezh, the stone itself, that she had; she could kill anything that moved or stayed still—but that wouldn't help her shift an inch along this trail. She could see almost anything she wanted to see, she could change stone to air, but she couldn't change it to bread and fill her stomach and shut down the hunger whirl in her head. *I HAVE to find a teacher. As soon as I'm out of this mess, Navarre can shunt me off, but he's going to HAVE to find me a teacher or I'll be such a plague on him, he won't know which end is up.*

> > < <

The wildings plunged into the stream, giggling and chasing each other; Faan watched, blinking, startled but amused to see flames play in water. A moment later a fish came flying onto the bank. She pounced on it, threw it onto the stone where Varney was building a fire, sullenly following her instructions to use only down wood. It's better for burning anyway, she'd told him, not so damp.

He looked round startled. "What?"

"My little fire friends, they're fishing for us."

"Better than nothing, domaji. This is the best I can do without tools. You want to come light it?"

Two more fish landed by her feet. *Patcha, my loves.* She laughed, gasped as a burn from her back washed through her. A third fish landed on the other two. *Enough enough, no need to wring the water dry.*

She dropped the fish by the first one, lanced a flick of fire into the woodpile, sighed with pleasure as the wood began to smoke then crackle as the fire took hold. "Where I grew up, they wrap fish in leaves, then cover them with mud and build a fire over them. Unless you know a better way...."

He shrugged. "Cooking's women's work. Do it how you please."

"Tsa! Stop sulking, Varney; you're acting like a brat."

He narrowed his eyes, then stalked off muttering.

She shrugged. "Potzhead." *Little ones, do you know where I can find some leaves that won't poison me?*

> > < <

Drinking in heat energy to replace what they'd expended on her that long painful day, the wildings were clustered like sleepy birds in the trees whose limbs hung over the fire.

She was stiff and cold; her back didn't hurt as long as she didn't move, but there was a dull ache that grew worse and worse the longer she sat. She'd asked Varney to bury the remains of their meal, but the bones and skin and other leavings still sat in an untidy heap beside the fire. *Women's work,* she thought. *He won't do it, not even to please himself.* He was watching her, his face thoughtful.

"Sweet," he murmured; he got to his feet, came

round the fire and knelt beside her, caressing the side of her face with the knuckle of his bent forefinger. "Little Sorcerie with big ideas." He began to kiss her and slide his hands over her.

At first she went along with it, the touch of his mouth melting her doubts, then he pushed her down and pain was white hot across her back. She tried to shove him away. "Don't," she said, "you're hurting me."

He didn't listen, didn't even seem to hear her. He was too busy with her clothes, his mouth nibbling at hers, smothering her protests.

> > < <

Drowsily he kissed her. "Make sure the fire doesn't go out," he murmured, then rolled over, curled up, and went to sleep.

She lay without moving, tears of pain sliding past her ears into her hair. A low-level agony burned in her back, stabbing deeper with every breath, a warning of what would happen when she moved. She drew shallow breaths, tried to collect herself so she could decide what to do. One thing she did know, in bone and blood she knew it, if he touched her again, she'd kill him.

She eased her trousers up, grinding her teeth as the movements woke new agonies in her back, pulled the laces tight, then tied them. After resting a moment, she rolled onto her side, gasping as spike after spike of pain pierced her. She managed to raise herself on hands and knees, then crawled to the staff he'd thrown down beside the fire. She used it to get herself onto her feet, climbing up it, hand over hand.

Varney snored. The firelight gleamed on his ivory skin, turned his hair red gold, ran like water on the clean planes of his handsome face.

She stood over him, gazed coldly down at him. "I wouldn't kill mezhmerrai and I won't kill you. It's not worth the shame I'd feel." She said it first with anger, then repeated, "Not worth the shame," speaking with grief this time as she felt the tug of what might have been. Hobbling and biting her lip to stifle gasps of pain, she walked away.

Chapter 9
Magus Unmade

Navarre strolled down Tirdza Street, enjoying the noise and bustle, in no hurry to get started on the Varney-hunt. He'd learned caution the hard way, restraint and the need to proceed slowly, testing the ground before each step. The blast from the curse had only reinforced those lessons. Varney wasn't likely to be killed, at least not anytime soon. The only deadline he worked against was his friend's rashness. If Faan succeeded in breaking them loose with her limited learning and dangerous power—and he thought she was quite capable of it—what happened then could be disastrous. In his unthinking hatred of the mezhmerrai, Varney was capable of doing something that would raise the Mezh against all outsiders and in her blind infatuation, Faan would surely back him and amplify the catastrophe.

He liked this land with its tidy, hard-working people, liked them despite their prejudices and their deliberately limited range of thought and interests. He hadn't tried to read the forward nodes—in any case, the curse guaranteed that they'd be dangerously distorted so he couldn't trust what he saw—but he was unhappily aware that his time here was closing out. Soon enough he'd be on the wander again, nothing certain, every path a possible snare. He sighed and turned into the innyard, meaning to collect his horse and head home.

The hostler was leaning against the doorpost, hands in his pockets. "Magus," he said.

A tall skinny man in leathers stepped into the doorway, strings and strings of painted wooden beads wound round his arms and legs, hanging about his neck, more beads threaded onto the thousand tiny plaits in his pale yellow hair. As soon as he appeared, he threw a bird's egg which broke on the ground in front of the Magus.

Alarmed, Navarre leapt back, but it wasn't enough, a bitter odor reached his nostrils, a fine fog billowed around him—and that was the last he knew.

> > < <

Pargats Vicanal stood scowling down at him when he came swimming from the fog. He was stretched out on a greasy table, his hands and ankles locked in iron cuffs riveted to the wood, a wooden plug forced into his mouth and bound in place with leather thongs pulled so tight they cut into his flesh.

"Velams is a clever fellow," the Lielskadrav growled, "but he's young and tender. Time will take care of that. Meanwhile, we've got a few questions for you, zemnik."

We? Navarre lifted his head, peered into the shadows. Dimly he made out the deeply lined face of Nestrats Turet, and behind him, the Kyatty wizard. *I see.* He dropped his head, cursing his carelessness. It was a lapse he was going to pay for. Women and slaves, he'd told Kitya, the only testimony the judges will take from them is what's given under torture. He should have included foreigners in that, and more than judges.

Vicanal turned his head. "Begin."

A growly voice from an area beyond Navarre's feet said, "When we take the gag out, if you try any powerwords, Magus, we'll strangle you a little, until you learn better. Slik, show him."

A noose around his throat tightened suddenly; he started to choke, then the ligature loosened and he could breathe again.

"Question. Where is Varney?"

Hands that smelled of sausage and smoke fumbled about his face, withdrew the plug from his mouth.

"I told all I knew ... ah!"

A limber cane slapped against the sole of his foot. It startled him more than it hurt, but he knew soon enough even a touch would be unbearable.

"In the Divimezh," he said; he began visualizing the timelines, then his brain whited out as the wizard spoke. A growl and a twitch from the Kyatty and he was awake again, fear sour in his mouth as he realized his helplessness.

"Question. Why did you sell him to the Devils?"

"I didn't."

Slap.

"I told the truth. He left and rode into an ambush."

Slap.

"I had nothing to do with it." Slap. "I didn't even know it was happening." Slap. "I don't go round looking for trouble."

"Question. Who bought you?"

"No one. I don't care which of you sits in that nadsic Seat. There isn't enough gold in this puny patch to tempt me. Megg sees to that. I fool around too much, I'm dead."

Slap.

"Question. Who bought you?"

> > < <

The torment went on and on.

Until the lightest touch was an agony that shot through his body and exploded in his head.

He wept and fainted.

They started on the other foot.

Over and over the same questions.

Same answers, words changing, but not the sense.

Screaming.

Cursing them.

Rambling on and on until he was unconscious again.

The questions stopped.

They forced a funnel into his mouth; its spout was curved and flexible and went down his throat.

The wizard poured in a Kyatty drug.

Voices buzzed in his ears.

He could hear himself talking, but couldn't understand what he was saying.

Then that stopped and they threw buckets of cold, soapy water over him, unlocked the cuffs, rolled him onto a litter, and carried him facedown up interminable flights of stairs.

He couldn't be sure how long the climb was because several times they knocked him against a wall as they went round a corner and the jar woke such agony in him, he dropped out for a short while.

They carried him into the stable court; he knew it because he could smell horse droppings and sweat.

He managed to turn his head.

There was a mule hitched to a divric, the wizard on the driver's bench.

The guards threw him into the back of the divric; he landed with his face buried in old musty straw smelling of horse urine and rat droppings. They locked manacles on his ankles and wrists, tied a tarp over the divric's cargo box, shutting him into darkness.

The wizard clucked to the mule and the divric started moving, jolting across the flags of the court.

He fainted.

> > < <

When Navarre woke, he was lying on his back, the tarp folded under his head, the plug in his mouth, the irons replaced with boiled leather cuffs linked by short thongs to a leather belt. His feet had been poulticed and bandaged, the chains taken away.

The wizard looked over his shoulder, laughed. "So you're with us again," he said, his voice dark, rich, with a buzz in the lower registers. He faced forward, clucked to the mule, slapped the reins on the beast's hindquarters, so it went along faster for a while, then dropped back to its steady shuffle.

When the wizard spoke again, he didn't bother turning around. The light wind blew his words back to Navarre. "Best get used to it, Bigous. That's your new name, Magus. A play on the old, eh? Bigous, it means Owned Thing. You're my Thing now." He hummed a snatch of tune in a minor key, slapping out the rhythm on his thigh. "Sh'ma then, Bigous, here's the way it's going to be. When you cooperate, you eat. That's just the beginning. You're going to have to earn every stitch on your back. If you want shelter, a fire, anything like that, you find a way to make it worth my while to provide it. Water and air, now they're free. Water is sacred. Sh'ma sh'ma, it's bad kwidd, very bad, to make even a Thing earn water. Besides, there's plenty of it round my place, no need to stint." He broke off, hummed some more, then slapped his thigh. "A little warning, bigou Bigous. You're smart, you won't have to have it repeated. You give trouble or try to run, I hamstring you, cut the tendons in your hands, you understand? No, don't fuss about answering. It's enough you know what to expect. We'll get on, bigou Bigous, I know it."

He went back to humming and whistling, sitting hunched over on the driver's bench, his long bony body moving easily with the bump and sway of the divric.

As the sun sank lower in the west, Navarre wallowed in despair as he had in the days after he learned the hard way the extent of the curse; he'd hovered on the edge of killing himself for months, working himself into exhaustion in his forge, making knives and axe blades and swords, using the sweat of his body, the precision of his hands to distract himself from the endless circle of regret, to wear himself out so he could sleep at night.

Even after the sun went down, the divric rumbled on.

Sometime after midnight, the wizard stopped at a guard post, showed papers to the officer in charge of the detachment manning it; neither of them referred to the prisoner in the back of the divric and Navarre lay quiet, knowing there was no point in drawing attention to himself.

The guard lifted the weighted bar and the wizard drove out of Valdamaz into Kyatawat.

A heaviness lifted from Navarre's spirit. Megg's prohibition was gone, replaced by a confusion of tugs and slaps, like the crosscurrents pulling at a swimmer in the bay. Kyatawat had no local god, only a churning brew of Entities with a melange of attributes shared and separate. The Wees were tiny Powers who drifted on the wind and nipped at lives like fleas. The Wieldys were huge Powers that guarded territories, capricious, often malicious, sly rather than clever. And then there were the Tweens, the between-sizers who were so varied there was no categorizing them. It was a realm made for wizards and witches who worked on things of the earth and operated within narrow limits. Inside his personal space, a wizard could be stronger than the most powerful sorcerer, but that sorcerer would be over the horizon in an instant if the wizard had a lapse of concentration. As would a Magus, even a crippled one like Navarre. If he weren't so tired . . . so very tired. . . .

Despite the dull ache in his feet and the bumping of the divric, Navarre slept.

> > < <

He woke much later, hearing the pit pat of rain on canvas, the sharper tings where it fell into metal bowls. The wizard had turned the tarp into a shelter of sorts, built a fire at one end. It was down to coals now, his supper dishes set outside to let the rain wash them. He was rolled in a blanket on the far side of the fire, awake, red glints reflected in his pale eyes as he watched Navarre.

After a moment, he spoke, softly, his dark voice like a wisp of night. "Sleep."

Navarre slept.

> > < <

When he woke again, he was stretched out in the back of the divric which was lurching, shaking, rumbling along at no great speed, the paved roadway having ended a short distance beyond the guardpost at the Valdamaz border. His body was bathed in a pleasant lassitude and nothing seemed to matter.

When the sun was high enough to shine into his eyes, he knew he'd been drugged, that the wizard had somehow fed and watered him in his sleep, and slipped in a stupifier while he was doing it. He couldn't collect enough energy to be annoyed about it. And it had a positive side—he couldn't feel his feet or the other aches and bruises of his expertly battered body.

The plug was gone from his mouth.

The only difference it made was to his comfort. His tongue was thick and his throat so numb he couldn't have cried out if someone were cutting off one of his legs.

Drowsily he considered his situation. *When I get out of this,* he thought ... and dropped off to sleep again.

> > < <

The wizard was lifting his head, pouring water in his mouth, water with a slightly bitter taste.

His head was lowered with rough care to the tarp, the straw rustled as the wizard checked the bandages on his feet.

Before the divric moved on, he was asleep again.

> > < <

There was a tickling beside his ear; he moved his head after a while, seeking to chase the thing away.

You want to get away from him, don't you? Listen to me, I can help you, all you have to do is say you'll serve me. He moved his head, irritation at the drill of the mosquito voice scraping away some of the drug-induced lassitude. He was in no shape for escaping anywhere nor, even drugged, was he such a fool as to trust a disembodied voice in his ear. After a while, he recognized the presence as one of the Wees that floated about Kyatawat making mischief wherever they could.

He ignored it despite the tickling and the exasperating whine. After a while it got annoyed, bit him, and went off to find a more cooperative victim.

The wizard looked over his shoulder, grinning. "Pesky little things, aren't they."

> > < <

They rolled deeper into Kyatawat, moving across the grassy hillocks on a trace that wound about like a worm with spasms.

Swaying on the driver's bench, shoulders rounded, hands dangling between his knees, reins pressed between his forearm and thigh, the wizard rambled on and on about the oddities of the land. "This is a peculiar place, Bigous, takes a lifetime to learn even a little of it. You try running it alone, you get yourself swallowed worse'n anything I can do. See that bit of glitter rock there? It's usually round here somewhere, but it isn't always in the same place. Same with the other boundstones. You can't see one from another, they're scattered that wide, but they move, too. They mark the Wieldy Dubdukawudy's holdland. You want to keep clear of that one, it plays games, crazy games."

> > < <

A while later he said, "That patch there, you can tell it by the haze that clings to the top of the grass, that's Hugwuhpady's holdland. One step inside that fuzz and you could be anything from a frog to an elk, if it's feeling kindly, or something a lot more disgusting."

> > < <

He stopped the mule and stood up, turning and frowning, eyes narrowed to slits as he searched the featureless grass.

He kept that up for several minutes, then shook himself, climbed down from the divric and took hold of the mule's halter. He led it through a wavy dance for more than an hour, then climbed back aboard, took up the reins and set the mule into a wide, shallow arc, heading obliquely westward. "That was Tugshadaddily's holdland, Tiyulwabarr be blessed for passing me some kwidd, it was asleep, not storming." He cleared his throat. "Ti-yulwabarr flows with my Ky'at. You're going to have to learn its little ways if you want to avoid making your life a misery."

> > < <

By the third day, things had settled into a greater calm; the most dangerous parts were behind them, though the wizard continued to negotiate with care the safest way among the holdlands of the Wieldys and at the same time choosing paths where he wouldn't meet hostile Ky'ats. All the time he dribbled words as if he'd had no one to talk to for years. Perhaps he hadn't. A wizard maintained too many secrets to trust to chance ears, had too many enemies who'd seize any opening he gave them to make his life a misery.

> > < <

He pointed his whip to the east. "That's the Sawqwa Ky'at migrating out there, going south with their herds, you could see them if you were sitting up. Satubelarr flows with them, it's a Tween Power, useful but nothing special. Still, the Sawqwa ancestors stole it from mine, so we're herited enemies. Long as we have room to keep apart, though, they don't bother me, I don't bother them."

> > < <

On the seventh day, the surroundings changed; the rolling grassland gave way to brush and scattered trees, small knotty trees with thick, dark green foliage, the leaves hard as rawhide with a strong acrid odor that was everywhere; even the rain smelled of it. The road, if it could be called such, was worse than in the grass; there were countless washes and narrow rocky ravines crossed by rope and plank bridges that groaned and sagged beneath the weight of the divric.

Navarre was sitting up now, leaning against the side of the divric's box, eyes busy, ears drinking in everything the wizard said. The Kyatty was talking too much, giving too much away, telling his secrets, trusting the drug to keep Navarre from paying more than cursory attention. But the long discipline of the Magus' learning was reasserting itself; his mind had started turning over again, though he still couldn't concentrate on anything for more than a few moments.

The mule labored on, the divric lurching and shuddering as they moved deeper into what couldn't quite be called foothills since there were no mountains, at least none visible, though the ever-present boil of clouds in the west obscured the horizon.

> > < <

"This part of Kyatawat ... the Wieldys don't like it ... too bristly for them ... it's mostly Tweens and Wees one has to look out for ... you'll have to learn the signs, Bigous...." The wizard was standing again, feet wide, balancing easily despite the jolt and sway of the divric, his head turning constantly, side to side, then a glance over his shoulder; he was tensely alert, his chatting interrupted by sudden direction changes or muttered chants as he reached into one or another of the pouches dangling from his belt and flung out powder ground from roots and leaves, adding to the pungency of air. "There's a ripple you can see ... not directly ... from the corner of your eye. You have to learn to look for it ... and to name the Tween once you see the sign. Since you've the Art, I expect you will be able to smell who's what soon enough. You just have to learn ... which is friendly ... which is going to bite you ... which you can ignore...."

> > < <

By the ninth day, the trees were no longer isolated as on a savannah, but were a dense woodlands. Navarre began seeing strays from the herds of the yeyeldi, the hill Kyatty's deerlike herdbeasts whose long silky hair had shifted already from Winter white to Spring beige striped with dark chocolate. It was calving time and the trees were filled with that moo-aaah's of the newborn and the bugling blats of their mothers.

Now and then he caught glimpses of the herdboys and herdgirls riding their small shaggy ponies, now and then adult men and women who were watching over the birthings, there to help any cow yeyeldi who was having trouble. Adults

and children alike glanced at the divric, then
turned and stared until it was out of sight. No one
greeted the wizard or made any attempt to approach him.

In the middle of the afternoon when the heat
was oppressive and the stench of the trees was so
heavy it weighed on Navarre like stone, making
it hard to breathe, the wizard sighed with relief,
dropped onto the seat and sat once again, hunched
over, hands between his knees, apparently half-
asleep. Navarre rubbed his thumbs slowly along
the stained leather of the confining belt, struggling to focus his hazed mind. *Home,* he thought.
He's in his own holdland.

They rounded a huge boulder with vines growing thickly over it, dipped abruptly down onto a
dirt road broader and better cared for than any
other tracks they'd traveled previously. Stone
walls rose up and cupped round a meadow with
a stream running down the middle. Dome-shaped
leather dwellings were scattered on both sides of
the stream, hobbled ponies wandered about like
family pets, nibbling at clumps of grass. Small
yellow dogs nosed about, played with children,
fought over bones or bits of chewleather. In a cor-
ral made from braided leather ropes and thin
poles with the bark still on them, several cow yeyeldi kept for their milk stood with heads down,
dozing in the afternoon heat. Small blond children played in the dust, chased each other round
the hutches, waded in the stream, none of them
older than four or five; watching them and working on bits of leather, knitting, twirling yeyeldi

wool into yarn with hand held spindles, doing all kinds of small useful tasks, old men and women sat on leather cushions sucking at long-stemmed pipes and blowing pungent smoke in twin streams from their nostrils, smoke that rose slowly into the motionless air and hovered about their heads.

Navarre drowsed as the wizard drove along the road, nodding wordless greetings to the elders, whistling a sudden trill to warn off a little boy who was rushing toward the mule while he looked behind him at other boys dancing and yelling at him.

Calving time, the Magus fetched up from the depths of his mind, his mouth spreading in a smile of satisfaction as he finished the thought. The rest out with the herds.

They passed into the trees on the far side of the meadow, the road deteriorating as they moved, stopped finally in a small glade with the stream curving along one side. Another of the domed leather dwellings was erected on a base of carefully fitted stone, slate, blue-gray and washed clean. Beside it was a small shelter of twigs and straw for the mule; a large brindle cat came out of that; it stretched, its rear high, tail waving, its white forepaws reaching out, kneading the bark-littered earth. Then it sat on its haunches, slitted yellow eyes watching intently as the mule slowed to a stop and the wizard jumped down.

As he hooked his fingers in the mule's halter and started leading him into the shelter, the cat walked over to him, mewing a welcome, stropping itself against his leg. He laughed. "Wi'ac,

Shishi. I brought us home a Bigous, go sniff at his knees, eh?"

Leaving Navarre sitting drug-chained on the dirty straw, he stripped the harness off, laid it away in a wooden chest waterproofed by a thick coat of wax. The cat jumped on the mule's back and rode there with his paws tucked in as the beast wandered off, heading without hurry toward the stream.

For several more minutes the wizard puttered about, bending over to make marks in the ring of sand about the slates, now and then dropping pinches of something from his belt pouches.

Dimly Navarre sensed the play of powerful magic, poufing up and then fading in an irregular rhythm. As the wizard completed his circuit, the Magus finally worked it out. The man was disarming the wards he'd set in place when he went south.

The wizard bent down and pushed past the skin door of his house, came out again a moment later with a roll of leather wrapped about thin sticks.

He forced the sticks into the ground beside the flimsy mule shelter, bent them over and tied them into a sketch of a small dome, then tossed the leather cover over them and began pegging it down. In less than twenty minutes he had a small hutch ready for its new inhabitant.

Doghouse for the family pet, Navarre thought. The drugs were beginning to loose their grip a little, either because his body was growing accustomed to them or because the wizard had been careless here on his home ground. He didn't move, tried to disguise his increasing alertness, but that proved useless.

The wizard came striding over to the divric, looked at him with narrowed eyes, then blew a pinch of powder into his face and the world dropped away.

> > < <

When he woke, he heard whistling outside the hutch where he lay on a thick pad of woven straw, a blanket drawn over him.

There was a nip behind his ear, like a fleabite but hotter. The Wee was back. *Say you'll serve me. Hey hey, say it and I'll tell you how to find what you need to burn the chilchil out of you.* Once again he ignored it. He knew more about Wees than the wizard—or the Wee—guessed, knew they were tiny tricksters, irresponsible and often tainted with malice. The day might come when he'd take that offer, but he couldn't even walk yet and he knew far too little about local pitfalls to chance it.

The wizard pulled back the doorskin and thrust his head inside. "Out, Bigous. It's time you started earning your keep."

The stiffness on his throat had loosened a little, but he knew the wizard could choke him with a gesture much as the apprentice spidznal Slik had done with a physical noose. Carefully he shaped the words. "Can' wal.'"

"You can crawl. You don't need to walk. If you want water, you have to go to the stream to get it. If you want food, you have to finish your job first."

"Wha' jo'?"

"Tell you later." He withdrew and went whistling off again.

After so many days of travel with no washing and only occasional stops so he could relieve himself, he felt as if he had filth encrusted on his bones. It wasn't something he liked, nor something he knew well. His family weren't rich, his father was a silversmith with a small shop, but they'd been comfortable, clean and well-dressed, all of them, his parents and his three brothers and two sisters. He hadn't seen them for years, but he always had a soothing sense that they were living much the same, quiet contented lives. His Talent had taken him a long way from them, brought him suffering and pleasures they couldn't possibly imagine, but he'd never felt such degradation as he had these past ten days, the babbling weeping worm on the table, then the stinking, crippled slave he was now.

It had taken such a short time to reduce him to this, such little things, a limber cane slapping against his soles, his own body filth.

He emerged from the doghouse on his hands and knees; it took him fifteen minutes to crawl to the stream, then he rolled into it and let the icy mountain water wash round him. After a short while he managed to raise himself on his knees and struggle out of his trousers and shirt. He scrubbed the worst of the muck off them with sand and a twist of dry grass, then tossed them onto a gravel patch and began cleaning his body.

"You are a hairy one." The wizard stood with hands on hips, watching him. "Mayhap I should've dubbed you Tibdab instead." He shook his head. "Bad Kwidd to change a calling. Sh'ma, bigou Bigous, it's time to tell you what name you'll give me, not my truename, certainly not, but my best usename. I am called Sabusé because I am the spring from which good flows. You will call me Sabusé without honorific because I need none; I am not dependent on the will of others for my worth like you people in the south." He nodded, a swift jerk of his head. "For my nose's sake, I will give you clothing, this morning and this morning only. You will keep it clean, which you can do after you've finished your tasks for the day; you may use those. . . ." He stirred the wet pile of cloth with his toe, a look of distaste on his face. "When you're mucking out or washing the others." He glanced at the sun, tossed a grayish waxy ball to Navarre. "Soap. Don't be long."

> > < <

Sabusé muttered under his breath as he tucked the ends of the copper wire under the elaborate knot that finished the binding of the great toe on his captive's left foot. Navarre winced as he felt a sudden surge of magic that burnt like acid as the knot melted together.

The wizard settled back on his heels, satisfied with what he'd done. "We'll start you off with little things," he said. "You perceive power wherever it flows, cikoud? Yes, of course you do. For the past several years while going here, there, wherehaveyou, I've picked up bits of stone, popped them in my whathaveyou sack and brought them home with me. What with one thing and another, I haven't had time, Bigous, to sort them, to label them and store them properly. Some, no doubt, broke and the virtue ran out, others had it sucked out, who knows how. Throw them away, they can be gravel on the stream bank, that's all they're worth now. As to the rest, sort them according to degree and kind, I'm talking about the power in them, not the form. When you've finished sorting them, study them until you know each like the fingers on your hand. Don't try to be smart. It'll cost you your toe."

> > < <

It was a tedious job. Navarre had to take each one, close it in his hand to shelter it from other influences, then tease out its secrets. Slow and tedious. He found himself enjoying it, which surprised him considerably. He like the smells and textures of the little stones, none of them larger than a bird's egg. Some of them were veined quartz and rather pretty, some were dull gray lumps, but there were aspects to please him in all of them, except the wasted ones, of course. He found those annoying. He detested waste.

None was exactly like another which made classification difficult; sometimes he shifted a fragment of crystal or shard of obsidian half a dozen times before he was satisfied enough to leave it for the moment.

The piles grew slowly, but they did grow, both in number and size.

He was startled when Sabusé called his name and he looked up to see an old woman holding a metal pannikin of something that smelled wonderful. With the wizard standing arms crossed and eyes narrowed, the old woman picked her way through the piles of stone and set the pannikin down beside him, along with a round of flatbread and a glass of herb tea. She left as cautiously and as silently as she'd come, disappearing into the trees as she went back to the Ky'at village.

"You have worked well, Bigous," Sabusé told him. "You may take a sun-finger to eat and move about, then you must return to your task." He read the question in Navarre's face, moved his shoulders impatiently. "It's obvious if you use your head a little. The time it takes for the sun to move the width of a finger. We don't have your southerners' mechanisms here, we don't need them. Sun, moon and stars tell us all we need to know." He stalked off to do whatever business it was that took up his daylight hours.

Navarre shrugged and began eating the yeyeldi stew.

> > < <

The days that followed passed the same way, Navarre absorbed in a small but painstaking task, the wizard vanished somewhere.

Now and then children from the village came to the edge of the trees to stare at him, too shy to venture out of shadow. And the brindle cat took to curling up against his buttocks, purring when she wasn't asleep.

His feet healed enough so he could get about with the aid of a crutch one of the old men whittled for him.

The drugs Sabusé continued to feed him, the endless small tasks, the kindness of the old people, the laughter of the children, the clean air, the peace—all of these things combined with his deep-seated dread of confronting the curse to keep him where he was.

He had a lot of healing to do, but he hadn't forgotten how he got here and he wasn't about to stay a slave ... he just needed time ... time and concentration ... time and. . . .

Time.

CABAL

They met again, late at night, in the dusty, cob-webbed catacombs beneath the Temple, gathered about a single candle flickering atop a stone coffin, four solid shadows in their black felt robes.

The squat man watched the others with a mocking smile hidden in the shadow of his cowl. Leduzma Chusker, welcome nowhere, Ledus Cikston's bastard half brother, got on a mezhmerrai slave, adopted into the Family by a doting father gone soft in the head, tolerated because he made himself useful, in fact irreplaceable; Cikston knew, if the others didn't, that the Family wealth floated on Chusker. What he'd done inside the Family, he was doing here and else-where; the time would come when every breath drawn in Valdamaz would belong to him, when he would say *tja* and one would live, *neka* and one would die. Only Nenova suspected the extent of his ambi-tion and she'd say nothing, not out of loyalty, but out of self-interest.

Vocats Oirs was fidgeting nervously, his boots scraping on the gritty floor. "Begarz is being treated like a hero since the fake attack on him." His voice was petulant, almost whining. "He's got men patting

his back who'd never have gone near him a month
ago."

Nenova made an impatient moment with her arm.
"It's what we did it for, isn't it?"

Kreisits Lazdey snorted. "What he means is, it
isn't him."

"Laz, you don't need to sneer. I've seen you looking sour, yourself. He's stealing your light; you're
the one who 'saved' him, but he pushes you back
every time."

Lazdey shrugged and turned his shoulder to Oirs.
To Chusker, he said, "Those rumors of yours about
Varney being the push behind this, they're going
down well with lots of folks."

Laughing, Nenova shook her head. "If women
could vote," she murmured, "he'd be in the Seat
tomorrow."

"Nu, they can't and he's been in too many beds
where he doesn't belong; he's made enemies."

Oirs rubbed his gloved hands together. "I heard
Vicanal's half crazy. He's found out somehow, they
say the Magus told him, that Varney's in the Divimezh. They say he's getting ready a raiding force
to go in and get him."

Lazdey nodded, his wall-shadow moving hugely
behind him. "It's no rumor, I know men in that lot.
He's going to move soon."

Chusker let them speculate on this for several
minutes longer, then he leaned farther into the light,
knocked his gloved knuckles on the lid of the coffin.
When they stared at him, surprised, he said, "Listen, there's more to it than Vicanal making a fool of
himself. You were worried about the Magus, nu? I've

*taken care of him. Some truths. One, Vicanal found
out about Varney from him. Two, he never has liked
Navarre, so it was easy to convince him the Magus
was the one who sold Varney. Nu, he seized him,
put him to question, then passed him on to a Kyatty
wizard. Three, Navarre's in Kyatawat now, crippled
and a slave. And I say to you, it's a good thing Vicanal is taking himself off; he has friends, he won't
be lining them up now, he'll be too busy. Laz, it's
time we dealt with Druz. He's gaining strength at
Begarz' expense. It's too obvious when you see
them together that he's what Begarz pretends to
be." He held up a hand. "Neka, don't play stupid,
Laz, I know you're not. We don't kill him. No need.
We just persuade him to put his foot in his mouth a
few more times. He likes you. Get him where doing
what comes naturally will appall the weak-stomached
and faint-hearted. I'll set up some occasions, I leave
the rest to you."*

*Oirs sniffed petulantly. "What about me? What
about an attack on me? Won't it be suspicious if
there's none?"*

*Chusker straightened. "Not yet," he said pa-
tiently. "Another missed hit so soon after Begarz
will stink like a beached whale after three days frying
in the sun. We'll beach Druz, and take out . . .
mm . . . Laro, I think, then it'll be your turn."*

"Tiesh tas, as long as it's done."

*Chusker turned to Lazdey. "How is Begarz doing
in Ash Tupel?"*

*"Lagging far behind Druz, even Varney has more
on his spiesh. His numbers have gone up a little
since the attack, but they won't stay up." Lazdey*

*played a tune on his fingers, a help to memory since
he didn't dare write anything down. ''The Jeredarod
of Tupelis, five hundred for Druz. . . .''*

> > < <

*The voices went on as the candle burned lower
and lower, numbers and dispositions, trends and
possibilities, arguing over strategies, arranging the
next week's activities.*

It was nearly dawn before they left.

Chapter 10
Kitya on the Move

Kitya stood on the roof of the tower watching Navarre ride along the Smithy Lane on his favorite horse, a big chestnut gelding with a long stride. In the distance she could see the shadow against the sky that was Savvalis; to her it looked ominous, a great beast in ambush waiting to eat him. She turned away. She'd warned him, but he didn't listen, he never did. There was nothing more she could do. She stopped, touched her long forefinger to her chouk, the eyespot between her brows. At least she could *know*.

Taking the lamp Navarre always left burning in his workroom, its flame having acquired shunga from its presence when he practiced his Art, she hurried down the stairs to the kitchen. Navarre laughed at her ways, but they worked—at least, when he wasn't around, they did.

She searched out the black iron frying pan he'd made for her, with the six bent legs that kept it just the proper distance from the coals, then she hurried to the forge, took charcoal from the wicker basket and returned with carefully counted steps, stretching out her long legs so the count wouldn't go too high; that would weaken the spell. It didn't matter that this was before the beginning of the a'to'a, the a'to'a knew what was what on both sides of its birth. In her mother's toopa, the charcoal was next to the firehole and needed no steps at all, so her mother's say'i'vaho was very very strong and the a'to'a was as detailed as a Sheshintook's dream painting.

She counted the sticks and piled them in the proper manner, then lit them from Navarre's lamp. "Ika nann ye, ika lek ye," she chanted as she blew the sticks alive, then set the pan over the fire and dropped a lump of butter in it. "Chakatuka oo blahaha." She sprinkled salt across the melting lump. "Ayoon a'go, ina laleh. Takeh wharet ayoon a'goheh."

Keeping up the chant, she bent over the pan, watching the melt intently.

At the proper moment, she snatched the pan from the fire, spilled the liquid butter and half-dissolved salt across the floor, screaming, "Towt!"

Breathing deeply, she bent over the spatter, eyes closed, the chouk between her narrow brows throbbing strongly. The smell of hot butter filled the kitchen, the only sounds were a faint sizzle and her rasping breaths.

"Not death," she muttered, "bad time, shackles, fate strong, force, pain, gods interfering. Ah ... ayeee!" She fell to her knees, arms crossed over her breasts, hands clutching her shoulders; for several minutes she rocked from side to side, then she sighed and relaxed.

She got to her feet and dipped hot water from

the stove's reservoir into a bucket, added a dollop of soft soap. Muttering to herself, she mopped the floor, then wiped spatters from cabinets and walls. When the room was clean again, she went outside and hoisted a flag on the pole, a small triangle of green felt.

She stood looking up at it for a moment, watching it shift sluggishly in the light wind. "Not that it will do any good," she said and went inside.

> > < <

Three days later Kaundar hadn't come, nor had Navarre. Kitya stood atop the tower once again, staring at the stain of Savvalis. He was gone, caught in his enemy's trap. She'd read it in the butter and his absence proved it. And he was wrong again, wrong about the mezhmerrai, the absence of Kaundar proved that.

When her father died, her mother grieved, but she didn't lie in the dark sobbing like some might have. She'd had her children, the herd, and her toopa to take care of. She wept for a day and and night, then she got to work. Kitya touched the tip of her forefinger lightly against the chouk, felt it tremble slightly. "Keo, the strike was set, the ill is done. I will not tremble here like a fledgling peggil in its hole."

She hurried to the bedroom on the second floor, gathered a few things she'd brought from her mother's toopa when she came away with Navarre, and set them on the dressing table—a thin curved skinning knife, the linked bone rings with

the claws on them that she wore on her left hand
when a raid was due or she was out alone with
the kuneag herd, the little bone phials of poison,
and some other things of the same nature. She
frowned at them, then looked down at the long
dress she was wearing, a dark green shift falling
straight from the shoulders with a slit up one side;
he liked her in it. After she finished her work,
she'd put it on every day since the day he'd left.
She ran her hand down the front, the soft velvet
clinging to her fingers. Then she took it off, hung
it carefully in the wardrobe, and brought out one
of Navarre's wool shirts. She used the knife to cut
off all but a handspan of the sleeves, then slipped
it on. It was far too big for her, hung nearly to
her knees, but she found a chain she used for a
belt, clipped it round her waist, then inspected
herself in the mirror. The shirt covered her ade-
quately; with leggings to protect her thighs she
could ride in it. She'd have to make the leggings,
but that wouldn't take long.

She took the shirt off, draped it over the chair
at the dressing table, laid the belt on it. She'd
need food and she'd better raid Navarre's stash
for emergency coin. Then craft a karetka to point
him—she'd need hairs from Navarre's brush, some
things he'd worn against his skin, and a piece of
clean bone. She stood a moment with her hand
resting lightly across the bronze chain and the
black wool, eyes closed, mouth compressed in a
thin line, then she pulled on a work shift and went
down to get started with her preparations. In the

end there was only one path for her, and there were things she had to do before she took it.

> > < <

In the last watch of the night, Kitya saddled the spotted dun Navarre called Tiggley, put a halter on him rather than a bridle, she disliked the idea of the bit; it seemed to her disrespectful to push a bar of iron into a horse's mouth, an admission of feebleness and ignorance. One shouldn't need such a thing to control the beast; she never had. She looked around a last time, then rode away from the smithy.

When she reached the crossing, she took out the karetka and held it in front of her face, dangling free at the end of its filament, one of her long black hairs. It was a pointed shard chipped from the leg bone of a bird, bound round and round with the curly brown hair of the Magus, strips of leather from his slippers, a wool swatch cut from his favorite robe dangling from it, sewed in place with special knots. It fluttered in the predawn breeze that teased the wisps of hair that escaped her travel knot and crept like icy fingers through every crevice in her clothing. For a moment it simply swayed erratically and her stomach clenched, then the sway settled and it pointed north.

He was alive. The pointing was proof of it. She sat a moment, head bowed, eyes closed, then tucked the karetka away and turned onto the Highroad.

> > < <

When she reached the cluster of soddies outside the Southgate, she stopped Tiggley and sat with hands crossed on the horn. Maybe he was in there and maybe he wasn't. She didn't want to go inside those walls unless she had to. "O Tiggley, O horse, shall we go round and try the karetka again by the Northgate?" She laughed as his ears twitched and he snuffled when he heard her voice, as if he were actually answering her.

> > < <

When they reached the double bridges across the Dzelskri, she stopped Tiggley beside the Highroad which was crowded with long lines of creaking wains coming to early market heaped with produce from the rich farmlands of the northern fistals. The horse dipped his head and snatched mouthfuls of river grass while she took out the karetka, held it up and waited for it to steady.

It pointed north. He wasn't in the city. She tucked the karetka away, then she slapped Tiggley on his shoulder with the ends of the reins, eased him into the traffic and took him at a canter across the bridge, his hooves clattering musically on the hard wood.

> > < <

She turned into a waystop an hour after sunrise, gave Tiggley grain from the saddlebag and water from the well, squatted beside him with stolid patience while he ate, drank, then grazed a while.

When he was rested, she mounted and continued north on a Highroad increasingly deserted.

> > < <

She could see the watchtower of the border post nearly an hour before she reached it; there was plenty of time for thinking what she was going to do; a woman alone out here, a foreigner—she'd seen the mixture of distaste and lust too often in Varney's eyes to have any illusions about what soldiers so far from home could get up to, given opportunity.

Tiggley was a hunter, used to rough travel and trickier obstacles than that weighted bar blocking the road. On the far side of the bar, the Highroad was flat and straight with grassy hillocks like haystacks on both sides of it. Not much cover, but enough, provided there were no riders coming after her.

She held the horse to a canter as they approached the post, shifted her weight slightly as one of the border guards opened a door and came out, carrying his clipboard.

Nearer she came, nearer—then she slapped the reins on Tiggley's shoulder, shouted in his ear, and sent him galloping toward the bar. He took off, cleared it easily, and thundered into Kyatawat.

She heard an angry shout as she pulled Tiggley
down to a walk, turned him off the road and into
the hillocks so that she was hidden from the tower
and the soldiers in it. In a few breaths she was
sure they weren't going to chase her into Kyatawat, and hidden as she was, they couldn't skewer
her with arrows from the tower. Breathing more
rapidly than usual, she leaned forward, patted the
dun's shoulder, then took him at a cautious walk
through the hillocks on a route paralleling the
road.

As soon as she could, she returned to the road.

> > < <

When the sun dipped below the horizon, she
made a dry camp beside the road. She was nervous now, tautly alert; Kyatawat was as chancy a
place as her homeland, maybe more so. She unfolded the horse's leather bucket, half-filled it
from the water skin and held it for him while he
drank. Afterward, she moistened her own mouth
with a few swallows, then ate bread and dried
meat a mezhmerrit had brought in exchange for
an arrowpoint.

When she was finished, she pulled the bone
claw-rings over her fingers, set the knife on the
ground beside the pad of grass she'd collected,
then wrapped herself in a blanket and lay a while
staring up at the stars. Navarre was alive; the karetka only pointed live things. That was good. It
was also good to be out here, senses alert, nerves
strung taut. She'd forgotten what it was like, when

you dozed with eyes slitted, ears set for any strange noise, with the smell of grass and dung in your nose.

After a while she slept.

> > < <

In the morning, the karetka showed that Navarre's direction had changed from full north to north by west.

She scowled at the rutted track; it rambled off toward the northeast, diverging farther and farther from where she had to go. Chewing her lip, she tucked the karetka away and considered her options.

She could leave the road and ride directly for him, counting on Tiggley's speed and her cunning to keep them out of trouble. After considering what she knew of Kyatawat—not much, but enough to make her go warily—she didn't think that had much chance of working. Besides, her chouk was throbbing again, reacting to the smell of power all around her, and her pum (the rudimentary tail encysted at the end of her spine) was vibrating inside its sac, itching and twitching.

Roads had their attendant perils, but traces like this in her homeland were made by people who knew the safest ways about. No doubt it was the same here. She scratched her toe in one of the ruts. Its sides were chewed and crumbly, there was no grass growing in it. Used often by wheeled carts and . . . she dropped to one knee, inspected the macerated surface . . . shod hooves, a few split hooves. It had rained here recently and she found prints of sandaled feet in a stretch of dried mud.

"Nu, Tiggley. We'll stay with the road for a while." She swung into the saddle, dug her heels into his sides, and settled into a comfortable slump as he loped along.

After half an hour of this, she pulled him to a walk. Navarre was alive. There was no hurry right now; better to conserve strength and keep oneself out of traps.

The road rambled on, shifting from side to side, never wandering very far from the general trend northward.

At sunhigh she came to a waystop, an area surrounded by lumps of blue-gray slate, with a well and a stone drinking trough. She smiled, patted Tiggley's shoulder. "I'm a smart niya, am I not? Rest stop time. It's been a warm morning, that water will be ahhhh...." Humming one of her mother's songs, she slid off his back and led him into the circle.

> > < <

Night brought her to another waystop. She put the hobbles on Tiggley and turned him out to graze, worked the well sweep and filled the water trough, then ate a round of waybread and a strip of dried meat. She dropped into a deep sleep as soon as she rolled up in her blanket.

> > < <

She woke to the intent gaze of half a dozen pairs of bright blue eyes.

She sat up, startled, surrounded by children who couldn't have been more than five or six years old. Boys and girls both, dressed much alike, the girls having long blonde braids with ribbons woven in the strands.

Her sudden movement didn't bother them at all. She twisted her head round. A group of adults were standing by the well watching; when they decided she was harmless, they went back to working the well sweep, splashing the water into a ditch beyond the boundstones. Others were sitting on horseback, moving slowly about the edge of a herd of antlered beasts that spread in a broad blotch across the grassy hillocks.

The children poked at each other, giggled; the tallest, oldest, and most daring (who happened to be a girl much like Kitya remembered herself being at that age) set her hands on her hips, shushed the others and spoke gravely, responsibility heavy on her shoulders. "Wi'ac kakoobikoo. Loolaboota adalap?"

She wrinkled her nose, then grinned as Kitya stared blankly at her. She poked the boy next to her, waggled her thumb at Kitya. "Rrikku rrik-kuu. Saaa. Bekabeka, eh?" She bent down, ran the tip of her thumb along Kitya's face very quickly then snatched her hand back, sliding her eyes under a fringe of white lashes toward the well and the adults busy there, knowing she'd gone beyond courtesy. When there was no reaction from them, she wiggled one arm in a vivid mime of a serpent. "Bekabeka," she chanted and the others followed her lead, chanting "Bekabeka, bekabeka," and dancing in a circle about Kitya.

"Akhu'day." It was one of the men at the well calling to the children. "Akhu'day dau'kx!"

The oldest girl cut off the dance in mid-stamp and went rushing to the well, the youngers trotting after her.

Leaving the other men taking turns on the sweep and dumping the bucket, the man who'd spoken walked toward Kitya.

She stood, pushing at the tangle of black hair that fell across her face, bothered because she'd been so deeply asleep she hadn't heard the noises of the approaching herd—and because she'd left the bone claws in the saddlebag along with her knife.

He bowed his head and offered a greeting. "Wi'ac, Kakubic." When he straightened, he waggled his hand as he brought his arm through an arc, taking in the herd and the people. He ended the gesture with his palm laid across his chest, roughly heart level. "Ky'at Tektaya." Hand still on heart, he waited.

She touched her brow with the tip of her thumb. "I am Kitya of the Moug'aikkin."

He drew his brows together, thin brows so pale they almost vanished into his face, then spoke slowly as if he had to dredge each word from old memory. "Why come...." He pulled his arm through another arc, a broader one. "Kyatawat?"

"Need." Her singularity was an asset for once. They weren't going to seize her; she'd be a disruption in the Ky'at. A raiding party would have been different, but their families were here and the herd; she had a strong feeling that, like her own people, they would do no ill in the face of the herd.

He didn't push the inquiry further, either because he didn't have the words for it, or because it was against Ky'at courtesy to throw too many questions at strangers. "Keep road," he said with another of his eloquent hand gestures, this one scribing the road ahead, hinting at hidden perils. Then he touched his chest. "Grass be of Ky'at." A flicker of his hand at the herd. "Sla of tattak-ulbiyoot." Hand slicing through the air. "Sla of Qelaloots." He frowned. "You say Pow ah ars."

"I hear, virs." She fitted palm to palm, bowed. When she straightened, he was walking back to his folk, a hint of a strut in his stride.

She got herself together as best she could with dozens of eyes staring obliquely at her, the men working at the well sweep, the women dropping water skins at the end of ropes, hauling them up again, giving them to older children to carry off to the wagons Kitya could just see on the far side of a hillock. The children stared more openly at her, giggling as she combed her long black hair, then wound it into its travel knot and pinned it in place. She rolled up the blanket, set it on the saddle, then looked around for Tiggley.

He was atop one of the grassy knolls, nipping placidly at the tips of the tall grass. She circled wide around the men at the well and climbed the knoll, whistling to the gelding so she wouldn't spook him and have to go chasing after him.

She clipped a lead to his halter, slipped off the hobbles, and led him back to the waystop where she found that the Kyatty women had filled her water skin for her and left it beside the saddle, along with a steaming mug of tea and some hot bread. She touched palm to palm and bowed to them, then dropped onto the saddle and began eating.

> > < <

Someone was following her. Her pum was tingling, but only a little. Whoever it was, he was a long way back and keeping his distance. He was focusing on her, though; otherwise her pum wouldn't have taken notice of him. A cockerel after her spurs, no doubt.

As the morning passed, he stayed roughly the same distance behind her, out of sight and hearing, riding his luck since the wind was blowing in his face which meant Tiggley wouldn't whiff his mount and get nervous.

Once again she had plenty of time for thinking. She couldn't kill him. Blood was bad business, whatever Land you were in. He'd be young and strong and accustomed to handling rope and struggling beasts. Nu, her mother had taught her a thing or two about cooling cockerels and Navarre had added flourishes. He won't come in sunlight ... unless there's more than one. Ch'! One I can handle, a flock of them. . . .

Brooding, irritated by this complication in an already knotty problem, she rode a while, then trotted along beside Tiggley. After the past several days she was sore in every inch, but already her body was hardening. Too long she'd lived soft. Sweating and panting, she ran a while longer, then swung back in the saddle.

She didn't stop at sunhigh; there was no shelter around and she saw a faint line of darker green between grass and sky, enough promised in it to justify pushing Tiggley a little harder than she liked.

> > < <

The green was a sluggish stream with trees on both sides, reflected in turgid water, pointed heart-shaped leaves fluttering in the hot breezes that wandered across the grass. The trees were wider than they were tall, with heavy limbs that curved down to rest on the earth; the trunks had thick rough bark with deep crevices in it, bark that smoothed out as it got farther from the roots. She tethered Tiggley to one of the low limbs, giving him enough of a lead to let him drink from the stream and nibble at the grass, then she ran up the limb and climbed as high in the tree as she could.

She waited.

It wasn't a long wait.

One rider. Only one.

He left the track after he'd been in view less than five minutes, rode into the grass. After that she saw him intermittently as he crossed the hillocks and finally vanished into the trees by the stream, a considerable distance east of her.

She climbed down and ate a cold meal, nervous as a kuneag at yeaning time with a pack of mo'ho on the prowl.

Tonight, she thought. *He's coming tonight. Late. When he thinks I'm asleep.*

She fed Tiggley the last of the grain, rubbed him down, then pegged him out in the grass so he could get himself a good bellyful before she started on. After this, no telling when she was going to find peace, grass and water, all in the same place.

> > < <

The hair was grass, the body under the blanket was more grass. When he bent over it, she landed on his back, the length of cord slapped about his neck, and pulled tight.

When he surfaced, she'd bound him like a fractious calf. She was kneeling over him, one hand resting flat on his chest. As she'd thought, he was young, couldn't have been more than sixteen, a pimple on his bony nose and a few straggling reddish-blond hairs under it, trying to be a moustache. "Ssssaaa," she hissed at him, curled her lip when she saw him shiver. "Nu, little cockerel, take a look at this." She closed her left fist and set the points of the claws against his cheek. "I doubt you can understand the words, but the pain will be clear enough." She pushed the tips of the claws into his skin, drew them slowly down his face, lifted them after about a thumbwidth of scratching, then she got to her feet and dragged him out of the dry camp into the grass.

"You can work yourself loose in a few hours. Go back home and boast the conquest you haven't made. Won't hurt me. I don't care what your lot think of me."

There was a whisper from the grass, barely louder than the sou-ffaa of the wind.

A cat the size of a calf flowed into the open, eyes of yellow fire, short sleek hair; the power reek around it was stronger than the musky, mordant catstink than the wind blew to her. The creature squatted on the other side of the youth, put a large paw on his chest, and extruded claws that shone ivory in the moonlight. It seemed to nod a greeting at her, then turned its massive head and snarled at the youth.

"Pishbadlarr," he whispered, his voice hoarse with fear. It was a power name, the name of one of the Tweens that wandered freely about Kyatawat.

The Tweencat stepped across the Tektayain, stropped itself against Kitya, absurdly like a kitchen moggie feeling affectionate, then glided away into the grass, silent as the wind.

Kitya stood, her knees aching, acid in her throat. "I hope you got the message, little man." Her mouth twitched into a brief smile. "I hope I did."

She left him there, fetched in Tiggley, got the gear on him, then alternately rode and walked until the sun came up and the track widened into

another waystop. Now and then she thought she
saw a long low shadow gliding along the road
ahead of her, but never clearly enough to know if
she was imagining it or not.

> > < <

As if the business with the cockerel had broken
some kind of spell, she began meeting people on
the road. Solitary women, mostly witches who
greeted her sister-to-sister. Solitary men, outcasts
from the Ky'ats, or foreigners with their own reasons for being where they were. Traders with
their wains. Peddlers with their packponies—she
stopped one and bought food and grain from him
with coin she'd taken from Navarre's stash, paying an exorbitant price, of course, but not disturbed by that; it was worth the cost to vary her
meals a little and keep Tiggley strong.

The waystops were crowded at times, but no
one bothered her after Pishbadlarr came from the
dark and curled up beside her, warm and purring,
the vibration traveling through her with a kind of
tenderness, as if the Tweencat had gathered her
in its arms and was rocking her to sleep.

> > < <

The karetka pointed directly west.

Kitya scowled at the cloudpiles that seemed to
climb for miles into the empty western sky. The
road behind her had become a narrow track, an-
gling more acutely toward the mountains in the

east that were just visible when she turned, a blue
scrawl against the lighter blue of the sky.

This waystop was a muddy waterhole in the
tangle of slowly straightening grass; there'd been
a herd here recently, a day or two before; it'd gone
on to the east and left a mire behind.

She tied on the water skin, swung into the saddle. For a moment she held Tiggley still, then she
leaned forward, patted him on the shoulder. "Here
we go," she said.

She tapped him with her heels; he snorted and
started round the waterhole, his hooves slipping
on the gelatinous mud.

Pishbadlarr flowed suddenly from the grass and
snarled at them.

Tiggley had grown used to the Tweencat, but
this was too much. He reared, screamed rage and
fear.

Before his feet came down, Kitya shifted her
weight to throw him off balance, yanked hard on
one of the reins to wrench his head around. She
didn't have as much leverage as she would have
with a bitted bridle, but her timing was on point
and she had the mud working for her. He slipped,
fell on his side. She was off him, at his head as
he struggled up.

As she soothed him with voice and hand, he
stood trembling and whuffling, shaking his head.
When he was quieter, she pulled up a handful of
dry grass and began cleaning off the mud. His
ears were up and he was looking nervously
around, but Pishbadlarr had vanished and taken
its odor with it. "Nu, Tiggley, looks like we don't

turn right here. We'll go on a bit and try again, see what happens. O horse, don't let Pish spook you. I think it's for us, not against. I think there was some danger there and it was warning us. I should've been listening to chouk and pum, but there's so much power here, they're always twitching and itching. Nu nu, that's the best I can do." She sighed and swung up, turned him onto the road.

> > < <

Half an hour later, Pishbadlarr stepped from the grass and stood between the ruts fifty yards ahead of them.

Tiggley shied, snorted nervously.

Kitya patted his shoulder, murmured soothing nonsense to him while she waited to see what the Tweencat was going to do.

Pishbadlarr strolled toward the grass, turning its head to stare at Kitya until it passed out of sight.

She sat without moving, stroking Tiggley's neck, waiting.

Pishbadlarr strolled out again, tail switching. It mewed, then said impatiently (the words scrolling across her mind's eye, rather than sounding in her ears): *What are you waiting for? You want to go west, don't you?* Kitya grimaced. "About time," she said aloud. She heeled Tiggley forward.

> > < <

Between pum and chouk, she was all itches and twitches as she followed Pishbadlarr on a winding, convoluted path through the trackless grass.

They circled an area where there was nothing visible but a low fog slashed through with jag after jag of lightning, another area where the air glittered with flies, flywings like shards of mica catching the sunlight, another where the grass had turned black and the stink was extraordinary.

All this while the Tweencat walked before them, pacing patiently along, never looking back.

On the tenth day the land began to lift into low hills, the grass thinned to an occasional clump and Pishbadlarr vanished, never having *spoken* again.

Kitya sat leaning on the horn, nearly as weary as the horse. "Navarre said the gods were mixing in this, Tig. That he had to do what he was doing. I thought he was just panting after that girl. I don't know now. I look out there, and I think what could've happened to me, and I think about Pishbadlarr coming to guide us, and I don't know. Maybe he was right. Or maybe it was caprice and nothing more. I don't know. Nu, horse. It doesn't matter, does it." She turned him and took him at a slow walk toward a clump of trees with birds fluttering about them; her chouk was cool, that meant water and the trees meant respite from the heat and the sun.

> > < <

In the morning, the karetka pointed west, deeper into the mountains.

She looked at Tiggley, his coat rough, his bones starting to show; she looked down at herself, then around at the shade and the clean cool water.

"Not today," she said. "Today we rest."

Chapter 11
The Magus Weaves a Dream Snare

There you are, pretty little slave, you've settled so tamely into your thrall, I begin to wonder if you lied when you called yourself a Magus. Not a Mage, no indeed, a tailless dog wagging his hindquarters to beg a meal. The Wee was angry at him for ignoring it, taking delight in tormenting him, mosquito whine in his ear day and night, rushing to Sabusé to tattle whenever it thought it saw Navarre doing something that would persuade the wizard to punish him. *You like it, don't you, no more prickly decisions, you were born a slave and have been pretending to be a man since, but it never was real, was it?* On and on it went, giving him no peace.

He turned his head suddenly, striking like a lizard at a bug, snapped up the Wee and swallowed it, dissolving it and drawing its speck of power into his blood. And went back to grating the tuber into the wooden cup.

As the Wizard loosened the spellbonds and decreased the strength of the drugs he was feeding Navarre so the Magus could use his "nose" to smell the threads of power, his hands to knot them, Navarre pushed cautiously against the limitations laid on him and worked out a sketchy map of what Sabusé did and didn't understand about the Art of a Magus. As slowly and carefully as he added to his knowledge, so slowly, so carefully, did he draw into himself infinitesimal trickles of power from the objects he handled for Sabusé, watching always to make sure the wizard didn't sniff out what he was doing. Suspicion was as dangerous as knowledge in his weakened state, for if Sabusé began to fear him, he'd burn away Navarre's knowledge, his intellect, all the things about himself that he cherished most. He'd be almost as useful if Sabusé made a golem of him, a flesh automaton with his gift intact and mind gone. And a lot safer to handle. It was only the wizard's pride that had left him intact thus far.

So he was careful. Very careful.

The stolen power was diffuse, scattered about his body, never still, flowing in his skin like an ameba's substance, shifting, coiling, climbing, falling, disguised by the heat of his body, by the resident exuvia of the wizard's own dealings.

With the contribution of the Wee, he had enough to begin weaving his own small web, a gossamer trap of dreams. It was exhausting work, with a mind dulled and slow from the drugs, a body withering, soft as the mush Sabusé fed him morning and night. During the day one thing was all he could hold in his mind in addition to the simple tasks the wizard set him. But his will to be free was strong and the rage that he was not permitted to feel ate at him beneath the masking numbness. And there was the fear that was greater than both.

He was undisturbed in his spinning.

Secure in his homespace, trusting his drugs, trusting the tether spells he'd spun about Navarre, Sabusé saw none of this.

> > < <

Night.

Navarre lay in a quiet that was deeper than sleep. He was listening. Not acting, only listening, absorbing into himself the wizard's dreams:
scraps   distorted images   snippets of memory   fragments from the day before   varying impressions Sabusé had of himself   mood-determined views of bits of his body   words, phrases, visions dredged from his studies and experiments   terrors shame-making moments   desires

All this was accompanied by a symphony of emotive refuse that sometimes jarred with the images, sometimes reinforced them.

That night and the next Navarre did nothing, simply absorbed what came.

It was quieter in the daytime, with the Wee dissolved and the children no longer coming to giggle at him because Sabusé complained to their parents, saying they distracted Bigous/Navarre from his tasks. Children being the same everywhere, now and then they sneaked back and had to be led off by a scolding mother or silent, irate father. But it was only now and then they came,

doing it on a dare or because they were angry
with their parents, and they were quiet about it,
peering from the trees, whispering and giggling.

> > < <

On the third night, Navarre touched a dream
and changed it.

> > < <

On the fourth night, Navarre nudged bits and
pieces from Sabusé's memories and fitted them
together in a brief but coherent play of images.

> > < <

On the fifth night Navarre did nothing. He had
not yet completed the penultimate dream, the bait
for the snare.

> > < <

On the sixth and seventh, again nothing.
Night and day Navarre worked at the tasks Sabusé heaped on him, forcing his dull and unresponsive mind to prepare the patterns and lay
down the mix of image, emotion, and spell that
would draw the wizard into the dream that would
hold him immobile night and day, day and night
until the spelltrance faded.

> > < <

On the eighth night Navarre began the bait.

> > < <

In the morning, Sabusé emerged from his house heavy eyed and morose. Navarre got to his feet, stood with shoulders rounded, eyes on the ground, waiting for Sabusé to set him his day's task. He was shouting inside, celebrating the triumph of his bait, but he kept his head down, his body soft.

"Fetch the offering," the wizard growled at him. "I would eat."

Each morning village women brought a hot porridge made from boiled grass seeds and ground nuts along with a dollop of yogurt, a pot of tea and a pile of the flat chewy bread they made from nutflour. They brought the food on a tray covered with a clean white cloth, left it at the edge of the glade. Sometimes the wizard collected the tray himself, but more often he made Navarre bring it to him, made the Magus crouch and watch him eat, then eat his leavings. It was a lesson meant to grind the slave's helplessness more deeply into him. And it worked.

> > < <

When Navarre had rinsed out the bowls and returned the tray to the road, Sabusé set a spelled leather leash about his neck. "You'll be my pack-pony this day, Bigous. No need for agility of hand or thought." He laughed, the wrinkles dancing in his face, then cast a handful of dust in Navarre's eyes.

> > < <

Sabusé thrust Navarre's arm through the handle of a heavy trug, then led him down the road, whistling and swinging the leash like a man taking a dog for a walk.

The Ky'at children giggled, tossed sticks and bits of stone at Navarre.

The elders looked at him, looked away, embarrassed. And frightened, a fear so strong that it penetrated the numbness that had seized his brain. Their wizard was their jewel and their terror. He tamed the Powers for them, gave them certainty and peace, but always there was the possibility he'd sour on them, turn from protector to tyrant. And now they saw him making a dog of a man. A stranger, but a man nonetheless. How long a step would it be to making them his dogs?

Sabusé and his slave walked along the beaten earth of the road, passed out of the canyon and climbed the slopes beyond.

Navarre's mind was wooden, his body clumsy as he lumbered after the wizard. He was sunk in revulsion, loathing himself; the dream snare seemed a dream only, a fantasy crafted to assuage his despair. He knew it wasn't so, that the snare was in place, waiting for night to close about the wizard and immobilize him. Still. . . .

Humming a monotonous drone, Sabusé squatted, scratched in the earth with a heavy wooden knife, bringing up odd plants that grew wholly or almost wholly underground. He tossed his finds into the trug that Navarre was holding, jumped to his feet and snuffled along, his nose twitching, his shoulders hunched, his eyes fixed on the dry red earth.

A long lean shadow flashing up from the ground, Kitya slid a knife between the wizard's ribs. At the same time her left hand slapped a poisoned thorn into his carotid, then she set her knee in his back and wrenched his head around. There was an audible crack. She kicked away from him, then squatted beside him, pulling the skinning knife from his side, wiping it on his shirt. "Kill a wizard three times to be sure," she said, her voice filled with satisfaction.

Navarre knelt with his hand outstretched, his mouth open. The drug had dulled him, his tongue was tied, the shout that had welled up in him was caught in his throat. He strained to move, to howl at her to get away before. . . .

The air shook.

The Tween Power Tiyulwabarr came rushing to destroy the deathdealer who'd killed its vassal.

Navarre fought against the hold of the drug, drove himself into a clumsy leap, closed his arms about Kitya, and held her hard against him. His Art paralyzed, it was all he could do to protect her. If a Great God was using Faan and him with Faan, even a Power couldn't destroy him . . . and that being so, his small immunity might shield her, too.

Tiyulwabarr yowled round them, throwing them to the ground, lifting them and slamming them against trees.

The trees turned to rubber and bounced them off, the ground softened and eased their fall.

It lasted forever, or seemed to, then the Power caught them high into the air and flung them in an immense roaring arc out over the grass.

They dropped in mud, hard enough to drive the breath out of them, but that was all.

Kitya struggled in his arms. "What. . . ."

He moved his mouth futilely, clung to her.

"V'ret, let me go. What are you doing?"

Abruptly she was a red-eyed serpent slithering from his grip.

And he . . . he stood on four sturdy limbs and snarled.

It was the beginning, only the beginning.

The moment he began to find his feet and work his brain, he melted into a slug wallowing in the mud . . . and Kitya was a red-eyed cat.

They oozed from shape to shape, drowning in the chaos of their ever-changing senses. In one of his momentary incarnations Navarre managed to remember name and attribute and know where he was—the landhold of the Wieldy Hugwuhpady who transformed things as its whim directed.

There was never time to grow accustomed to one form before they took another, snarling at each other or coupling in a heat that turned to revulsion as they changed in mid-coitus. Roaring with soundless laughter, Hugwuhpady repeated that scene over and over in endless variation.

Sometime later ... he was never sure how long that first phase lasted ... he felt an agony in one paw then a rush of energy.

He looked down, saw a thorn in his knobby green skin and a moist tentacle withdrawing toward a shapeless red-eyed thing that crouched over a leather sack that he dimly remembered Kitya carrying.

An excitant on the thorn, something to give him strength. Kitya! She. ...

He started to change again and rejected it.

Strength flowed into him.

He heard Hugwuhpady grumble but ignored it.

He whirled a time-sac about himself, withdrew from the landhold into the shapeless elsewhere where the *timelines* flowed, where Hugwuhpady couldn't reach him. Clumsily at first, then more easily, he slid back through the transformations until he came to the point of first arrival. He hovered there, reshaping himself, the image of what he was stretched out before him, frozen in that instant.

When his body was finished and right, he sat cross-legged in midair, hauoming and emptying his mind of rancor and fear.

Time passed and did not pass.

The hauom filled the sac.

He breathed and did not breathe.

Silence filled the sac.

> > < <

He cycled back, snatched Kitya-thing into the sack and took her to her true-image, wrought on her until she was herself again.

She blinked dark red eyes at him, brushed a delicately scaled hand across her face. "What. . . ."

"Hush. It's not wise to speak here," he murmured. "Hold tight to me."

He returned to the now/moment, sucked in a breath, gathered himself, dissolved the sac and *leapt* before Hugwuhpady could seize him. . . .

. . . . and whirled in a vortex beyond his control

. . . . winds howling at him

. . . . words he couldn't understand echoing hollowly, metallically about him

. . . . forces twisting and contorting him, threatening to tear him into bits so small the wind could blow him like dust

. . . . mouth wide, he screamed and made no sound

. . . . *THE WRYSTRIKE, THE WRYStriiiiike.* . . .

. . . . he felt nothing, not even pain

. . . . he was alone, torn from Kitya

. . . . the roaring, wrenching flight went on

. . . . and on

. . . . and

. . . . on

. . . .

Chapter 12
HONEYCHILD in Chaos

Leaning heavily on Varney's crude staff, Faan stumbled through the dark after the knot of wildings she'd charged with finding shelter for her—and with taking her along ways that she could manage. They were doing the best they could, but every root, every rock in her path bruised her, caught at her feet, threatened to trip her. Her misery was complete, or so she thought, but she struggled on, knowing that if Varney followed her and tried to take her back, she'd probably end up killing him and she didn't want to. She no longer saw him shimmering in a golden haze, but she didn't hate him; her anger had died with the fading of the light from the little fire. He wasn't clever, nor a deep thinker, but a good enough man in his own terms, honoring his word to other men, brave, skilled in things his peers valued. The trouble was, none of that applied to her. All she could do was get away and stay away. *When this business is done, I HAVE to find a teacher,* she told herself over and over, *I HAVE to find a middle ground between killing and surrender.*

"That lump of misery, that's your Shenda? Tsa!"

The acerbic small voice sliced into her cloud of woe; she jerked to a stop and stared up at the tree ahead of her, blinking to clear her eyes. "Ailiki?"

A glow sat on a low branch with the mahsar snuggled up against it, looking sated and drowsy. Ailiki yawned, scratched at the fur on her chest. "Fafa."

Faan pushed at the hair falling across her eyes, scowled at the glow, gradually making out the form contained within it, a form something like Ailiki but with an aura of maleness about it, she didn't know why she thought that, but she felt it strongly. "Who. . . ."

"You can call me Heeyail, Shenda."

"What's Shenda?"

His glow shifting with his movements, Heeyail spread long thin arms, as if to say there was no way he could explain the fullness of his meaning.

Ailiki produced her flight skins and came gliding to the ground, landing neatly by Faan's feet.

The wildings fluttered back, their fires tainted with stains of blue and green. Like rooks mobbing an intruder, they flew at the glow, screeching in their highest, most piercing voices.

Faan clutched at her head. "Don't" she cried. *Don't. Please.*

Honey Chickee, you need we not he.

I need whatever help I can get. It doesn't mean I value you less, but I am in deep trouble, little ones. I don't know how I'm going to get out of this, don't make things worse for me.

We hear thee, honey chickee, but don't trust he. Seem to mean then fly the scene. We see we see.

I hear and understand. We'll see what happens. Ailiki is my friend and . . . she smiled down at the mahsar who was ignoring all this and combing out the fine white ruff that flowed down her chest. *And my family.*

The wildings gathered in their cluster again, then went floating off, looping back over and over to see if she was following.

Heeyail sniffed sarcastically, then wrapped his arms about his narrow body and walked along a tree limb above her head, following her with an ease that made a mockery at her stumbling, limping progress. In his peculiar way, he was a help; his attendant glow was stronger than the moonlight and helped her move with more sureness because she could see where she was going.

She struggled along for another hour, then heard a loud dull roar, a noise that gradually swallowed all others; when she emerged from the shadow into the light of the descending crescent moon, she understood.

A small river dancing with whitewater emerged from a canyon and danced over boulders, racing past her feet, spraying her, drowning her in the noise of its progress; at the back of the canyon she could see a great waterfall, plunging down a cliff that seemed half a mile high, though when she thought about it a moment, she knew it couldn't be.

Mist began rising from the river. The noise got louder and louder, the gravel under her cold feet seemed to twist and shimmy—and she was falling. . . .

Falling heels over head through a chill seething mist. . . .

Gripping the staff so hard her hand hurt, because it was the only solid thing she touched. . . .

Screaming as the cries of the wildings pierced her head like needles. . . .

Ailiki bleating and clutching at her legs, claws snagging in her skin. . . .

Heeyail roaring his dismay and reeling in a drunken spiral around her, skinny arms and legs spread wide, his glow almost torn from him. . . .

> > < <

They landed in a pool of liquid, warm and thick as blood.

> > < <

Buoyant as puffballs, the three of them who were more or less solid popped to the surface and floated there while the wildings surged about in drunken loops until they, too, regained their balance.

The pool was fairly shallow; Faan used the staff to push herself to the edge, then give her purchase as she struggled up the bank. As she straightened and tried to look around, she was startled by the ease with which she moved; whatever other virtues that pool had, it had certainly healed even her smallest aches.

Fog thicker than any she'd seen before swirled

round her. The ground felt spongy under her feet. Unnatural.

"Where is this place? What happened?"

Ailiki emerged from the cottony swirls, sat on her haunches pressed up against Faan's leg. Heeyail followed her and crouched on the unsteady ground, arms wrapped about his knees.

"What? I'll tell you what," he said. "It's Ysgarod's Closet."

"Who's Ysgarod?" She sniffed. "Or what? A god? I thought Meggzatevoc was the End-all around here."

He shivered; he looked like a wet cat, though the pond hadn't wetted any of them; she was dry as she'd started out. "Not a god. Worse. A god you can argue with. Sometimes. Ysgarod ... I don't know how you'd even talk with it. It's the Divimezh. I'm a piece of Ysgarod. They are." He pointed at the heavily bobbing wildings, then pulled himself in, grew weightier as Ailiki began grooming him, her small black fingers working through his shimmering, ghostly fur. "You are, now. As long as you stay in the trees. You were making problems for it, so it tucked you away till it decides what to do with you. And us with you."

Faan lowered herself to the ground, sat with legs crossed as she poked at the half-immaterial ground with an exploring finger. "Anybody ever get out of here?"

Heeyail shrugged. "Not that I heard of."

"How long does that cover?"

"Since before the Valda came."

"Nu, that is not a happy thought." She scratched

at her nose. "Obviously you haven't been here yourself."

"Obviously."

"Jauk! One jegging god after another pulling my strings."

"Not a god."

"Same thing. I refuse to let it happen again."

"So what do you plan doing about it?"

After a minute she laughed, shook her head. "I haven't a clue, Heeyail."

> > < <

Time passed oddly; she felt it tripping over her in a series of hiccups as she focused on the substance on which she sat, using what she knew of *transformation* to try discovering its essence. There was nothing there to her othersight, though she could feel the spongy, moist resistance against her hands. She concentrated hard, struggling to grasp what it was that held her up.

After several more of those jolting hiccups, she began to get a sense of flowing forces.

She couldn't manipulate them yet, but she had hopes.

Ailiki came and went, exploring in her own way. Heeyail sulked for a while, got bored with that, and drifted off after the mahsar.

Frightened by their surroundings, the wildings had fled to her; they clung to her, half buried in her flesh.

She blinked, suddenly ravenous. Without thinking about it, she waded into the pool and crouched there, eyes closed.

When she felt sated, she went back to her investigations.

> > < <

"Nu?"

Ailiki blinked at her, then chattered to Heeyail.

He was denser, his glow thickened to a yellow soup; his acerbity was blunted and he seemed sleepy. He twisted his rubbery face into a comic grimace, then dropped his hand on Ailiki's back, fingers moving softly slowly in her fur. "She says there are walls all round, a few hundred yards out, fog everywhere. What you see is what you get."

Faán rubbed her fingers up and down the shadowline between her nose and the corner of her mouth, stared blankly at the rolling fog.

"Walls," she said finally, dragging out the word then letting it die; the wildings stirred uneasily, then sank deeper into her.

"Ysgarod's Closet," he said.

"Tsa!" She got to her feet, the vigor of the movement a rejection of everything about her. Without saying anything more, she charged through the mist until her hand slapped against the wall.

She leaned into it, tasting it as she had the stone she'd transformed. As she'd suspected, though it seemed solid and immovable, it was much like the "ground" here. She looked over her shoulder and

down, her eyes on Ailiki and Heeyail. "Feed me,"
she said.

Heeyail hung back until Ailiki pinched him and
drove him toward Faan.

She crouched, drew her hands down the wall
as she lowered herself. Ailiki and Heeyail pressed
up against her, both of them clinging to her, their
hands wrapped in her tattered shirt.

She focused on the wall and began forcing a
transform on it.

The "ground" beneath her convulsed wildly, the
fog boiled. The wall throbbed and tried to draw
away from her. She pushed harder, drawing
power from the wildings and her two small companions.

Ysgarod's Closet everted suddenly, vomited her
and the others onto a sandy slant with thornbush
and clumps of dead grass scattered over it, directly in the path of a hundred men riding at the
forest.

> > < <

When Faan hit the sand, her feet shot from under her and she was on her back again, sliding
down the slope, scratched by the thorns, stung by
nettles and other aggressive weeds. The horse racing at her squealed, did a quick dance with his
four feet and almost missed her completely, one
back hoof grazing her arm, pinching the skin
against the ground.

She staggered to her feet in the middle of the

confusion and noise, knocked silly but not really hurt.

A man with wild eyebrows, a drooping mustache, and a purple face was yelling at her.

She ignored him as she rubbed her hands down her sides, then ground the heels into her eyes; the attack on the Closet wall had drained her, the abrupt change of place had unsettled her.

There was a sudden weight on her feet.

She dropped her hands, looked down.

Heeyail and Ailiki were crouched there, back to back. She smiled. "Nu, that was a. . . ."

A riding crop slashed across her face. Pain. Sudden. Sharp.

Her attendant flamelets flared high, started to arc.

Horses squealed in terror, men swore.

"Nayo!" she cried, "I won't have it." She reached into the fire, closed her hands into fists as if she could hold them that way.

Oddly enough it seemed to work. The fires subsided, only danced excitedly on her shoulders, whispering pleas in her ears, *Let us go, let us have him, O dearling, O honey*.

"Nayo," she said. "Behave yourselves. This is no time or place for killing." She sighed, loosed them, brushed again at her eyes, then touched gingerly at the whip-cut on her cheek.

The riders had their mounts under control again; they were clustered together a short distance off, two of them holding onto the arms of a third, the man with the purple face who seemed to be in a steady state of rage.

She brushed at her tattered sleeves, then walked slowly toward him, the twin fires like wings on her shoulders.

They stood their ground, controlled their horses, though there was some eye rolling and halfhearted bucking.

She stopped a horselength away from them and frowned at the old man. "Why did you hurt me?"

He spat, the glob of spittle landing near her toes. "Foreign bitch."

She raised her thin black brows. "Any of the rest of you more sensible than the crazy man there?"

"You try anything, Witch, and you're full of holes." The long, lean type beside the old man made a quick slicing gesture with his hand.

She looked past him. Several of the riders had arrows nocked, bows drawn. She snorted. "Hadn't I held back, you'd all be ash. Listen, if you've got the sense to, I didn't pop down among you by my own will, I have no malice toward you, no intent to harm. At the moment. But don't push me, I've had a bad week and I'm not in a tolerant mood."

"Taisin! Get over here," the old man howled.

The man who'd been talking to her edged his horse closer to the old crazy and talked to him in a low urgent voice.

She couldn't make out the words and she didn't try. She was so tired she could've melted into a soupy puddle without even noticing the change.

> > < <

Taisin backed his horse a few steps, then brought him around until he was facing her again. "Forgive the Lielskadrav's hasty act, O Witch; he is driven by fear for his son."

"Varney?"

His pale brown brows drew together. "You know him?"

"Tja. You don't need to worry about him, he was alive and feeling good the last time I saw him."

"You saw him."

"We were taken together." She pushed wearily at her hair. "You're going after him?"

"Tja."

"Why you bothering about me, then? Go."

"Where is he?"

"In the Mezh. Otherwise, I don't know and I don't care." She hesitated, looked slowly from face to face. Reyna and Tai had raised her with love and taught her with tenderness; every day of her life—at least that she could remember—she'd watched them caring for hurts and doing their best to make hard lives a little easier—and they never asked that anyone deserve what they did. It wasn't something you forgot, even when a god made a destroyer out of you. She was annoyed, she hurt, she didn't know these men, they stank of blood and anger, but in the end she couldn't let them go unwarned. "Going in there, that's a bad idea. The Mezh is roused. You won't come out again."

There was a commotion behind Taisin; he ignored it. "Show us where Varney is. Take us there."

"I . . ."

There was an odd chirring sound and she trembled as heat built up around her, a heat the man didn't seem to feel. The smell of magic intensified until she was panting; the Mezh was there, straining to get at her, Meggzatevoc was there somewhere, raging, yet curiously restrained. Heeyail and Ailiki pressed hard against her legs, curling round her, in their own way protecting her.

She heard a rustle in the dead grass behind her.

She tried to turn.

Something crashed into her head.

She dropped into fire.

Then darkness.

Chapter 13
Ferment

1. Navarre

Navarre stopped whirling and landed feather light on a dusty dim red-brown plain that stretched endlessly on every side melting into a sky whose color was nameless but tending toward gray. He stood flatfooted and empty for a time, drained of everything including thought.

After a while he turned, slowly; the only way he knew he was turning was by the scrape of his bare soles on the ground, whatever it was, stone? concrete? It was the same everywhere he looked.

He stopped turning.

He was neither hungry nor thirsty; he couldn't tell if he were breathing or not.

His physical body was there, but it was in a curiously quiescent state, as if his flesh were dreaming along with his mind.

He started walking. He didn't bother using his Art to find a direction to walk in. It was the Wrystrike that sent him here, how could he trust anything except what came in through his five ordinary senses? And what did direction mean here where every place was like every other?

Each step seemed to be miles long. The dull red-brown floor fled beneath him. It made him feel oddly breathless—though he still didn't know if he was breathing.

He walked on and on.

After some indeterminate time, he saw a dark lump rising ahead of him. A small lump, a person sitting there.

A few steps and he reached it.

He edged around it, found himself almost to the horizon beyond it. He had to back and fill for a frustrating time before he was actually standing before the silent sitter.

She lifted her head and looked at him, a big woman with an ancient wrinkled face, iron black and collapsed on the bone; the smell of age hung about her, musty and intimidating. She sat there, wrapped in layers of wool and silk, relaxed, amused, her once-beautiful hands curled over her knees, a jewel on her thumb shimering blue and green and crimson, a black opal that echoed the bright lights in her black eyes.

He said: Where am I?

She laughed silently, the wrinkles shifting, her lively black eyes narrowed to slits.

She said: Oh, vain man, only concerned with yourself. Is that all you can think to ask?

He said: Who are you?

She said: I am Sibyl.

He said: Faan's teacher?

She said: One aspect was.

He said: Where am I?

She said: Otherwhere.

He said: Why am I here?

She said: I may not speak on that subject.

He said: How may I leave?

She said: Any time you desire.

He said: That is not what I asked.

She said: Contemplate the Wrystrike.

He said: I have for years contemplated the Wrystrike.

She said: And you have learned nothing.

He said: Nothing.

She said: Contemplate the Wrystrike.

And she vanished.

He sat where she'd been sitting and did what she said to do.

All his life learning had meant control and clarity. He'd sought that with the Wrystrike, trying to understand its degrees of deviation; once he knew that, he could adjust and ignore it thereafter. For years he'd experimented with the Great Art, watched how it went wrong—and learned nothing, found no perceptible pattern. Now and then he was troubled by the harm he caused, yet he never stopped testing himself no matter what it did to the folk around him, pushing away the rubble he'd made of their lives—or running from it as he'd run from Kitya's people.

Always he sought control.

Sitting in the warmth the Sibyl left behind, he had a new thought. For the first time he wondered what would happen if he let go and simply rode the wave of the Strike.

Rode?

Before this moment and this idea—which had appeared suddenly and without precedent—he'd seen the Art as a kind of machine, one incapable of independent acts, the same pattern producing the same result always and inevitably; even the Wrystrike shared this quality, despite its randomness; it was the randomness he couldn't penetrate, not the curse itself.

He'd seen the forces he manipulated as inanimate and infinitely malleable. Every teacher he'd known, every Magus he'd intersected, they thought that way. It was the natural way for them. And him. It was the reason their Talent took them into Magery.

What if he thought of it as a beast to be trained but not broken?

As a smith he'd had to learn how to handle horses and he'd watched good trainers teaching the beasts; they gentled them, understood their natures. With time and patience, they got what they wanted, guiding natural behaviors until they had mounts so responsive that they worked to little more than the rider's thought.

What if he did that with himself?

Could he endure that eternal uncertainty, that possibility that like a beast the Power would assert itself and go astray?

He contemplated the Wrystrike and his Art.

"It won't come at once," he said aloud. "Habits are hard to break. I'll slip into the old way . . . and destroy . . . and try again. And run from the souls whose lives I've ruined. And try again. . . ."

Time passed.

He could feel Time like a wind.

It grew sluggish and thickened, flowing first like water, then like gruel, then slowing yet further.

And still he sat, brooding on the Wrystrike and his Art.

2. Pargats Velams

Velams frowned at the Diviner. "Every one of them?"

She pushed the hair back from her face, long blonde hair, so fair it was almost white. "Yes. Every one. In one bed or another when Dinots Laro fell off the roof."

He took her hand in his, rubbed his thumb across her palm. "Payanin, you're sure of that?"

"They were sleeping the sleep of the unworried, V'la. You know I wouldn't lie to you."

He leaned across the table, touched her cheek. "I know."

"I've had a thought, though." She closed her fingers about his hand, kissed it and set on the table, her own resting lightly on it. "If any of them are involved, they must have met with the other plotters. There has to be more than one. You see that, don't you?"

A muscle twitched at the corner of his mouth. "They'd have those meetings smoked so thickly nothing could break through."

"That isn't what I mean." She leaned forward, her eyes on his. "Think about it, V'la. Unless the leader is very clever indeed, one or more of them will vanish from my vision for an hour or two. It isn't the meeting I'm after, it's that absence. Or rather, a pattern of absences."

"Nu, that is a thought." He pulled his hand free, got to his feet and started pacing back forth. Over his shoulder he said, "How long would that take, Payanin?" He threw out his arms, groaned as he stretched his spine. "Since they're dead, their innocence painfully proved, you can forget Apsis and Laro. And Varney, of course. I know my brother. With only Druz, Begarz, and Steidz to trace, it shouldn't be too difficult."

"You include Begarz? Wasn't he attacked also?"

"He's alive." He sniffed. "One asks oneself why."

"How long? Three days, perhaps. Perhaps longer." She hesitated, dragged the corner of her mouth down. "You'll have to pay for my time, V'la. I'd give it freely, but I'm not free."

"I know. I'll send the coin tomorrow." He stopped at the window, stood looking out at the flickering dark. Thee was another name he could give her. Leduzma Chusker with his Devil mother. Forest Devils had taken his brother. Who else would they listen to? But he respected that man's brain too much to go near him yet, even by proxy. A step at a time. He couldn't help his father and his brother if he were dead or tangled in a blood feud with Family Ledus. He sighed. Vicanal had probably killed Varney's best hope with his obstinacy and twisted hates, but he couldn't abandon his father to his stupidities. He couldn't abandon his brother.

>> <<

On his way out of the Temple he stopped to light a candle to Jah'takash to ward off ugly surprises for his family and himself.

3. Pargats Varney

Waving the torch in a wide arc, Varney charged at the darkness where yellow eyes glimmered at him and seemed to be getting bolder; he heard snarls and grumbling threats as the unseen beasts backed off.

He added more wood to the fire, breaking it into easy bits with the axe he'd stolen from a Forest Devil village, dropped to a squat, and waited as the night hours crawled past. Several times more he charged at the darkness as the beasts grew bolder. They wouldn't let him sleep. They wouldn't come into the firelight so he could see them, but they made noises out in the dark that told him they were there and he could see their eyes gleaming, yellow eyes, green eyes, eyes as red with hate as his were from lack of sleep.

The light gradually grayed, then brightened to true morning. He put out the fire, gathered the wood that was left and bound it on a bundle he could carry on his shoulders. There was a binding on him too, as the old Devil had said that first day. He wouldn't leave the trees. He hadn't be-

lieved it then, but he did now. Whatever direction
he took, he ended up deeper in the Mezh. They
stole Faan from him to make sure of that, stole
his chance away from him. Nu, they were going
to pay, for that as well as the rest. The first village
he'd found, he'd only taken the axe and some food.
That was stupid, he should have held the Devils
hostage till they let him out of here. The next
village, it would be different. Sooner or later, he'd
find another one, and then they'd see.

4. Kitya of the Moug'aikkin

Torn from Navarre and flung into a red nowhere, taut with rage but with nothing to fight,
Kitya whirled away and slammed down into the
kitchen at the smithy.

"Koo'maik!" She slammed her fist into the wall.
"Circles! It's all to do again." She looked down
at herself. She was stripped naked, scratched,
bruised, filthy from that ooze they'd wallowed
in—and in spite of everything, still clinging to the
leather pouch; somehow she'd held onto it through
all that mess, maybe because it had in it just about
everything that remained of her ties to her
mother.

Thinking about her mother made Kitya laugh.
Burning your fat for a nonsense, she'd say. What
did I tell you, ligik, hai-yah? When you feel good,
your head's good. Make a mess of yourself, make
a mess of aught else. Kitya scrubbed her hand
across her face, sighed, and began pulling the pins
from her filth-encrusted hair.

> > < <

After a bath and a hot meal, she settled herself in front of the fire in Navarre's parlor, rubbed oil on her hands and arms, then her legs, then buffed her nails, pampering herself until she felt relaxed and at ease once more within her skin. She lifted her feet onto a hassock and lay back in the chair, watching the dance of the flames, sipping at the ruby wine she'd brought up from the cellar.

"Wrystrike," she murmured. "Took him who knows where. It's Varney's doing, getting him mixed up in this ooyik, poor old Magus, he can't say no. Ts. Nu," she took a sip of the wine, let it trickle down her throat, a warmth burning down her middle, "I have to find that girl. I'm not strong enough by myself." She wrinkled her nose, dragged down the corners of her mouth. "Much as I loathe the thought. Hai-yah, I hope Tiggley's all right. The Kyattys must have found him by now. Do I ride tomorrow or do I walk? The mezh-merrai eat horses. But if I walk, it could take for-ever. I suppose I should cast another a'to'a. And spin a kechkech to point the girl, since there's no way I can make a karetka for her. Faan. Tja, that's her name. Silly name." She yawned, emptied the glass. "I'll need fresh mazhru and ashera for the kechkech. And fishbone." She ran her tongue across her lower lip. "None of it here, that means Savvalis. I am forsworn for sure, hai-yah." She yawned again. "Sleep now, let the hard things wait."

> > < <

Kitya almost forgot her votaj; she had to dig
into her trash drawer where she'd thrown it the
last time she returned from Savvalis, so incensed
she swore she'd never go back. Navarre had
laughed at her and gone off to the smithy, leaving
her to put away the slop she'd been forced to buy
to keep peace and get away from the market with
a whole skin.

She wrinkled her nose, slipped the thong over
her head, counted on her fingers the things she
needed and didn't have so she could convince herself once more that this trip was necessary. Her
mother said, better be ready than sorry. It wasn't
one of her more trenchant pronouncements, but
no one could be at the top all the time.

> > < <

Morning dawned gray with a thick blanket of
clouds obscuring the sun; when she left the house
it wasn't raining yet, but it would be soon. She
swung into the saddle, slapped the reins against
the black's shoulders and laughed as he surged
into a gallop and clattered half-wild from the
smithy court. She let him run down the long hill,
but when they reached the flat she brought him
to an easy canter and they rocked along while she
looked about her, astonished to find the land as it
always had been. So much had happened to her,
it seemed to her that everything should reflect
that upheaval, but it wasn't so.

> > < <

The civiel looked at the votaj, looked up at her, eyes squinted, rain dripping from his nose and chin. "It's near expired," he said.

Kitya's eyes narrowed to crimson slits. "But it's still good."

"Tja. . . ." He drew the word out until it was an insult, then he tossed her the bronze square. "Get it replaced before you leave." He stepped away from her, thumped the weight so the bar swung up. Once she was through, he went trudging back to the shelter, muttering loud enough for her to hear the sound if not the words.

No doubt cursing foreigners who brought him out on a day like this, she told herself.

Despite his earlier run, the black was restless and ready to play the idiot at the first excuse. She used body and voice to keep him in hand and had little attention left for what was happening around her.

She did note a few children playing in front gardens, splashing happily in puddles and chasing each other across swatches of grass, and she passed a woman or two trudging along with market baskets draped in oilcloth. Otherwise the street was empty, the houses silent behind half-open shutters.

She frowned. There was something wrong in Ash Pargat; more than the rain was keeping people inside. She could smell fear, feel eyes following her. Ooyik tripled! Varney in the middle of it, she was sure of that. She'd never liked him, didn't like the way he looked at her, didn't like that arrogance that assumed every woman was available to him if he decided he wanted her. Kowt.

She glanced toward Pargats House, clucked to the black. The sooner she left this Ash, the better she'd like it.

A group of men in blue tabards trotted into the street ahead of her, spreading in an arc that blocked her. A glance over her shoulder showed her another line behind her.

A burly old man stepped in front of her. "You will come with me."

"Why should I? Who are you?"

"Pargamaz Teiklids, woman. Pargats Velams wants to see you."

She crossed her hands on the horn, scowled down at him, considering this turn in her lifeway. "Why?"

"That's the Heir's business, not mine. You can go on your feet or on your back, up to you."

"And do I come out again?"

He shrugged. "That's the Heir's business, not mine," he repeated and stepped back.

Swearing under her breath, she swung down. "The horse belongs to Magus Navarre. On pain of his displeasure take good care of it." She dropped the reins and stalked toward the street that led to the entrance arch of Pargats House.

> > < <

When Kitya walked into Pargats Velams' study, he stood at a window, looking into the garden beyond. He turned, nodded at Teiklids, and stood without speaking until the head guard withdrew.

"Your name is Kitya, I believe."

Nostrils flaring, mouth compressed, she nodded.

"Sit down, Kitya. You needn't worry about this, I merely wish to talk to you."

She ran her eyes over him, slowly, insolently, getting some of her anger out—suddenly disarmed when he grinned at her, eyes crinkling, a slightly discolored tooth and a hook at the right end of the grin giving him a skewed charm that was far more effective than his brother's flawless beauty. She came forward and lowered herself into the chair by the small round table. "Nu, what is it?"

He smiled more sedately, settled across the table from her, rang a small silver bell. A moment later a girl came in carrying a tray heaped with cakes and delicate sandwiches. A second brought in a smaller tray with cups and a steaming pot.

"My father...." He filled a cup, pushed it across to her. "You have to understand, he's a man of great heart and ..." His smile turned wry. "Though he loves all his sons, Varney is especially dear to him." He paused, gazed at her as if he expected some kind of comment.

She sipped at the tea and waited for the Heir to go on. What she knew or didn't know was her business and she wasn't gifting it to anyone, although ... his eyes were green, not blue like his brother's ... and shrewd ... she had a feeling that her pose wasn't fooling him much. She set the cup down, folded her hands. Her mother said, what doesn't come out your mouth won't get you in trouble.

Velams sighed. "Why are you here?" he said, breaking a painful silence.

"I'm housekeeper and cook; there are herbs I need."

"Then Navarre has returned."

"Neka."

"Do you know where he is?"

She pressed her lips together and stared past him at the rain coiling down the window. "Neka," she said finally.

He was annoyed but controlled it. What he wanted from her, she didn't know, but he was certainly wiser than Varney. "More tea?" he said.

"Tja, patcha."

He filled her cup and pushed it across to her, sat back in the chair and laced his hands over his stomach. "Do you know where he was?"

She hesitated, then she nodded. "Tja." She couldn't think of any reason not to answer, other than her own reluctance to tell him anything. He seemed a sensible man—of course, that could change in the blink of an eye and she could disappear with no one to wonder about her. One of the quiet ones, but a man accustomed to getting what he wanted, that was what Varney said. You don't want to cross him, Varney said. I don't know what he'd do, Varney said, but I guarantee it would be sufficient and effective. She set herself to give him the least possible response, watching to see how he took her answers.

"And that was?"

"Kyatawat."

"But he's no longer there?"

"Neka."

"He escaped?"

"Tja."

"How do you know?"

"I went there."

"You say you don't know where he is now."

"Tja." She chewed her lip, spoke again after a moment. "Do you know his curse?"

"The Wrystrike?"

"Tja. It took him, shed me. I don't know where he landed."

"But you're working to find him."

"Tja."

"How?"

"I am of the Moug'aikkin. We have our ways."

"When you find him, say to him this: You have reason for anger, Magus, but not at my brother. Or me. I ask you to forgive an old man his folly. It would be beneath you to vent your fury on him and unjust to harm my brother and me for what we could not help. I know you understand this. I count on your good heart." He stood. "Will you do this?"

"Tja." She stood also. "Not for you or your brother. For him."

"That is enough." He rang the bell again. "Is there anything I can do to further your search?"

"The civiel ordered me to replace my votaj. Will you take care of that for me?"

He looked startled, then smiled. "With plea-

sure. You'd best wait here, Kitya of the Moug-
'aikkin."

>><<

Despite the rain Tirdza Street was swarming
with people; there were half a dozen new ships
offloading along the wharfs, hundreds of shoppers
had come from the other Ashes, cart trains
creaked along, heading for the market area near
the North end of the street, cadets in variously
colored tabards jostled each other, yelling insults,
a few fights broke out, black-tabarded civiels
shoving between the youths, sending off one
group, then the other, only to have them trickle
back once the civiels had moved on to deal with
another lot.

The noise was deafening, the crowd thicker
than she'd expected after the emptiness and silence of Ash Pargat. She slid down from the saddle and led the black into one of the side streets
until she came to an inn where she negotiated the
use of a stall for a few hours.

>><<

The herbalist was a dark little man as wrinkled
and shaggy as the roots in his bins; he'd drifted
here from some land so far to the east that Kitya
hadn't even heard of it. She'd dealt with him a
few times the first years she'd lived in this place,
found him irritatingly vague but skilled at squeez-
ing coin from his customers—and gossip. She lo-

cated a crock of ashera, crushed a leaf, sniffed at it, wrinkled her nose. "Picked the wrong time, I'm sure of it, nearly spoiled. Hunh. Nu, I won't be needing much so I suppose I can use it. Four nidjes for a quarter spoon, and I'm being generous at that."

"Two chelk. Word's around Vicanal took agin Magus, had him shipped out."

"Ts. Dream on. One chelk. Word ... you know what word's worth. Magus doesn't get shipped out. Magus goes where he feels like."

"One chelk seven. Word can be right, can be wrong. Don't matter, trouble's there. A person might be wise to stay short and keep low."

"One chelk five. A person might give blessings for a timely alert. A wise person will follow a pointed trail."

"One chelk six. Word is too that Magus is caught in a godweb, that who strikes at him will miss, the strike coming home on him who made it. There is a postern door here. A person could leave by that door and avoid watching eyes."

"Done. A person could do that, when a person's business is completed." She watched him wrap the small heap of ashera leaves, said, "I'd like a quarterspoon of grated mazhru and some fresh fishbone. Heads if you have them."

> > < <

When Kitya had the herbs and bone tucked into into her pouch, she followed the silent shadowy little man through the odorous storerooms at the back of his shop and stepped into the alley that ran behind the row of houses. It was empty of all movement and sound except for the gentle patter of the rain. She nodded to the herbalist and hurried away.

> > < <

As she turned into the sideway that led to the stable where the black waited, a hand dropped on her arm.

She swung around, eye narrowed, hand on her knife, saw a stocky, fair woman with fine brown hair and sunspots sprayed across square cheekbones and hooked nose.

The woman dropped her hand. "No need for that," she said. "My name is Desantro. I'm a friend of Faan's."

"Nu?" Kitya straightened; she recognized the name from what she'd heard of Faan's story. These two were bound in a bloodsearch; she might be a help in locating. . . .

Desantro pointed with her chin to a man a few steps back. "Dreits says you're Navarre's woman. She went to see him, didn't she? At the Gul Bazelt the innkeeper says she hired a mule and rode out. Where is she? What happened to her?"

Kitya looked quickly around. No one seemed to be interested in them, but one could never tell who might be watching with all these houses hemming one in. "We can't talk here."

"Tiesh tas, that's true. The Gul Bazelt has a din-ing room, we could sit over a cup of tea and seem no different than half the others there."

Kitya smiled. "You fall very naturally into cabal."

Desantro shrugged. "I was a slave."

"Nu, I see." Kitya glanced at the servant. He was standing relaxed, with a sureness in his center she'd seen in no one, not even Navarre. "What about him?"

"Dreits is Faan's friend and will help if he can."

"She seems to have a horde of friends."

Desantro shrugged. "Are you coming?"

"Nu, I am."

> > < <

Kitya stirred a drop of honey into her tea, watched it dissolve. "Navarre is . . . I don't know . . . in difficulties . . . lost, one might say. From what he said to me, he and your friend are bound in a. . . ." She couldn't find the word, set the spoon down, and spread her hands.

Dreits nodded. "She has said it also. She read it in Qelqellalit's Pool."

Desantro wrinkled her nose. "And in the Diviner's dish. The last time I saw her, she said she'd seen something; she wouldn't say what it was, but as soon as Dreits told me about the Pool, I was sure she saw the same thing in the dish and it had something to do with Navarre."

Dreits nodded. "And I. She wanted all I could tell her about the Magus. As we discovered, she rode out the same afternoon on a mule she hired from the stable here. Navarre brought it back the next day and paid the fee. There's more that happened that day, I'm sure of it, but the hostler won't say."

Kitya sipped at the tea; the honey made it taste revolting, but gave her a tiny boost of energy. "First, you'd better know this. Varney claimed the right to escort your Faan back to the city; he was taken with her and she with him." Her mouth twitched. "Taken is the right word. Before they reached the Highroad, a band of mezhmerrai captured them and carried them off." She went on to tell them the rest of it.

> > < <

Dreits sighed. "And Vicanal didn't believe him. Of course he wouldn't, he hates Navarre. Everyone knows that."

Kitya spread her hands again. "Whatever. When I came up with him, he was a slave to a Kyatty wizard." She grimaced. "I killed the wizard and things happened, ts! He's trapped somewhere and I can't find him. So I need that girl. Faan." She straightened, fixed her crimson eyes on Desantro. "You know her well?"

"Well enough. Why?"

"Among the Moug'aikkin, there are ways of pointing. They work best when one knows well the person one searches for. I know Faan almost not at all. Come with me. Help me find her."

Desantro's fingers tapped erratically at the tabletop while she stared past Kitya's shoulder at something only she could see. "Faan is more than able to take care of herself," she murmured. "Sooner or later she'll come out on her own." She blinked, sighed. "I'll do you a deal, Kitya. I'll help you anyway I can to find Faan and pry your Magus loose from wherever he is; in return, you see if you can point my brother for me. And you do that first, before anything else."

Dreits coughed. "May I add, what binds Navarre to the girl is this quest for Desantro's kin, so if you help Desantro, you'll be helping yourself."

"Nu, let it be so. I will do the thing, I swear it, if you come now, without wait or hindrance."

"Agreed. Dreits, tell Tariko I've found another route to our brother and have gone off to try it. Tell her to take care of my things . . . and Faan's . . . no, you hold those, that's better . . . in case I'm gone a while . . . um . . . but not to worry, I'll be back when I've finished this."

He got to his feet. "Tungjii's blessing on the pair of you," he said and limped out.

5. HONEYCHILD burns

Faan stumbled along in hissing hostile shadows, bumped by the shoulder of Taisin's horse. Her hands were tied behind her, there was a plug in her mouth, held there by leather straps, and there was a choke chain about her neck. Taisin held the loop of the leash, drove her along the trail. He didn't jerk her about unnecessarily, but he gave her no slack at all.

Hissing hostile shadow and trees that moved though there was no wind.

The horses were nervous, snorting, shying at shadows and dead leaves that blew suddenly before them.

The air stank, a miasma that moved with them despite the lack of wind.

Small black biters swarming thicker and thicker until it was impossible to breathe without snorting them in.

Birds flew overhead and splattered them.

With the stench, the pain, the constant jerking of the choke chain, cutting off her breath until Taisin shook it loose, Faan was very near the limits of her strength.

Thorn canes snaking around tree trunks, slashing at her legs, wrapping like barbed wire about the horses' legs.

She fell.

Taisin jerked the chain, dragged her up, choking her painfully.

She fell again. This time she was out cold.

Sometime later she woke, belly down across his legs, jerking and twitching to the roll of his mount. A lassitude heavy as a leaden cloak weighed her down, her mind seemed frozen.

She closed her eyes and let go.

> > < <

"Strip the bitch."

The words penetrated the haze in her brain and she tried to protest, but the gag held her tongue down and the poison from the thorns that had torn her legs had spread through her, leaving her weak and feverish. She way stretched flat on the ground in a small clearing; the sky was dark with a gibbous moon glowing through a haze of cloud.

She whimpered as knives cut through her rags and hands wrenched them off her; the faces of the men bent over her were intent, curiously impersonal. That frightened her more than all the rest.

When they were finished, ropes were tied to her ankles and wrists and jerked tight, spreading her legs wide, nearly pulling her arms from her shoulders. The gag was cut from her mouth and tossed aside.

Vicanal stepped over her left knee and stood between her legs, glaring down at her. "Where is he?"

She stared up at him, licked her lips. When she tried to speak, her throat closed and the only sound that came out was a harsh rattle, then she screamed as he brought the short whip down across her stomach.

"Where is he?"

She tried again. "Don' kno'," she managed to groan.

The whip came down again, this time across her breasts.

"Where is he?"

"Don' kno', don'. . . ." She screamed again as the whip cut down, crossing one of the first splits.

"Where is he?"

She writhed within the limits allowed by the tether ropes, fought to find words to persuade him to listen to her; at the same time she knew that no words would convince him, that he didn't want to believe her.

Again the whip whistled down.

"Where is he?"

Shouting the question at her over and over, not even waiting for an answer, he whipped her bloody.

With one long endless scream, she loosed the fires and slid into blackness.

> > < <

When she surfaced, the earth around her was blackened; even the dirt had burned. The trees at the edge of the clearing were charred skeletons.

She struggled up, pressed her hand against her mouth, the end of the tether rope fluttering from her wrist, as she saw the contorted humps that had been men and horses, the white splotches where the bone had been burned clean.

"Shouldda let 'em burn the first time, saved yourself this trouble." Heeyail sat alone on the limb on a dead tree, his glow gray as ash.

She gazed at him, blinking slowly, opened her

mouth to say something—and found she couldn't speak. Her tongue was locked, her throat wouldn't move. She got clumsily to her feet and began picking through the dead, going she didn't know where, going away from here.

CABAL

Vocats Oirs fidgeted restlessly about the dusty tomb, his feet cracking the grit until Kreisitssev Kreisits Nenova gave a small scream, closed her hand about his arm.

"Sit down before you drive me crazy," she whispered at him.

He let her lead him to one of the unsteady chairs, cleared his throat, whispered back, "Why aren't they here?"

She shrugged, settled across the table from him. "Laz is getting above himself," she murmured, more to herself than to him. "I think he's close to pulling out on us."

"Fool!"

"Maybe. If he thinks he can sell Chusker. . . ."

Oirs snorted. He looked round, his pale eyes moving restlessly over the dusty niches with their rotting coffins. "You bring some wine?"

"For later." She lifted her head. "Someone's coming."

Oirs paled, got hastily to his feet, knocking over his chair.

Leduzma Chusker came in, Kreisits Lazdey following behind, his cowl up, his hands tucked in his sleeves.

Oirs picked up his chair, pulled his cowl forward and sat leaning heavily on the table, his shoulders rounded, his hands clasped, the strain in them visible even through the heavy gloves.

When Chusker spoke, his voice was cool and easy, ignoring the stolid resistance of Lazdey, the skittishness of Oirs. "It's going very well. Druz has put his foot in his mouth enough times to make his supporters start thinking twice about what he'd do as Augstadievon. Laro's cousin is too weak and dithery to cause trouble. In addition, with Vicanal and Varney both out of reach, Varney's support has plateaued—we've got Velams to thank for holding it as high as it is. Tsa! that man's clever. By the way, word has come to me that Vicanal has gotten himself killed along with all his men. A stupid man who died in a stupid way taking a hundred idiots with him. Where was I? Tja. Begarz is pulling ahead farther every day." He turned his cowl toward Lazdey, who nodded, started tapping a gloved finger on the worn gray table. "Nu, if the election were to be held tomorrow, he'd have a convincing win. Tja, tja, Oirs. The attack on you is set and I've arranged a convincing save. I'm not going to tell you when or how it'll happen, it'll be more natural if you're surprised and upset. Much more persuasive. Questions?"

Oirs grunted, pulled his hands off the table.

Nenova rubbed her thumbs together, turned her

head to look from one to another. "Velams," she
murmured.

"Leave Velams to me, in a few days he will cease
to be a problem. With Vicanal and Velams dead and
Varney gone, Valdosh will hold the seat. Any of you
know him?"

Lazdey nodded. "When I was brought in to teach
the cadets some strategy, he was in one of my cad-
res. Hothead and not very bright."

Oirs snickered. "A replica of his father, one would
say."

"Exactly." Chusker leaned back. "Now, Oirs,
this is important, I want you to stir up your coterie
and assemble them all at the next council meeting
and I want you and them to agitate for a commission of investigation into these deaths. Mostly you.
For one thing, that'll be a most persuasive reason
for the attack, for another, it'll bring you to people's attention in a most positive way. I'll meet with
you later, go over your speech so we can get it
right. Nu?"

"Tiesh tas. It sounds good." Oirs sighed and relaxed.

"Nenova, can you get Turet there?"

"No problem."

"Laz, about Begarz. I want him on his feet, sec-
onding the call loud as he can manage. You'll have
to prepare him, but do it as obliquely as you can,
hmm?"

"No problem." Lazdey's voice was dry, distant.

"Then let's have a drink and celebrate our suc-
cesses. Nena?"

She brought out the wine and the glasses, moved about the table filling their glasses.

　"To the Seat," *Chusker said.*

　"To the Seat."

Chapter 14
Search and Run

1. Kitya of the Moug'aikkin

Kitya dropped a pinch of ashera on the coals, passed the headbone of the fish through the thick aromatic smoke. She chanted:

Illeeyuga nah'meh nam'meh
Rakil Rakil inalayyah
Owha okanoah ana okah
Desantroah
Keecha koh kai kanayeh

She threw a pinch of mazhru onto the still bubbling ashera, adding a musty acrid bite to the sweetish odor of the leaves. She chanted:

Naga ney a whana hey
Ahey kuna Desantroa
Keech kaneeyeh owha koa
Illeeyuga Rakilloa

Desantro held out her hand; Kitya used a sharpened edge of the headbone to cut a forefinger, then rubbed the woman's blood over the bone. She chanted:

Owka owka otouka owka
neeya illeeya
kechkech kaneh eeya eeya

As a last step in making the kech, she took the fine cord she'd braided from Desantro's hair and tied it through the eyehole of the headbone, passed the whole several more times through the diminishing trails of smoke. She set the bone carefully on a bit of stone, took the small brazier to the door of the kitchen, dumped the coals and the ash onto the flagging outside. She left the brazier by the door—it'd have to be cleaned later, before she built the second kech, but she wasn't ready to work the purification right now. She was tired, her throat was sore from the strain of shaping the words into the proper rhythms and there was still more to do before this tukkrum was wound up.

Desantro knelt on the tiles, sweat beading a pale face. Kitya had warned her not to speak before the proper time, but her anxiety was apparent without need for speech.

Kitya lifted the kech with the tips of her two forefingers, let it drop lightly into Desantro's cupped palm. She chanted:

Ohla esshon a-oka
Neeya anna a-noka

She cracked her hands together as loudly as she could.

Desantro started, then she took the hair cord between thumb and forefinger, lifted the kech until it hung free. "Pa-Rakil," she said.

For a moment the kech swayed aimlessly with shaking of her hand, then it plunged about like a fish on the hook, finally whipped around and froze, pointing west and a little north.

Sweat beads popped out on Desantro's face. "Tuzra," she said.

The strain went off the cord, the kech went dead.

"Pa-Rakil," she said.

Once again the fishhead pointed west.

"Tuzra."

She took the clean linen square from Kitya, wrapped the kech in it. "Patcha," she whispered. "Everything we tried . . . I'd almost given up. . . ." She coughed. "What now? Anything you want, I'll do my best."

Kitya yawned, stretched. "Bath. A nap. Food. Then we talk. You tell me everything you know about Faan."

> > < <

Three days later, Kitya stood beside the black with her hand on the saddle looking up at a tattered green flag still flapping against the pole. "You see that?" She pointed.

Desantro twisted her head around and up. "Nu?" She brought her attention quickly back to the beast under her as the mare sidled nervously, her hooves ringing on the flags.

"That's a warning, Desa. Take it to heart. Who gave us that was once a friend. Not now. The Mezh is hostile. We won't be welcome."

Desantro leaned forward cautiously, patted the chestnut mare on her shoulder. "What's new in that?" She laughed suddenly, recklessly. "Trees," she said. "Mountains. Geddrin be blessed, how long's it been?"

Kitya frowned. "You do understand?"

"Oh, tja. Don't worry, I've seen a forest angry. When the Hennermen burned us out and carried off m' kin."

"The Divimezh isn't like other forests."

"How many have you seen, Kat my friend? I thought not. All forests have have dangerous hearts. Nu, if Geddrin will listen to me and my memory holds, I can do a thing on my side to smooth our passing. Spedj-ne spedj-ja. Let's go." She glanced at the lowering sky. "That's a mean storm coming."

> > < <

Desantro drew in her breath as she saw the dark, forbidding line of trees breaking suddenly from the sandy heath; it was more ominous than she'd expected. Wind whipping her hair about her face, she whistled to warn Kitya, pulled the mare to a nervous stop.

Kitya rode back to her. "What?" she shouted,

raising her voice to break through the howl of the wind.

"Give us a minute." Desantro slid from the saddle, grunting loud enough when she hit the ground to make Kitya smile.

"Need me?"

"Neka. Just wait." Desantro pulled off her boots, rolled up her trousers, kicked a clear spot in the sand and dropped to sit cross-legged, hands resting lightly on her knees. She closed her eyes; her childhood was very clear to her these days, Zens and Parraye were fascinated by it, pestered her whenever they got a chance to tell them more stories. The old protect-rhyme was etched in her mind, though she hadn't thought of it in decades.

She closed her eyes, cleared her throat, began snapping her thumbs against her midfingers. "Gohair wa Pamu," she sang, her voice cutting strongly through the wind. She let the sound fade, then added a translation into Valda speech.

Gohair wa Pamu, O Forest Groomer
Auchair ki Mamu, I enter your heart
Au Hern ta Pina, I honor your truth
Au Mern ka Kina, I intend no harm
Gomaung wa Pamu, O Mountain Comber,
Hakair awwama, hear me,
Matahai eMamu, Father of my heart.

She kept the clicking of her thumbs and fingers going as she felt the wind like questing fingers brushing over her. There was no acceptance in it, not yet. She started singing again, no rhyme this time, nothing from memory, only a plea to be remembered and restored to the family of the forest. "Geddrin Groomer of Trees, I am your daughter. Hear me, Gentle Giant, take me to your bosom, a stranger coming home. I and She who rides with me, we will take a festering thorn from the heart of the Mezh, do not shut out us out, do not attack us. We mean no harm, only good. Give us passage, let us in and let us leave."

She let her hands fall, her head droop and all the while she held in her mind's eye the image of Faan, her intent to bring the girl out of the Mezh, her buried memories of the Whauraka and the trees of her ancient homeplace, her deep joy at the times she'd seen the Mountain Groomer walking his watch.

Immaterial fingers brushed through her once, then again, then they were gone.

The wind dropped, the pressure on her softened. It wasn't exactly a sanctioning of her intent, but a wrathful semineutrality that surrounded her and seemed to say: Very well, come in, but stay strictly to what you claim is your purpose; if you stray, except that we will crush you.

A raindrop splattered on her nose, startling her into opening her eyes. With a groan of effort, she caught hold of a stirrup and pulled herself to her feet. More rain was starting to fall. She wiped her hand across her face, bent to pick up her boots. Without waiting to pull them on, she swung into the saddle. "Let's get under the trees," she said. "It'll be all right now, I think."

> > < <

They rode at a slow walk in the shadows, the
rain dripping around them; the air was heavy, motionless, a remnant of a stench hanging about.
Now and then Kitya took out Faan's kech and set
it on the girl. By late afternoon the slight but constant shifting of the point told them that Faan was
traveling steadily south, as if she meant to walk
the length of the Divimezh.

Desantro glanced around at the thickening
shadow, the growing chill. "It's time we looked
for a place to camp," she said. "Is there any way
you can tell from that thing how far off she is?"

"Neka." Kitya scraped water from her face.
"What about a fire? Will it mess things up if we
build one? It's going to be a cold, wet night and I
don't want to fool with pleurisy."

A wind began to blow, suddenly, without warning, coming at them from behind, pushing at them;
the trees on both sides of them shuddered and
shifted their branches, opening up one path,
weaving together to block all the others.

The two women looked at each other, then Kitya kneed the black into a canter along the open
way. Desantro followed; she wasn't that accustomed to riding and anything above a walk made
her uneasy, but she was even more uneasy about
being left behind.

> > < <

A few moments later, they rode into a charred clearing and stopped, sick, as they saw the lumps of incinerated flesh, the fragile bones like lace woven through and around the blackness, washed white by the steady rain.

Desantro swallowed. "Faan," she said.

Kitya's head whipped round. "What do you mean? What's the girl got to do with. . . ."

"I told you. She dances with fire."

Hand pressed across her mouth, once more Kitya inspected the clearing. Some of the lumps were too big for men. Horses. Horses were terrified by fire. She felt a surge of anger against the girl, dropped her hand. "Why did she have to burn the horses?"

"I don't know. I doubt if she meant to, it's just she can't handle it, not really. You think this is Vicanal and his lot?"

"It'd take a Diviner to tell for sure. But tja, I think it's them. Let's go, Desa, I stay here any longer, I'm going to erp up every meal I've had the past ten years." She clucked to the black, began backing him so she could ride round this place of horror.

Desantro hadn't the skill to back her mare, but she brought the chestnut slowly around, the beast stepping delicately through the ugly debris as if she knew what it was.

She followed Kitya around the edge of the burn, shivered as the wind picked up again and began pushing them away from the direct line to Faan. For a brief time, Kitya fought against the push, but when Desantro was about to protest, the younger woman muttered under her breath and let the wind guide her.

> > < <

By the time the rain had diminished to a chill mist, they came to a stream that cut across a stretch of black rock. Their camp had been made ready for them there; they saw on a flat section of rock beside the stream, a pile of wood under a hat of plaited straw, a string of fish, a heap of tubers on a wooden platter, two loaves of bread.

Kitya laughed, a short sharp bark that had little humor in it. She eased herself in the saddle, looked over her shoulder at Desantro. "Patcha you, eh, Desa. Nu, let's not waste the light." She slid down, began stripping the gear from the black.

Desantro started to answer, then her mouth dropped open and she stared at the clouds that piled up in the west, salmon pink and liquid gold. "Geddrin," she gulped.

An immense form filled with light—made from light—came striding across the mountains. Curiously distorted, his bright shadow like rays of sunlight through a break in the clouds, Geidranay Groomer of Mountains bent over, reached toward them; immense glowing fingers brushed through them, leaving a warm tingle behind, an effervescent fountain of joy—that vanished as soon as the Great God passed from sight.

Desantro shivered, rubbed at her eyes. "I . . ." She coughed, cleared her throat. "I've just come

home," she said. "I ..." She shook herself, slid
from the saddle; her knees threatened to give way,
so she clung to the skirt until she felt strong
enough to stand. She let go of the leather and
leaned her face against the sleek chestnut hair at
the mare's withers, the movement of the large
muscles and the strong horsey smell comfortingly
real as she watched Kitya fitting hobbles on the
black. She closed her eyes and let the warmth of
the horse soothe her for a moment, then she
stepped away, crossed her arms. "Nu," she said,
her voice gone dry. "It's not me, it's what Faan
did, what she is. I've a strong feeling the Mezh is
itching to rid itself of her. You ever come across
boring ticks?"

Kitya straightened. "Tsa! that I have. And cut
them out of me." She tapped the black on his
hindquarters, watched him three-leg-it to the
stream, then she turned. "Tell you what, get the
fire started and I'll strip the mare."

> > < <

The rain stopped completely the moment Desantro took the cover off the wood.

> > < <

Kitya came back from the stream, wiping her
hands on a twist of dry grass. She halted at the
edge of the firelight and stood watching the older
woman a moment. Desantro was gazing into the
fire with something like the same look she'd had

when Geidranay passed. She was nothing like Kitya's mother, her face was too broad and bony, her
body too square, but she had the same aura of
strength and sensuality and Kitya felt a surge of
affection for this stranger that surprised her with
its strength. But after all, why should it? They
were two women alone, both a long way from
home in time and distance.

Kitya pulled a blanket around her shoulders and
sat across the fire from Desantro. She took a
skinny, crooked branch from the woodpile, began
poking gently at the fire, pushing the unburnt por-
tions of the sticks toward the center. The heat felt
good, moving from her face and hands into the
rest of her.

After a while, she said, "What are you going to
do after this is over?"

Desantro blinked, pulled her blanket closer
about her. "You mean this right now? Or later
after I find my brother?"

"Both, I suppose. No, after. What will you do
when you find your brother?"

"Go home." Desantro looked startled. "I hadn't
thought about it before, but seeing Geddrin like
that. . . ."

"What if your brother's happy where he is and
wants you to live with him?"

"I'd have to think about it, but it's a long time
since I was a child, Kat. I think . . . I'm almost
sure, I'd just go home. I find I've a hunger to see
Kappawhay the Cloud Breaker, Rawhero the Sun
Spear, Whentiaka the Land Guard."

"Hmm?"

"The mountains round where I was born. I didn't want to think of them while I was a slave, I couldn't bear it. It was hot where I was, hot all the time. Made your blood thick, your head, too. Safer to think in the body and the moment, leave what happened to chance. Sometimes, though, I'd see the ugly black peaks outside the garden and remember my own. . . . I want to go home, Kat. I want the smells, the feel, I want the cold and the heat, I want to hear speech I was born hearing." She touched her fingers to her mouth, dropped her hand. "I have to be sure Rakil's not hurting, but after that. . . ." The fire deepened the creases in her face, darkened the sunspots and painted a red film across her pale skin. "And you? If you don't mind my asking, are you going to stay with the Magus?"

"I'm in no hurry to breed, if that's what you mean, and my homeplace is . . . closed to me, until the wheel turns for a certain person and he goes to wait his rebirth." She drew back her lips to expose pointed eyeteeth. "And I'm not about to move aside for some itchy little virgin."

"Faan's a good child."

"Who's just killed a small army."

Desantro giggled. "Nobody's perfect."

Kitya opened her eyes wide. "Tsa!" Then she started giggling also.

They laughed until they were exhausted, then stretched out and slept beside the fire, content to leave their safety to the forces that seemed ready to tolerate, even help them in their search.

2. Pargats Velams

Velams walked into the garden late in the afternoon; the grass was wet from the rain that had stopped for the moment, the dark rich smell of the earth in the flowerbeds mixed with the sweeter perfume from the blooms. He lingered a moment, enjoying the freshness, then crossed to the summerhouse and went inside.

Payanin moved the kettle onto the brazier and stood. She dipped into a low curtsy and stayed down, eyes on the floor, waiting for him to speak.

Velams closed his eyes, closed his hands into fists. He'd been expecting this, but expecting was different from knowing. It was a moment before he could speak, and when he did, his easy tenor had turned rough with the control he was putting on himself. "This means he's dead, doesn't it. When does the word come?" Moving slowly, carefully, he settled himself into the rustic chair. "That's enough official decorum, Nestrazma Payanin. Sit. Talk to me eye to eye."

She rose with the easy grace that he loved to watch, took the chair across the table from him. "The High Holy Nestrats Turet had demanded an Official Lazushet from the Diviner Primars. It will be handed to him tomorrow. You will be summoned to the Temple at sundown and informed of your coming investiture."

"Decorum still, Payanin?"

"This is your unofficial official notification, V'la. Tja, your father's dead. Do you want the details? They're not pretty."

"I've never considered ignorance either a strength or a virtue, not like some of my peers." He looked down at his hands, straightened his fingers, held them steady on his thighs. "Tell me."

She did so, with a quiet neutrality that made no judgment of Vicanal's acts or of the girl who was responsible for his horrible death. "It was after a cut across her face," she finished. "The girl screamed ... something ... it wasn't a language any of us knew. Her eyes rolled back and her body went limp. At that moment fire demons rose from her shoulders and raced around the clearing, the sounds they made were like laughter, they burned to cinders every living thing except the girl, then they raced upward in a crimson helix, into the clouds, into the sky, then they were gone. Completely gone."

"And the girl?"

"We don't know. Most times we can't penetrate the Shadow under the trees. Ysgarod the Mezh let us see what IT wanted us to see, then IT shut against us. IT was saying: see what happened, now stay out."

"And Varney?"

"Nothing."

The water began to roll inside the kettle, the lid to dance with a metallic rattle. While Payanin busied herself with the ritual of tea making, Velams rubbed at the crease between his thin blond brows and stared at a knot in a floorboard without actually seeing it. "I loved my father," he muttered. "He wasn't an easy man or even a good one, but I loved him. I want her dead, that stupid girl. Why did she have to come here?"

"V'la ..." Payanin spoke hesitantly. "There's something you have to know. Primars made us swear not to speak of this, not even whisper it to our most trusted friends. I'll be counted forsworn when I confess, but perhaps I'll be forgiven when I explain. The girl. . . ."

He jerked his head up; his face was pale, his eyes shallow and shiny as if a shutter had been closed behind them. "That wasn't for your ears."

"I know. This is important. Listen to me. You can't kill the girl."

"At whose orders?" His voice was very soft, his body rigid.

"I didn't say you were forbidden to kill her. I said you can't. No one can kill her until she finishes what she's being shaped to do."

"Maybe she won't die, but she can hurt." A whisper nearly lost in the soughing of the wind. "You saw that. She can hurt."

"Tja. And we saw what happens to those who hurt her."

He closed his eyes, banged his fist against the arm of his chair until it began to bleed.

She sat and watched. There was nothing she could do but wait until the rage had cooled enough to let reason surface.

> > < <

He leaned back in the chair with his eyes closed, one hand rubbing the other, his face shut against her.

She poured his tea, lifted the cup and saucer across the table and set them down with a small click. "The girl was only an instrument," she said, speaking in a murmur so he could hear her or not as he chose. "An unknowing tool. If you want the ones who used her. . . ."

"Nu?"

"I finished the scan two nights ago. Whoever is the leader, he's almost as clever as he thinks. All of them vanished from view, including Varney and the dead ones."

Velams cracked his eyes; after a moment he sat up, reached for the cup. "So that line's dead."

"Not quite."

"Nu?"

"After the Augstadievon died, it was like that. On the last night of the scan, I had another thought and read the month before the poisoning. And I included Oirs and Samaz, along with Kreisits Izvarits, Ledus Uncil and Tupelis Celabirs because they're next in line. They were all in plain sight the whole month, V'la. All but one. Oirs. He vanished not once but five times."

"That fool. Who would trust. . . ." He blinked. "No one. They're not working to put him in the seat, it's someone else, someone they think they can use. Druz, Begarz, or Steidz . . . and I'd say Begarz, why else that fraudulent attack? It fits. Oh, tja, it fits."

"What are you going to do?"

"I think you'd better not know that, Payan."

She shrugged, said nothing.

A corner of his mouth curled up, the hard lines of his face relaxed. "I owe you more than I can ever pay."

Reassured, she reached across the table and touched his hand. "You owe me peace in the land and pleasure in my bed, nothing more."

"Were it possible. . . ."

"Neka, love, I know. But I'm half-blood and Temple-bound." She smiled; it was painful at first, then easier. "In any case, I don't think I'd make a good wife, V'la, my mind would be elsewhere all too often and you'd be left making excuses for my absence. It's probably better the way things are."

She stood, again with that instinctive utter grace, came round the table, kissed the wrinkle between his brows, and swept out.

He sipped at his tea and listened to the diminishing rustle of her robes, the patter of drops on the roof as the rain began again. After a few moments, though, he slammed the cup down so hard it broke and set himself to plotting ways of getting Oirs into the question chamber deep below the House without bringing a blood feud on Pargats House or alerting Leduzma Chusker. Without a wisp of evidence, only from what he knew of the man, he was almost sure Chusker was the driving force behind these deaths.

> > < <

When it was too dark to see the far side of the room, he got to his feet, the beginnings of a scheme worked out. Grief hit him suddenly. Body shaking with gusts of rage and anguish, he clutched the back of the chair and wept for his father.

The eruption was as brief as it was wrenching. In a moment he had himself together. He rubbed his sleeve across his eyes and went into the Heir's wing to await the summons of the High Holy Nestrats Turet.

3. Navarre

Navarre stirred. His musings had begun turning in on themselves; the paths he took were paths he'd taken before. The only thing that led to was self-flagellation, and a more useless activity he couldn't imagine.

He got to his feet, ran his hands through his hair, scratched vigorously at his scalp, as if he meant to scratch away the futility he'd started sliding into. He laughed, the sound booming out, delighting him. He laughed some more, just to hear the rumble of it. "I AM I," he cried, his deep voice magnified, filling the vast space under that leaden sky. "I DENY YOU," he cried.

The sky wrinkled and ripped apart, the hard reddish stone beneath his feet melted to powder and blew in a wild vortex about him.

> > < <

When he could see again what was beyond his nose, he found himself in a place of . . . what?

Streams of light, painted light as if it had passed through a stained-glass window like those he'd seen somewhere, he couldn't remember where right now, rays crossing and mingling with each other, color melting into color, emerging pure again. Nothing solid there but him. He looked down at hands like pinkish-brown glass and lost even the certainty of his own weight.

"What is this?" he shouted—and saw his words stream away, little shimmers of black edged gold . . . little shimmers . . . his words were diminished here to fleas running through the light lattice.

Light flickered around him; the beams shifted, changed, took on a shape vaguely familiar . . . with him a little dark beetle in the center . . . a hand so huge the fingers were longer than rivers, the thumb a tower as immense as . . . he couldn't think of anything that big. . . .

He bent his neck and looked up. A face was sketched out above him, hinted at by shifting planes of light and color. The mouth opened. Words dropped like golden rain, he felt them rather than heard them. "GO BACK. ACT. BOAST NOT."

The hand slipped from under him and he fell through a chaos of nameless, shapeless forces that flung him erratically about until he was completely disoriented, until he could only cling to that irreducible, indescribable essence of who and what he was, that hard center of himself which he never thought of but which was always there undergirding every act, every thought, every response.

Twisting and turning, swooping and tumbling, he fell through chaos, he fell and fell. . . .

> > < <

A long-fingered white hand came from the fog and cupped under him, holding him as gently as he'd seen Kitya hold a mouse on her palm before she let it go. A huge but eerily beautiful face loomed over him, great green eyes with slit pupils like a cat gazed down at him. More of her took shape, firm breasts with pale green nipples, a long supple tail with fishscales like slices of green jade, flukes that flipped about with an insouciance that made him smile despite his terror.

"Godalau," he said and saw the word rising from him in a bubble, along with the other bubbles of his breath.

Tungjii emerged from the weedy tresses that floated free about her head. Heesh sat on her pale shoulder, comic little figure, with hisser heavy breasts and fringe of hair about a shiny bald head. Heesh slipped a strap from hisser shoulder, pulled a wineskin into view, tossed it down to Navarre. "Have a drink," heesh said. "After Perran-a-Perran you NEED a drink." Hisser's words emerged as bubbles that burst one by one in Navarre's face.

He drank and was filled with warmth and laughter and nothing seemed tragic any longer. He wanted to drink again, more and more, but he knew better so he shoved the stopple home and tossed the skin back.

The Godalau pursed her perfect lips as if she blew him a kiss, then she took her hand from under him and melted in the fog.

And he fell again.

Endlessly.

But he didn't care any more.

He was content to wait until this journey found its end.

After a while he slept.

4. Honeywild

Faan walked without stopping, sustained by the rain and the sun like the plants around her.

Her mind was turned off. She neither thought nor remembered, all she knew was what came dimly through her senses, all she felt was the urge to get away—she didn't know from what or to where, only away.

A glow followed her through the trees. She was aware of it like everything else around her. Now and then a small gray-brown animal brushed against her ankles. She was aware of that. She put a name to neither phenomenon and forgot each two seconds after she noticed them.

Sometimes mezhmerrai hunters followed her, staying carefully within shadow, watching her, whispering together, but they wouldn't go near her even when Ysgarod the Mezh roared at them to drive her east and out of the trees.

When the sun dropped away, she slowed and groped along, but she never stopped. Day and night, night and day she moved south through the

Forest, always inside its bounds though sometimes she had to turn aside to go around an im-
passable ravine or find a place where she could
ford a creek. There were times when Ysgarod the
Mezh Itself tried to push her to the east and out
of it, when trees fell over in front of her, thorn
canes whipped at her, but she scarcely noticed Its
efforts, always returning to her southline and her
blind forge forward.

> > < <

On the seventh night she stepped into one of
the larger meadows and began trudging across it.

Two smugglers were camped beside a trickle
that ran along one edge of the meadow, their train
of packponies unloaded and grazing free since the
little beasts were too afraid of the trees to leave
the open.

They'd dug a hole and built a fire in it to cook
their supper, a fire reduced to coals and invisible
a few yards away; one man was bending over the
hole, the glow reddening his face, his eyes squinting against the threads of smoke as he thrust a
twig into the coals to give him a light for his pipe.
The other grunted and got to his feet. "I dunna
what it is, Marsh, but since I drunk that brew
Stort was passing out, I've had the runs something fierce."

"Hunh. So you keep telling me." He waved the
twig, checked the coal at the end, then settled on
his heels and applied it to the weed in his pipe-
bowl, sucking vigorously on the curving stem.

"Running at both ends," he muttered as he watched his temporary partner push through the brush to the sump they'd dug for the purpose.

"Sai! Marsh. C'm 'ere. Hurry."

"What is 't this time, Trev?" he called.

"You gotta see 't for y'sef. C'm on."

Marsh set his pipe on a flat stone and got to his feet. "Last time I take a greener this trek," he growled and pushed through the brush.

Trev was crouched by a scraggly bush, staring across the meadow. When he heard Marsh drop beside him, he pinched his partner's arm. "See that there." He pointed to the pale naked form plodding across the grass. "Pretty thing. Y' think ol' Mezh it's gi'ing us a present?" He started to get to his feet.

Marsh clamped his hand on the younger man's shoulder, shoved him down. "Don't y' ever listen, fool! I told y', don't touch anything inside the Mezh."

"Y' say don't touch merrys. That's no merry."

"Don' matter, fool. Look't her. She's a crazy. Mezh mad."

As she got closer, they could see the bruises on the pale body, the whip cuts, the bloody scratches, the wild matted hair, sticks and leaves threaded through it. A small beast walked at her heels, a glow rode her shoulder.

When she came even with them, she stared at them from white-ringed eyes that seemed to see only horror, then she walked on.

Trej shuddered, then cursed and felt at his crotch. "Shat m'sef, merdenn femme."

Marsh sniffed, pinched his nose. "Ya so, go dump y'sef in stream, cool y' off lotsa ways." He got to his feet and went back to the fire.

> > < <

Faan saw them dimly, but paid them no more attention than she had the mezhmerrai who followed her. Sunk in horror, running from a pain she could no longer bear, she continued her flight south.

Chapter 15
Returns

1. In the Divimezh

Navarre woke.

He was plummeting through clouds, moonlight shimmering around him.

He willed himself to slow and was gratified to note that the small powershift worked without the heat that usually marked the stirring of the Wrystrike. Cloudstuff curled about him, cool and diaphanous, as illusory as the chaos of Otherwhere; gusts of wind tugged at him, vanished as he dropped into another stratum.

When he glided through the last of the clouds, he saw the Divimezh below him like dark wool spreading across the rounded mountains of the coast range.

He landed easily at the edge of a meadow flat and stood in the shadow of a tree wondering why he'd been brought here.

Half a dozen ponies were scattered across the grass, grazing placidly, undisturbed by his sudden arrival. On the far side of the meadow where a thready stream ran through brush and rocky outcrops, he heard men talking in short staccato phrases; he couldn't make out the words, but the ponies were evidence enough to tell him a pair of smugglers were moving north along the Greenway. The breeze brought him the pungent smell of pipe leaf; it jolted his body to life again, his stomach clenched, saliva flooded his mouth, and he remembered how long it'd been since he'd had anything to eat.

He started to step into the moonlight, stopped when he saw a pale form emerge from the trees on the far side of the meadow.

Naked and battered, black hair wild, a glow riding one shoulder, the mahsar running silent at her ankle, Faan trod toward him with a heavy weariness, hands moving as if she groped her way through a fog only she could see.

He was distracted for a moment by a stirring in the brush by the stream. The smugglers? He took a step forward, raised his hands, ready to protect her.

Nothing happened. Faan turned her head and gazed blindly toward the brush, then continued slogging along.

Navarre waited for her.

When she came even with him, she turned her head and looked at him, then looked away and went on walking south. Her eyes were empty. She must have seen him, but what it meant to her was impossible to read.

"Sh'dug," he whispered, "What happened to you, child?"

He followed her, frowning.

Pulling her out of this looked more complicated than he'd expected . . . as that thought struck him, he laughed aloud. Complicated! That was an understatement worthy of Kitya at her tartest.

Ailiki came trotting back to sniff at his ankles. For a moment, the mahsar paced beside him, looking up at him, speculation gleaming in her eyes, then she ran ahead, took her place beside the girl.

This situation was as inchoate and disturbing as the soup he'd been falling through; it was something he had to change as soon as he could, but he needed an open area, relatively free of trees and other threats.

He could feel Ysgarod the Mezh cringing from her, continually trying to deflect her without touching her, to turn her east so she'd pass out of It.

In the shadow under the trees he caught glimpses of mezhmerrai gliding parallel to her, keeping well away; he could smell the fear in them, and a kind of dreadful expectation.

She walked through all this, untouched and—perhaps—unaware.

> > < <

When the Wounded Moon's fattening crescent was low in the west, Faan came to a burn that was several years old. The regrowth was as yet barely shoulder high and the dead trees had mostly fallen with here and there a skeletal remnant rising black and angular above the thickets.

He closed in on her until he was walking at her heels, and when they reached a rockslide with a mudflat beyond it, he caught hold of her arm and held onto it though she tried to pull away. "Faan," he said. "It's Navarre. Listen to me. It's Navarre." A flicker of memory—he thought he knew how to reach her. "Massulit. Remember? The sapphire with the star at its heart? I've got to talk to you about Massulit."

She stared at him, her mouth drooping open; there was nothing in her eyes, neither fear nor anger, no recognition of him or the words he was flinging at her.

He'd forgotten how strange her eyes were; even in the leaching moonlight, the difference in their color was apparent. It gave him an oddly disoriented feeling as if he saw two girls before him, the one imperfectly merged with the other. "Faan," he said more softly, making a croon from her name, thinking of her at that moment as a young wild thing, wondering aslant if that was the origin of her name.

As that thought flitted through his mind, heat suddenly glowed round them.

A form began taking shape over hers, a white doe with bi-colored eyes, translucent, growing more solid the longer he looked at it.

He wrenched his eyes away, tried to shake her loose, fought against the heat and all it meant. . . .

Then he froze, unable to move.

Wrystrike had him, he knew it and despaired for both of them.

"I am the White Hind," she sang, in a voice that was almost falsetto, far from her usual deep tones.

I am the White Hind
Blind and fleet
My feet read the night
My flight is silence
My silence summons to me
Free and bold
The Gold Hart.

"I am the Gold Hart," he sang, the words forced from him.

I am the Gold Hart
Artful and fierce
I pierce the night
My flight is wildfire
Desire consumes me
She looms beside me
Fleet and unconfined
The White Hind.

His words ended in a challenging bugle. He thrust his cold black nose against her neck, nuzzled at her.

> > < <

The hart with the coat of rough, raw gold and the great rack of antlers trotted beside the dainty hind with the bicolored eyes. The Mezh heaved a great sigh and the forces that had been concentrated here melted away.

2. Pargats Varney (1)

A piercing squeal and a steady bump bump bump brought Varney groaning into awareness. He started to sit up and the world tilted. He rolled against bars and stabilized enough to look around. He was in a cage of green saplings bound together by braided grass ropes, a grid on the bottom, a grid on the top, vertical bars around the sides with ropes knotted about them and woven between them. He caught hold of the bottom grid, pulled himself back into the middle, the cage straightening as he did so. He looked up.

The cave was hanging from a thick cable that came over the top of a cliff within armreach if he chose to thrust his arm between the bars. He looked down, snapped his eyes shut.

There was nothing between him and the ground but the grid he was sitting on and the ground was at least a hundred yards straight down, and worse, it was covered with sharp-edged rocks and clumps of thornbrush.

Eyes still shut, he eased himself around and set cross-legged in the middle of the grid, trying to figure out how he'd gotten there.

The last thing he could remember, he was in the middle of a Forest Devil village, holding the local shaman by the hair with one hand, the axe raised in the other, yelling at them to lead him out of the Mezh or he'd chop the man's head off and start on the rest of them. He had his shoulders against one of their huts, they couldn't have gotten at him that way ... he dragged his fingers across the back of his head, felt a small sore place like a bug bite, and swore.

They'd pricked him through the wall with one of those darts.

He fumbled at his chest, felt the lump of the aizar stone; weren't for that, he'd be dead. He contemplated his surroundings and wondered if that was such a blessing after all.

A small gray bird came swooping into the cage, drove its beak into his face, nearly piercing his eye. It was gone before he could react. There was a flock of them outside the cage now, squawking and skreeing.

He turned his head cautiously, saw litter and feathers on ledges and poking from holes in the stone. Nesting range. He cursed again, the Devils must have dropped him here deliberately.

Another bird came at him.

This time he caught it and wrung its neck. About to throw it away, he stopped and looked at the small gray fragment. His stomach turned over, but he tucked the dead bird into the front of his shirt and set himself to catch as many more as he could.

3. Pargats Velams

In the Krontzall of the Alkazal, the Investiture was beginning.

Simmering with resentment, Leduzma Chusker

sat on the back bench in the Leduz Sector among lesser cousins, a clear space on each side of him. The only reason he was here was because his half brother didn't have the face to order him to stay away or the intelligence to create a believable difficulty that would keep him busy elsewhere. Chusker knew the true basis of his half brother's disquiet—though his eyes were his mother's, Devil black, his hair a red so dark it, too, was almost black, his skin a greenish ocher as if Isayana had worked a compromise between Devil and Valda, his face was an exact duplicate of Cikston's. Old Ientules put his stamp on all his sons, legitimate and otherwise. Cikston couldn't bear to be in the same room with him if there was anyone else about to see that likeness.

Face impassive, he watched Velams pace along the golden way, an elegant white figure reflected as in a shallow pool by the polished metal. White tunic, white trousers, woven from winter yeyeldi wool, virgin shearing. Around his neck, the Heir's Chain, plates of chased gold an inch square alternating with half-spheres of dark jasper. Red slippers on his feet, embroidered with gold and pearls. White, gold and red, the Heir's Colors. Colors Chusker would never wear, though he was Ientules' first born son. Nor would he ever wear his House's equivalent of what Velams was going to receive, the Pargats Ring (which Vicanal must have left behind when he went chasing off into the woods) and the ancient Pargats Pectoral.

He watched Velams with reluctant admiration; the man knew how to make the most of an occasion, walking with a firm step, head high, face grave.

He saw House Daughters turn their heads to follow Velams, speculation and ambition plain in their eyes; Velams had left the womanizing to his beautiful brother, taking to himself a single lover, the Diviner Payanin, staying true to her from the night he first brought her to bed. Chusker had heard his half sisters, their maids, and other silly girls sighing over this "tragic" love and yearning for a paramour of their own who'd be as true and as handsome.

The High Holy Nestrats Turet stood on the tall, round dais at the east end of the Hall, there in double guise as Caretaker and Priest; while the Temple Glitodj intoned their formal chants from the curved stand behind him, he waited for the Heir, the Objects on a table beside him, his ringed hands crossed on the heavily embroidered front panels of his best robe.

As the ceremony commenced, Chusker rested his back against the pilaster, his face in shadow, his eyes half closed, his wide mouth curling at the corners as he waited for the surprise he'd crafted to enliven the occasion.

> > < <

The chorus swelled for the third time, the questions were asked and answered. . . .

Who are you who come before me with the Chain of Pargats?

I am Pargats Velams mtya Nestrats, Valda
of the pure blood for fifty generations.

What is your rank?

I am Heir to the Pargats Lielskadrav.

What is it you desire?

It has been declared and certified that my
father is dead, that the Pargats Lielskadrav is
no more. I ask that the House continue undis-
turbed. I ask to be declared and certified Liel-
skadrav of Pargats House, swearing homage
to He-Who-Commands-the-Land, the Great
and Caring Meggzatevoc.

Do you so swear?

I kneel before his representative and place
my hands between his and I say, I will serve
the god Meggzatevoc in sadness and in joy,
through all the turns of my life.

Let it be heard in the Akazal and the Ashes,
I, the High Holy Nestrats Turet, Caretaker of
the Valda and of all Valdamaz do declare that
here before you is Pargats Velams mtya Nes-
trats, Valda of the pure blood for fifty gen-
erations, now Lielskadrav of the House of
Pargats.

The voices of the Temple Glitodj soared again
as Velams knelt and bowed his head. Nestrats
Turet lifted high the heavy square pectoral with
its crusting of jewels catching the light from the
lamps, glinting red, green, and blue. When he was
through posturing, he reversed it and laid the
chain on Velams' shoulders, then placed the Ring
on his left thumb and lifted him so he could stand

before the Valda and accept their applause in the form of a stormy clatter of wood on wood from the claquers brought for the occasion.

Velams stood, arms outstretched, head high....

Chusker concentrated on keeping his face relaxed, his hands still ... now, he thought, get on with it, now!

High over the rest of the Hall a pane in one of the clerestory windows had been eased from its lead canes. At the opening crouched a shaman-shrouded crossbowman from the Mezh, a special bolt in the slot, shaman-cursed to bring it home without fail; Chusker found it a delicious irony that the iron point had been crafted by Navarre with his own magic wrought into it, the magic that was supposed to whisper the point home to its target.

He alone heard the twang of the cord, and then only because he was listening so hard for it; the claquers were still going, drowning most other noises, even the chant of the choir.

He let his eyes droop half-shut and forced his mouth to stay relaxed as he caught sight of a yellow streak, the bolt darting for Velams....

Then with everyone else he was on his feet, staring.

A Kyatty wizard appeared in midair, caught the bolt, and came crashing down with it to land on his knees before the dais, the deadly missile held flat on an outstretched palm.

Velams plunged down the steps to the kneeling man, shouldering aside the Valda who'd come pouring off the benches, bellowing, "Get back, get back! The man just saved my life. Druz! Get them away."

Druz grinned at him, large square teeth gleaming between a dark gold mustache and beard, then he spread his powerful arms and began sweeping the others back.

Behind Velams, on the dais, Turet was turning from side to side, looking for someone he could order to do something, his face wrinkling sourly as he was ignored by Velams and everyone else.

Velams took the bolt, looked at the wicked edges of the triangular point, then at the Kyatty wizard. Around him Valda men muttered, but he scarcely noticed that because he recognized the face and form of the man Vicanal had bought to smoke his more dubious acts.

"Sabusé," he said.

The wizard got to his feet. "Vicanal's son," he said.

"Patcha for my life. Where did this come from?"

Sabusé pointed, his long bony arm slanting up at the clerestory on the left. "He's gone now."

"Who?"

"I may not say."

"How do you come here?"

Sabusé shrugged, brought his hand around in an expressive curve. "Not in this place."

Velams took a deep breath. "Nu, you're right." He swung round, bowed to the High Holy Nestrats Turet, straightened. "Pardon, High Holy, for this disruption. If you will call for the sounding of the gong and set the garidj to clearing out the Hall," he added tactfully, "you can feel free to have your sardzin search the roof for traces of the assassin."

> > < <

Velams came into the room tucking in his olive-brown workshirt, his feet in worn sandals, a lock of light yellow hair falling across his forehead. He nodded to the wizard perched uncomfortably on a straight-backed chair. "It's stopped raining. Let's sit in the summerhouse. The servants will have made tea for us and we won't be disturbed there. Not until it's time for my sealing. You understand, we've only an hour to talk. After that I must remain silent and alone for the next two days. It's our custom." He smiled suddenly, one end of his mouth hooking up higher than the other. "Meant to induce the habit of thinking before we act. It works sometimes." Without waiting for a response, he crossed to the long windows, pushed one open and stepped onto the slate walkway outside.

> > < <

Velams filled a cup for himself, then poised the spout over another, lifted a brow.

"Naught for me, Vicanal's son."

Velams frowned. He took a moment to set the delicate porcelain pot on the tray, then lifted his cup, sipped from it and set it down. "Poison in these circumstances would be a stupidity hard to excuse."

"You could not poison me; this body is not mine, only taken for the moment."

Velams sat very still, breath caught behind his teeth, then he relaxed. "Whoever you are, be welcome. Sabusé or not, you saved my life and I pay my debts. What do you want?"

"One entered my domain and injured me. I seek a proper redress."

"From me?"

"Neka. I will do all that is necessary. What I ask from you is housing for the body while the spirit roves."

"In search of whom?"

"That is my business."

"Neka, Power—as I assume you are. You are in Valdamaz now, you are in my House. I am Lielskadrav, Father to my Blood and Vassal to Meggzatevoc. If your quarry is kin to me or subject to Him, we have something to talk about."

The wrinkled lids of the wizard lifted and Velams found himself staring into an abyss, black and whirling, depth upon depth, sucking. . . .

He blinked and turned pale, but he refused to look away.

The lids lowered again. The wizard's hands lifted and lay flat on the table, palms up. "Not your kin. Not anyone's kin. Nor That One's vassal. By the Coign of Yah'du which is the heart of my being, I swear it."

Velams' lips twitched, the humor that lay so close beneath his skin tickled by this oath and its futility. Coign of Yah'du. It meant nothing to him. Whether it meant anything to the Power. . . .

"That being so, I give you the freedom of the House." His face hardened. "Perhaps we can make a further bargain after the Retreat is over." He rang the bell without waiting for an answer. "If you'll follow the maidservant, she'll show you to a room where you can stay undisturbed while you do what it is you have to do."

The pseudo Sabusé stood. "I know what you want, Lielskadrav. I will consider my price."

4. Kitya of the Moug'aikkin (1)

Kitya pushed her thumb through the loop at the end of the kech's dangle cord, lifted it so both of them could see it. "Pa-Faan," she said.

The kech jerked and pointed south.

"Tsa, hasn't changed for three days now. Tuzra." She tucked the kech back in her belt pouch, drew her hand across her brow, wiping away for the moment the sweat beads collecting there. There was no breeze, even though they kept moving, and it was very hot.

Desantro yawned. "Never thought I'd get tired of trees," she grumbled, "but this lot. . . ." With those words they rode into sunlight, leaving the heaviest part of the canopy behind; they were entering the mouth of a stony canyon where there were few trees but a lot of thornbrush and rock-piles.

Desantro rubbed the back of her neck and twisted her body about to ease sore muscles, then she blinked. "Kat, do you see that?" She pointed.

Kitya wiped at her face again. "I don't see how

you can stand this. I feel like I can't breathe." She followed the line of Desantro's arm, frowned. "Looks like a cage hanging off the top of the wall."

"Something in it, too. I can't tell from here, but the way those birds are acting. . . ."

Kitya's mouth tightened, then she shook her head. "Not our business, Desa. I wouldn't say it's something I like to see, but. . . ."

"But we're here on sufferance."

"Nu, you know it."

Desantro shrugged. "I've seen worse," she said and clucked to the mare to make her move faster.

> > < <

When they were almost even with the cage, Kitya looked up, startled, as she heard her name called.

"Kitya, it's Varney. Give me a hand. Help me get out of this."

In spite of the conciliatory words, there was a rage and violence in the voice that made her shiver. She looked at Desantro.

The older woman eased in the saddle, folded her hands on the horn. "Up to you, Kat."

"You're a big help. Tiesh tas, I can't ignore him, he's Navarre's friend." She tilted her head back, frowning up at the cage. All she could see was a particolored blotch on the bottom grill. "He's always making trouble, that twok."

"Nu, what do we do?"

"As little as possible." Kitya jerked the thongs

loose that held the long thin rope she'd tied to the saddle. "Find me a skinny rock, will you? I need it for a weight, but it'll have to go through those bars." She unsnapped the saddle knife, sliced off a length of rope and recoiled the rest, then began knotting the cut end of the shorter piece about the hilt and guards.

Desa nodded and slid from the saddle. In a minute she was back with a stone the size of two fists which some accident of weathering had given a narrow waist. "This do?"

Kitya sniffed. "Varney's Luck. Like it was made for it." She measured wrist to elbow from the knife, tied the stone to the rope. "Nu, let's see if my arm's still good. I used to be able to chunk a mo'h in the head halfway round the herd. . . ." She slid from the saddle. "Desa, take the horses on a ways, I don't want to chance hitting them with this."

> > < <

She waved when she thought Desantro was far enough from her, then began swinging the stone and knife in a circle, gradually lengthening the rope, turning it faster and faster until the two weights blurred as they whished through the still air. When she felt ready, she released the rope.

The stone flew up, curving just a little; it struck against the bars, but it didn't have a chance to rebound. Varney was waiting and caught hold of the rope. "Patcha you, Kitya," he yelled down to her as he began drawing the knife and stone into the cage. "Won't take long now. Wait for me."

"You can hope," she muttered and trotted for the horses. A moment later she was in the saddle. "Let's go. He can rescue himself."

Desantra raised a brow, a twinkle in her light brown eyes. "You don't like him much." She heeled the mare into a fast walk, matching the black's gait.

Kitya snorted. "He's misery in a pretty skin. Thinks the sun shines out his dangle." She stood in the stirrups, shook herself and settled back more comfortably. "I'll be glad when Navarre's had enough of him and this place."

5. Pargats Varney (2)

Varney watched Kitya swing into the saddle and ride off with the other woman. "Whore," he muttered. "Scales on your hide, snake in your soul." He blinked. "What's she doing out here anyway? She mixed up in this?" He looked after her until she vanished around a bend in the canyon, swore again when he realized that the bit of rope she'd tossed to him wouldn't reach a fraction of the way down. "Have to go up." He inspected the grid overhead. "If I can get through that without collapsing the cage. . . ."

He settled himself in the center, waited until the swinging stabilized, then began working on the knots about the stone weight; after getting rid of that, he'd have to make some sort of sling for pthe knife so he could use both hands without fear of dropping it.

> > < <

It didn't take him long to cut through several of the branches that formed the top grid; the knife had the edge of a razor and stayed sharp despite use and misuse, probably one of Navarre's making. He was careful not to touch the cording near the edge; once it started unraveling, there was no telling where it'd stop. When he was finished, he checked to see the knife was firmly attached to the loop of rope about his neck, then pulled off his boots and shoved them out of the cage. There was no point in hauling them about; he could always retrieve them if he didn't kill himself climbing out of this thing.

Carefully not looking down, moving in small, controlled increments so he wouldn't start the cage tipping or swinging, he pulled himself through the hole he'd made and stood with a foot on each side of the cable. He flexed his fingers and tried not to think how far he'd fall if he missed his grip.

Alarmed by this new manifestation, the little gray birds launched themselves from their nests and flew about squawking and swirling, working up courage to come at him again.

He shouted at them and they went whirling away. There was no time to waste. Gripping the cable in both hands, he swung his feet up until they hit the stone, then walking and hauling himself hand over hand, he began the climb.

> > < <

He gave a last shove, flung himself up and over the lip, and rolled away from it until he crashed into a tree. He lay there, clinging to the tree until the shaking stopped, sobbing with the sudden relaxation of the terror that had consumed him.

> > < <

As he used the gnarled trunk to pull himself to his feet, he heard a crashing not far from where he stood. He froze, relaxed a breath later as more sounds told him it was some large beast lumbering off, nothing to do with him. Not Devils come to mock his weakness.

Anger put stiffening into his body. "Boots," he said aloud. "I'd better get my boots. More than one kind of snake in this sewer."

> > < <

He began walking east, stubbornly, obsessively, cursing Kitya as a treacherous bitch, cursing the Forest Devils, cursing the murdering plotters in Valdamaz, cursing Navarre . . . even Navarre. Half starved and more than half mad, he suspected his friend of selling him, why else would that whore dare ride off and leave him? Friend, piest! Da was right, can't trust anyone but the Blood. He slapped at the trees with the rope ends, the sound as well as the feel of the rebound draining off toxins dumped into him by fear and anger so he was finally able to slow down and think more coherently.

He called Faan to mind and smiled. Sweet child, silly thing, too softhearted to survive long . . . what a woman should be . . . tender and . . . he sighed. Nu, too bad, but by the time he saw her next . . . if he ever did . . . she'd be over the shine and probably annoyed at him. That happened lots of times. Never mind, there was always another one. . . .

His heart jolted as he saw three dark figures gliding through the trees. He turned to face them.

Black eyes stared into his, opened wider till they were ringed with white, then the Devils howled with terror and ran from him.

He threw back his head and roared with laughter. "The Man-you-can't-kill, is it?" he bellowed after them. "That's it, run, you Devils, run, you filthy savages." He clicked his teeth together. "Run or this ol' man is going to eat you raw!"

He stood staring into the shadow under the trees until the last sounds of their flight had faded into the ordinary noises of the Forest, then he sighed with satisfaction and strolled along, keeping an eye on the sun, sure that it was only a matter of time before he was in his own rooms, resting in his own bed, luxuriating in the smell of clean sheets and the herbs from the hot bath he'd soaked in for a full hour until everything that had happened in here was steamed out of him and he could feel clean and whole again.

> > < <

Midmorning on the third day, when his confidence had begun to wear thin and his belly was wrapped round his backbone since he'd had nothing in it but water for who knows how long, the earth beneath his feet jumped as if the mountain had hiccuped and the air seemed to blink—and he found himself on the coarse sand of the wasteland beyond the rim of the Divimezh. When he looked north, he could see the Smithy compound atop Djestradjin Hill rising black against a cloudless blue sky.

6. Kitya of the Moug'aikkin (2)

Kitya's chouk throbbed and her pum tingled more and more as the days slid by, five, six, seven. . . .

On the seventh night they made a dry camp in a small clearing with no help this time from the hovering mezhmerrai.

> > < <

Kitya poked at the fire, scowling. "Something's building up to blow," she muttered.

"I don't know magic. . . ." Desa drank the last bitter swallow in her mug, set it aside. "But maybe it already has. The trees feel different."

Kitya looked up quickly. "How?"

"Hard to say. Kind of like they've relaxed; they're still nervous but not so afraid as they were. Same time, they're madder'n ever." She coughed, looked around. "I don't know. It's been a long time away. I could be wrong."

"I don't think so. My pum's still giving me fits. Ever had an itch you couldn't possibly scratch? We'd better find Faan soon or I'm going to turn into a hoop trying to bite m'self in the backside."

A huge gold hart raced from the darkness, leapt the fire, and vanished into the darkness again.

"What was that?" Desantro rolled up from the sprawl she'd thrown herself into when the beast charged them.

Kitya was already on her feet again, hand on the hilt of her skinning knife, her eyes searching the dark, the oval swelling between them throbbing visibly. She turned slowly toward Desantro, her mouth open, her eyes shining a molten crimson as they caught the firelight. "Navarre. . . .

"Huh?"

Kitya touched her cheek, licked her fingertip. "It was. That was Navarre."

"That was a deer. A stag."

"It was also Navarre. I'll show you. Look." She dug into the pouch at her belt, brought out a thing both like and unlike the kech Desantro was used to seeing. "This is the karetka I made to find him. Watch."

Without hesitation the karetka pointed after the hart. It was drawn so strongly, it strained against the hair cord like a puppy on a leash, pulling it out straight from Kitya's fingers. She wrapped her other hand around it, holding it gently as one would a baby bird that had been shoved from its nest, blew on it, then put it back in the pouch. "You see?"

"So what do we do now?"

"I follow him."

"And Faan?"

Once more Kitya dipped into her pouch. This time she brought out the kech. "Like you said, she can take care of herself. And you don't need her any more. You have the Rakil-kech. Follow her, follow me, whichever you prefer." She tossed the Faan-kech to Desantro.

In mid arc the charm swung about and went darting after the hart, making a tiny keening as it flew.

Desantro chuckled. "Problem solved," she said. "Looks like they're together."

> > < <

The next three days, the gold hart—and a white hind they saw the second night—ran circles round them, teasing them in an exasperating game of tag the deer never lost.

On the third night, Kitya scrubbed down the weary black before she fed him the last of the grain, swearing in three languages with every stroke of the brush. She turned him loose to browse on the twig ends, weeds, and the tufts of wiry grass growing in the small clearing.

"I'm a fool." She threw herself down beside the fire, watched Desantro stirring their improvised soup in a pot precariously balanced on three small stones.

"Why say that now?"

"I just discovered it." She pulled her legs up, wrapped her arms about them. "I keep thinking that stag's Navarre, but it isn't, it's a beast, mind and body. It'll play with us until something distracts it and it goes off where we'll never find it. They'll go off, I should say, because he'll take her wherever he goes."

"So what do we do?"

"Do what I did from the day I was born." She pulled a pin from her travel knot, used it to scratch her head. "I rode to herds from my first breath. Neka, it's true. I came at the wrong time, Spring instead of Winter; the kuneag were calving and every hand was needed. My mother buried the afterbirth, wrapped me in wool, stuffed me into a sling next her skin, and went to do what she could. She was a wonder, hai-yah."

"She's dead?"

"Neka." Kitya chuckled. "She always said it'd take an axe to kill her, cold wouldn't do it, or work, and certainly not me." She passed her hand across her mouth, closed her eyes a moment. "The *was*, that was for me, for the years I haven't seen her. Navarre tells me she's alive and well. When I ask. What was I . . . ah tja, we have to drive them before us. Herd them out of the Mezh. A chase is no good, we'll just wear out the horses and get nowhere."

"I won't be much help, Kat. I know plants and earth, but they stay where you put them."

"Nu, I'll tell you what to do. No problem there. But we won't do it tomorrow. There's grass here and water. We'll rest tomorrow. Come the next day, though. ...." A sharp nod and a snap of her fingers, then she sniffed. "Is that burning?"

Hastily, Desantro pulled the pot from the fire.

> > < <

On the morning of the second day, the chase began as soon as the hart appeared, the hind running at his side.

Kitya snapped the end of her rope under his nose, rode at him, shouting. Desantro angled away from her and between them they drove the two deer eastward toward the edge of the Mezh. With rope and shouts and Kitya's handling of the black, they kept the pair running in a panic, plunging through brush and thickets, driving them in blind flight. ...

Until the trees thinned and all four of them broke from the Mezh into the wasteland beyond. ...

The gold hart and the white hind stopped. Abruptly. As if full sunlight had turned them to stone.

The forms began to sublime like mist when a morning heats up.

In moments two bodies were sprawled on the coarse sand, Faan curved to the right, Navarre to the left.

Kitya swung down, ran to the Magus and pushed her fingers up under his chin. Then she sank onto her heels and squatted with eyes closed, breathing hard.

When she looked up, Desantro was getting to her feet. "Her, too?"

The older woman nodded. "Alive, but out." She glanced around. "Any idea where we are?"

Kitya stood. "Highroad should be that way." She pointed east. "It runs north and south the length of Valdamaz. We can make a dry camp here and get some rest. If they don't wake by morning, we'd better load them on the horses and start walking. It's all I can think of to do. Once we get back to the smithy, maybe then. . . ." She didn't bother finishing, but turned to the black and began working on the cinch buckle.

CABAL

"What happened? What went wrong?" Oirs was still pulling his robe about him as he rushed into the crypt; he was pale and sweating, close to panic. "What about me? You said. . . ."

Chusker brought his hand down flat on the stone lid of the sarcophagus, the slap echoing through the low irregular chamber. "Sit down. Be quiet. There's nothing to panic about."

Nenova closed her hand about Oirs' arm. "Hush, friend. He's right. It's a small glitch, that's all. It happens. You should know that. There's no danger, the bowman got away without a trace."

Oirs dropped into a chair, wiped his sleeve across his face, his arm shaking, his breath unsteady. He pulled the hood over his head and huddled in the black folds, staring gloomily at the dusty stone of the sarcophagus they were using for a table. The figures carved into cartouches were so worn as to be unrecognizable and what was left of the inscription was in old Valda, with even less meaning.

Nenova traced one of the enigmatic letters, scratching at the traces of lichen in the grooves. "Laz is late," she murmured.

"Laz is busy with something I asked him to do," Chusker said.

Her hood shifted; he could feel her eyes moving from his hands to what she could see of his face. She didn't say anything, but he knew she didn't believe him. That didn't matter so much, it was Oirs he had to calm back to a reasonable state; that was the major purpose for this meeting—and it was working. Oirs' hands emerged from his sleeves, his shoulders straightened, his head lifted.

"I suppose Velams doesn't matter that much," he said. *"He wasn't one of the original targets."* He leaned forward. *"Chusker, when's my attack going to happen? It should be soon. Turet's issued a call to set up the commission, he pulled me aside, congratulated me on having the wisdom to suggest it and said he was going to suggest I chair it."* There was more than a touch of self-satisfaction in Oirs' voice, his panic retreating before his vanity.

"Splendid. Couldn't be better. Listen, Oirs, you're still young and vigorous, you can start building support now, twelve years from now the Seat moves on and it could be I'm looking at the new Augstadievon. It's just as well Laz is busy, we can keep this between ourselves, mh? Your attack, it'll come in a few days. We want to ride the wave. You understand? Good. You should get back now. You have to keep yourself on view as much as possible."

> > < <

When Oirs was gone, Chusker pushed his hood back, pulled out a handkerchief and wiped the sweat from his face.

"Nu, what happened, Chus? The truth this time."

"The truth is, I don't know. Rumor is that there was some connection between Vicanal and that wizard, but you know what that's worth."

"Turet was fussing about it last night, trying to convince himself to call Velams to explain his trafficking with foreign magic. I doubt he will. Velams scares him. In case you're interested, Master Zebiesko kept his sardzin poking about all night and harrying the Diviners, but none of them got so much as a smell, so you're clear on that. We're clear."

"You too, Nenova?"

She shrugged. "I'm with you to the end, Chusker. Have I any choice? Don't answer that, threats would make me itchy and I might do something I'd deeply regret until the Hangman's Noose cut that off." She got to her feet. "Oirs will be steady for a while now. There's no more point to this, is there?"

In the doorway, she turned her head so he could see her delicate profile cut cleanly from the darkness. "Don't forget Laz, my friend, or underestimate him. He's not dangerous yet, but. . . ." She didn't bother finishing, just pulled the door shut and walked away, her steps quick and light.

He sat for several minutes watching the candle stub flicker in the drafts that wandered about the room, then he blew it out and left.

Chapter 16
Spells Wound Up

1. Savvalis

"Oirs? Just because he vanished for an hour or two?" Nestrats Turet scowled. "He was the one yelling loudest for an investigation; more than that, he was attacked yesterday, nearly killed. You should know about that, Velams, seeing what happened to you."

Velams glanced at Master Zebiesko who stood a pace behind the Chair; it was him he'd have to convince. The head sardzin's face was expressionless. The balance hadn't tipped yet. "I don't claim I've got hard proof of his guilt," he said patiently, "only that there's reason to question him. It wasn't once he vanished, it was five times and nothing in his days or nights to explain why." He drew a roll of parchment from his sleeve, tapped it lightly against his thigh. "Nu, I'm sure enough he's in it that I'll chance that I'm wrong." He held up the roll. "This is a sealed and sworn agreement to life-exile if Oirs doesn't confess."

Nestrats Turet leaned forward. "Already drawn up?"

"Tja. All it needs is your seal and signature, High Holy." He drew in a long breath. "I ask two things before I give it over. One: You hold your Hand above Pargats House against the vengeance of Vocats Jelum when I seize Oirs and put him to Question. Two: You provide Fairwitnesses from among your sardzin. If the confession is made and is convincing, you'll have in your hands the true murderers of your brother and you will return this document to me."

Turet rubbed his thumbs along and along the edges of his hands; his eyes flickered uneasily about, avoiding Velams, resting briefly on Master Zebiesko, shifting to the tapestry banners rippling gently on the walls.

The silence stretched out—uneasy, aching minutes clicking inexorably on.

Velams waited, knowing that Turet would be pushed to a decision when he couldn't endure the silence any longer. Yes or no, the chances were even.

Turet closed his hands over the arms of the Chair, turned to Master Zebiesko. "Nu, what do you say?"

"If Oirs confesses, you're covered." Master Zebiesko's voice was husky, insinuating. "If not, Velams is kicked out and still you're covered. You might take some darts from Jelum, but he gets distracted easy; find him a girl and things'll cool down. Up to you, High Holy, but I don't see how you could lose."

Turet chewed on his lip, then he nodded. "Let me read what you've writ, Pargats Velams. If it's what you say, then we're agreed." His hand shook as he reached for the roll.

He pulled it open and read slowly, his lips moving, stopping, moving again as if he tasted as well as viewed the words; he was going to be sure that he knew what he signed. Finally he nodded, reached for the bell.

Master Zebiesko spoke quickly. "High Holy, better not. I'll fetch what you need and witness the sealing; the fewer who know, the safer we'll all be."

"Nu, do it, then."

> > < <

Turet tapped restlessly at the Chair arms. Abruptly he turned to Velams. "It seems a wispy sort of evidence."

"Indirect perhaps, but I find the Diviner's report sufficiently convincing to wager my Place on it."

"Tja. . . ."

> > < <

Master Zebiesko returned with two of his men. "Witnesses," he said to Velams. "Take them with you when you leave."

When the document had the last signature, the last seal affixed, Velams hurried out, the sardzin following silent behind him. Varney and Teiklids should have Oirs by now; the sooner the Question began, the less chance there was for the other plotters to smell a trap.

2. Smithy

Kitya sliced through the rope that tied Navarre's legs to the saddle, called to Desantro to help her. "He's a tough shrik, but I'd rather not bounce him off the tiles."

Together they got him down, then brought Faan to lie beside him.

The horses stood with heads down and ribs showing. Kitya stroked the black's neck. "Poor old boy, you've had a hard week. Now it's stable time and you can rest till you're feeling sleek and sassy." She looked up at the sky. "When we could have used some shade, there's not a cloud." she said, clicking her tongue at the vibrant blue. "Nu nu, my mother said you can always count on the weather to do the wrong thing."

Desantro wrinkled her nose. "Tja," she said curtly. "Let's get to it, eh? I'm hungry enough I'd barbeque the mare here if she hadn't become part of me."

Kitya chuckled. "I know what you mean. Tell you what, you take care of the horses, I'll go light up the bathhouse salamandrit so we can have ourselves a long hot bath with herbs in it and plenty of soap."

"What about them?"

"Nothing's going to bother them for a while anyway; if you feel like worrying, drop a blanket over them. We'll carry them into the kitchen when

I get back." Kitya strode off, scratching at her arm
where a thorn cane had caught her; the petty irritation wouldn't heal until it was washed and
salved. She gave a muffled hoot of laughter. Like
a lot of things, she thought. Like a lot of things.

> > < <

*Faan dreamed she floated in melting yellow-white
light, Navarre dark and secret beside her, a golden
cord joining them heart-to-heart.*
*There was no pain here, no choices that tore at flesh
and soul, only the heat and the light.*

> > < <

Kitya eased Faan's shoulders down, clicked her
tongue because she hadn't noticed Navarre's
braid. She pulled it loose, tossed the frizzed end
onto his chest and froze as she saw a faint trace
on the tiles, the side of a man's boot printed with
a thin, almost invisible film of mud. She sprang
to her feet, the skinning knife whispering out as
she turned, moving in slow arcs as if it too had
eyes. "Someone's been here," she breathed. "Stay
here. Don't let. . . ." She darted from the room.

> > < <

She sauntered back in a short time later, pulling pins from her hair and dropping them in the
pouch at her belt. One of Navarre's black wool
houserobes was folded over her shoulder. "Had a
visitor, but he's gone. He went through Navarre's

bedroom like a band of kappits. Varney, I'd say. Mezh must 've popped him out like it did us but closer and sooner, so he came here to clean up before he rode into Savvalis. Pretty boy wouldn't want his stubble showing." She tossed the robe over a chair, threw after it the long blue dress that had been out of sight under it. "Salamandrit won't have the bathwater hot for a while yet, so we might 's well do some scrubbing on our babes here."

Desantro rose from her squat beside Faan. "What about something to eat?"

"Nu, I'll do those honors, Desa. You're about as good a cook as you are a rider and I won't say more than that."

She set Desantro to pumping water into the stove's reservoir, with instructions to get a fire going as soon as she'd topped it off, then went to see what Varney had left in the pantry.

> > < <

Desantro was bending over her, washing her face, drawing the cloth gently along her arms, putting salve on the cuts . . . it hurt a little . . . it was a good pain . . . it meant care and tenderness.

She began to worry dimly about the odd state she was in where she saw everything with wonderful clarity, lines sharp as knife edges, the colors bright, every stain, every dent, as vivid as if it were printed directly on her eyes—yet it was also far, oh so far away from her, as if she lay in one world and looked into another. Looked through glass. She felt the soft-

*rough brush of the wet soapy cloth, Desantro's strong
nervous fingers, and yet. . . .*

> > < <

"Why bother with sandals? He's not going anywhere."

It was hot in the kitchen from the fire, the water that was nearly boiling, the soup pot slowly
cooling, only a scraping left in it. Desantro wiped
the sweat from her face, grimaced at the muddy
film on her hand.

Kitya glanced up, then went back to what she
was doing. "My mother says do something, do it
right or it'll bounce back at you when it hurts
most."

"Your mother ever sleep?"

Kitya grinned up at her. "Nu, I lived with her
five full hands of years and she was a determined
woman."

"Evidently."

Kitya pulled the strap through the last buckle
and got to her feet. "Lovely pair of corpses, nu?"

The dark blue dress was too long for Faan, falling over her toes in graceful folds, the velvet
changing color with the shifts of light. It was tight
over her shoulders and rather loose about the
bosom, but the texture of the cloth brought out
the fineness of her golden skin and set blue lights
in her black, black hair. Desantro had laid the
girl's hands, one atop the other, on her dia-
phragm; they were long, slim, and lovely despite
the battering they'd endured.

Navarre was shaved; his hair was combed into a halo of light brown curls about his pleasantly ugly face, his braid brought forward to lie on his chest, the curving end like a quotation mark at his waist.

Desantro frowned down at thm, shuddered. "Don't say that, Kat. Round here, words have a way of coming true whether you mean them or not."

"A little salt will cancel that." Kitya stepped across Navarre's legs to the chopping table; she took the canister of salt that was sitting there, turned with it in her hand, a wide grin on her face—a grin that changed to shock as the door crashed open and Sabusé stood there, glaring at her from eyes like dark glass.

Kitya wrenched the lid off the canister and flung the salt at him, scattering some of it across Navarre and Faan, then she leapt at him, knife in her hand, screaming, "I killed you, oochiero, stay dead. . . ."

The Revenant recoiled, the salt eating at its flesh, then it roared and raised an arm, black light whirling in its open palm.

> > < <

Agony . . . burning . . . fear . . . hate. . . .
POWER!
The glass that sealed Faan from the world shattered and she gasped as she felt/saw Navarre come awake at the same moment, surge up, grab Kitya's ankle, and send her sprawling.

Faan rolled onto her knees, got tangled in the dress as she tried to stand and at the same time keep an eye on the Thing in the doorway.

Navarre rose calmly, then stood brushing salt grains from his face. "Wrong place, Tiyulwabarr." With a gesture and a WORD that filled the kitchen with an enormous SOUND the mind couldn't hold, the Magus killed the black fire and drove the Power back. Heat swirled round him. He ignored it, caught his breath, said "You've done your worst and lost. Now get out of here."

"Neka, I will not."

As Magus and Power began their battle, a battle of will against will, of barrier pressing against barrier, Faan grabbed at the dress, jerked up the heavy blue velvet and got her feet clear. She stood beside Navarre, delicate tongues of blue fire flickering along her arms, her body aching with remembered pain, her mind a stone rejecting the hybrid THING that was trying to inflict more. Smaller fires danced across her face and dress, burning away the flecks of salt. She looked around. Ailiki was nowhere about. *I've lost her,* she wailed silently.

The Revenant sensed her anguish and struck at her.

She screamed. Blue fire roared from her, went whirling about the room, driving at the Power, repulsed by it, returning to the attack....

> > < <

Mouth set in a grim line, Desantro crawled away from the fight as fast as she could without drawing attention to herself. Her memories of that murderous Goddance of their last days in Bairroa Pili chilled her to the bone despite the torrid temperature of the room. When Faan was like that, people got killed.

She knelt beside Kitya, clamped her hand on Kitya's mouth when the younger woman's eyes snapped open and she started to say something. "Quiet," she whispered, "and keep your head down. This is going to get nasty." She took her hand away.

Kitya sat up; the skinning knife she clutched in her right hand made this more difficult, but she wouldn't put it down or slide it back in its sheath. Her long black hair hanging loose, shining with blue lights from Faan's fire, she caught hold of Desantro's shoulder and squatted beside her, balanced on her toes, ready to attack if the THING tried to come at her again.

> > < <

"Give me the woman." Sabusé's voice howled through the roar of the whirling fire, with echoing overtones from the Power within.

"No." Navarre felt Faan's hand close on his arm, then gasped as her fire poured into him—corrosive, caustic, raw power that pushed him to the edge of his control. His flesh turning translucent, his body a lamp that glowed darkly, he lifted his hands, gave one last warning. "The Wrystrike will take us all if you force this."

"Give me the woman. She is mine. She killed my vassal and violated my space."

"So be it." Navarre SHOUTED words that blew like icerain about the swelling Power, weaving a net of cold and time about the animated body, freezing it while Navarre pried at the force within. . . .

But only for a moment.

The Power needed the body to exist in Valdamaz despite the DENIAL of Meggzatevoc. Maintaining Its roots within Sabusé, It extended Itself to its full dimensions, bursting the walls of the house, scattering the fires, consuming the WORD-sleet, enveloping Navarre and the others, drawing the air from them, smothering them. . . .

Navarre shaped Faan's fire and seared a hole through the intangible; he couldn't reach the body, not yet, but he could discommode the Power and stop the smother. . . .

The Power screamed, a soundless drill that burst stones, turned them to dust drifting on the wind. . . .

Navarre muted the noise, began reweaving his time net, waiting for the Wrystrike, riding the wave of its rising heat. . . .

> > < <

Faan was rage and denial, was everything Valdamaz had shaped her to be, was cold and hot at once, was Weapon. She struck and the Power screamed. . . .

> > < <

NOOOOOO ... THIS IS NOT THE
WAY.....
GO O O O GATHER....
The immense voice boomed
through them, shaking them
like terriers shake rats....
PERRAN-A-PERRAN, GOD OF
GODS
SPOKE
and
ACTED

The Power-in-Sabusé, Navarre, Faan, Kitya, Desantro—
all of them were caught in whirling wheeling
forces ... vortex ... the soundless
voice of Perran a Perran
roaring
commands
that
Navarre and Faan
ignored ... Tungjii's laughter ...
smell of hisser wine ... intoxicating,
strengthening ... Faan's fire eddying about
Navarre
... her wild furious outcry echoing in his ears....
Immense immaterial hands reached, shoved....

The vortex swept across the land, through the
city and plunged....

3. Question

"Chusker, it was Chusker, he did everything...." Oirs screamed and writhed in the restraints that locked his wrists and ankles to the table as the spidznal cut another fine line across his chest, then began to paint it with tincture of natri, an irritant without equal.

Velams stood at his shoulder waiting until the spidznal had completed an inch of the cut, then held up his hand. The apprentice slapped a wooden plug into Oirs' mouth, held his head still. "Nu, Chusker was the lead. Who else was in it? And don't waste time screaming, little Oirs. I might just get bored and go away. The spidznal enjoys his work, too bad to deprive him of that pleasure." He nodded at the apprentice who pulled the plug out.

Behind him, Varney watched, grim-faced and golden, his beauty restored by sleep and pampering. In the shadows beside him were two others, watching, listening, the sardzin Fairwitnesses.

Panting, blinking, and squinting against the sweat streaming into his eyes, Oirs opened his mouth to speak. Nothing came out but a blat like a sick calf. His mouth worked, his eyes darted from side to side, then he gabbled, "Nenova, Lazdey, that's all, that's all, it was Chusker's idea, he did it, I didn't do anything...." He broke off, whimpering.

"Tell me about it," Velams murmured, "tell me about it step by step. Who were you aiming for the Seat? You?"

"Neka neka, Begarz was the one, my following wasn't big enough, besides, that was why Lazdey was in it, he could't be a Candidate with the smudge on his line, but he thought he could run Begarz ... and ... and Nenova, she was Kreisits married to Kreisits and she had Begarz panting after her, his tongue hanging out, his second wife died in childbirth, she was going to wed him once he was Seated, even if she was his close cousin. And Chusker explained it wasn't safe for one of us to go for it, not this time anyway, as long as we kept back, no one would suspect us...." He laughed, laughter turning to hysteria.

The spidznal lifted the brush where Oirs could see it; his laughter broke off instantly and he was whimpering again.

"Who did the killing?"

"I don't know, I really don't, Chusker maybe ... he's always been strange since he ran away when he was twelve ... he doesn't talk about that...." Oirs' voice was starting to trail off in the relaxation that comes after intense strain, his eyelids slid down until he pushed them up again, frightened that he wasn't satisfying his tormenters, that if he didn't keep talking the pain would start again. "He never told us how he had them killed, he said it wasn't safe, not safe for him, he meant, we all knew that...."

"Describe your first meeting."

"We wore masks and long robes, black felt, gloves ... we didn't know who the others were, only Chusker knew. Nobody said anything at first, except for him. None of us wanted to say anything that could be used against. . . ."

4. The Final Moves

A roaring noise like a great wind swallowed his
words . . . the walls seemed to explode outward . . . forms hurtled at them . . . swung
away . . . came round again . . . blurred . . .
blue fire wheeled about them . . . forces
whirled about the chamber, currents of
RAGE HATE ANGUISH FEAR thick
as warm honey glided through everyone watching . . . on the table
Oirs was moaning and bab-
bling though noone was
listening not
even the torturer
. . . the roaring got louder and
louder, rose in tone until it was a
piercing
squeal. . . .
then POPPED!

Navarre half-fell against the table, Kitya dropped to a squat, hands over her eyes, Desantro stumbled away from them, bumping into Velams, backing off again. Faan drew the blue fire back into herself. She met Varney's eyes, her nostrils flared, and she turned away.

He shrugged.

Sabusé screamed and flung himself at Navarre, but the Power inhabiting him had been contained and he was thrown back against the wall, then forced down, his forehead pressed to the greasy stinking flags, his hands clasped over the back of his neck. The body went slack. It was submission.

Velams looked from one weary face to another, finishing with Navarre. "What is this?"

Navarre scowled at him. "You know exactly what it is, Lielskadrav." He turned, contemplated the quivering Oirs who lay where he'd been not so long ago. "For that, you were going to let this worm," he nodded at the crouching Sabusé, "take my companion."

Velams didn't flinch from the accusation. "For the good of my House, for the good of my Land, for the good of my brother, tja. A woman and a foreigner, she's nothing balanced against all that."

"She's worth the lot of you." Navarre turned his head, listened to a muted boom that meant nothing to the rest.

It was to the sardzin he looked when he spoke again. "The Caretaker sent you?"

The elder of the two men nodded. "He waits in the Vertejazall."

"That one, he's talked?"

"Named the names."

"Say the names. I have a reason."

"Leduzma Chusker, Kreisits Lazdey, Kreisitssev Kreisits Nenova."

"Nu, let's get it finished." To the spidznal he said, "Throw some water over that and get it on its feet." He prodded the prostrate Sabusé with the toe of his boot. "You, take everyone here to the Vertejazall, then bring those three named to join us. Good for good, I will loose you and give you leave to go."

The body of Sabusé stirred, gave a resonant eerie growl, a sound that grew louder and more powerful, shook the air ... then they were seized and *SHIFTED* to a vaulted room, the banners on the walls fluttering with the wind of their passage.

Navarre spoke to the elder of the sardzin. "Bring the Caretaker."

As the man turned to leave, Nenova appeared, fell to her knees with the force of her landing. She got to her feet, shook out her elaborate tea dress, and smoothed her hair. "What is this?" she demanded. She paled as she saw Oirs cowering naked and battered beside the spidznal, but made no other concession to the fear that had to be churning in her.

When the Caretaker came rushing in, followed by the sardzin witness and half a dozen others from his guard, she swung round, her head up, a challenge in her pale blue eyes. "What is this, O Holy Turet?"

He stared at her, his mouth dropping open, a greenish tinge to his skin. He looked away from her without speaking, marched to the tribunal's High Seat and settled himself. "Where are the others?"

Navarre smiled. "Coming."

Lazdey was next. He looked swiftly around, saw Oirs, drew his sword. Varney leapt at him; a hammer blow to the neck, a twist of an arm, and he had the man down and disarmed.

Chusker appeared, flung down on the flags before the High Seat, the Power-in-Sabusé standing beside him.

Navarre spoke, a soundless WORD that shook the air.

Sabusé's body crumbled to dust, the Power fled with a high keening of fear and rage.

"Bring them to me," Turet screamed. "Set them on their knees before me."

Nenova moved with dignity to kneel beside Chusker. Oirs went weeping and cringing, hardly able to walk, stinking from his own wastes, his sphincters having opened early in his torment. Lazdey struggled, cursing the sardzin, calling Velams and Varney calumniators who should be on their knees not him. He had to be forced down and even then he didn't stop talking.

"Where's your proof? Word of a worm like that? He hates me because I'm a man and he a sniveling zurk. I demand a trial. I demand a judge without prejudice. I demand. . . ."

"Shut the trumkaz up." Turet's hands clutched the chair arms so hard, his knuckles were white. There were white patches beside his nose, sweat on his forehead as he moved his eyes slowly from face to face. He lingered on Nenova. "Why?"

She smiled. "Because it pleased me," she said. "Because men were dying and I had a hand in it. Because your brother forced me when I was little more than a child, then he arranged my marriage to that pig so he could keep on having me. Because he infected me and I'm dead anyway." She lost her calm with the last words, spat them out.

"You've been with your brother's whore, High Holy, you've lain with your brother's death. How do you like that?"

It was he who looked away.

Lazdey jumped to his feet, backed away from the others and the sardzin. "I don't care what these launsigs say, I wasn't in it, I didn't do anything, it was me saved Begarz's life from them when they hit him. Don't listen to them, they lie. . . ."

Nenova turned to gaze at him, nostrils flaring. "Laz the brave soldier, listen to him whine. Wasn't even tortured like little Oirs there. Tsaaaa. Chusker's the only one with nerve, the only real man among you all."

"Be quiet, you whore!"

She laughed at him, but paled again when a sardzin caught her by the hair and jerked her head back, showing her the blade of his long knife.

"Chusker," Turet said hastily. "You were respected, powerful, your House was in your hands. Why?"

Leduzma Chusker smiled. "Why not?" he said. He bowed, straightened. "I curse you; by curse of my mother and the power that lives within me, I curse you and your kind. My blood is on your heads, my ghost shall haunt you howling through your nights and days, nothing you do will be unknown, nothing you say, nothing you think." He brought his hand up and with the blade concealed in his palm, he slashed his throat, the blood spurting to spread across Turet's feet and legs before he crumpled, his veins almost emptied, still a calm smile on his slackened face.

> > < <

As the blood halitus filled the room, a head pushed up through the largest pool, followed by shoulders, a pudgy body. A plump baby of a man stood on the tiles looking around at them, hair the color of moonlight, eyes the clear green-brown of a mountain tarn, flickering with shadow like the dapple of blowing leaves. Huge eyes. Owl eyes. Meggzatevoc's Speakingform.

It stepped from the blood and stared at Faan.

Faan looked back, her bicolored eyes colder than stones. God or not, she paid the Speakingform no reverence.

It let her challenge fall unanswered and smiled, the archaic smile that curled the lips and left the eyes untouched. "I am the Answer and the End," It said. "I am the god in the last act of the play who brings Order out of Disorder."

It turned a degree further, put out its hand, touched Varney on the brow, leaving him with a round, ridged red mark. "Small things first. Pargats Varney, I claim you. Light man, you will learn weight. Fifteen years service to the Temple and ME. You can shorten the time by growing character, but I doubt you will. No Augstadievon you. You would destroy the Land and I will not have that. Be silent until I give you leave to speak."

Red in the face, sweating with sudden fear, Varney opened his mouth. . . . And closed it again when no sound emerged.

Another shift, owl eyes lighting on Velams.

"You, Pargats Velams, you have allied yourself with an intruding Power. For this Pargats House must forgo having a Candidate in this election. Since the wrong is small, the punishment is limited. Rejoice that I ask no more of you and be very careful to serve ME well."

A third shift and It faced the plotters, living and dead. "I confirm the guilt of these agents of Disorder. Hang them high and throw their bodies to the sea. I will not have them in MY Land." Again that eerie smile. "High and Holy Nestrats Turet. You have not failed to serve ME, but you might have. I will not allow this. A Eunuch you henceforth, your Holiness enforced."

It made one last turn. "You flouted ME, Magus, because you knew you could. I may not touch you or yours, but I can cast you out, which I dooooo . . . all of youuuuu. . . ."

The room dissolved about the Four-who-were-Linked, the Ouuuu of the last word became vortex winds whirling them away. . . .

EPILOGUE

If they flew across land or sea, they did not know
   it, east, west, north or south, they didn't know
    where they were being swept, they could nei-
     ther escape the vortex nor change direction.
      Round and round, endlessly
         wheeling through a roaring chaos,
        Navarre, Faan, Desantro
        and Kitya,
       round and round,
      facing each other
     with their backs
    to the howling
    gyrating
     gray wind. . . .

which set them down on a bleak and barren
shore, icy spray lashing them, sand driven by the
north wind scouring their faces.

They had nothing but the clothes on their
bodies—except for Kitya who had her belt pouch
with its small treasures, her skinning knife, and
the lethal hairpins Navarre had crafted for her.

Curling her arm across her brow to keep her

hair out of her eyes, Faan turned a half circle, inspecting first the ragged chalk cliffs with the straggling patches of wiry grass like fringe along the flat tops, then the seashore and the sea. For an instant she thought someone was watching her, but the feeling blew away before it was more than a shiver in the spine.

Fire burned through her body, heels to head, but she ignored it, using her free hand to haul up the overlong skirt as she kicked at the sand, sending a small crab into a desperate scuttle for shelter. "Gonna gonna kick and scratch," she sang. "An't gonna catch me ee." When she saw the tan grains flashed to glass by the heat in her toes, she changed the words. "Gonna gonna kick and burn. An't gonna catch me ee."

Her voice was lost in the wind, so she let the song die and went back to looking around. Out in the tossed gray water she thought she saw the flukes of a jade green fishtail. She jumped back, caught her foot in the dress and nearly fell. "Potz!" She hauled up the heavy blue velvet, twisted around so she could see down her back, straightened with a little bounce. "Kitya, loan me your knife, huh? I'm going to break my neck if I don't get rid of this extra cloth."

Kitya raised her thin brows, pinched her mouth together. Silently she handed over the knife, then dug in her pouch for a comb and began dressing her long black hair into its travel knot.

Faan wrinkled her nose, popped her lips in a mock kiss at the woman's back. *You put it on me, it wasn't my choice.* She slashed at the skirt of the dress, shortening it to mid-calf so she could walk without tripping.

Ailiki the mahsar appeared on the beach south of them and came picking her way fastidiously along the shore, avoiding the fingers of the advancing tide, the dead fish, and sprawled sea weed. "Aili my Liki," Faan called, sudden happiness bubbling up through her as she saw the one creature who'd been with her all her life, the one who'd never gone away for more than a little while. "My wandering sister, welcome back."

Ailiki sat up, waved her pawhands, then returned to her leisurely stroll.

Holding her hair again, kicking the ragged circle of blue velvet away from her, Faan ran along the sand to meet the mahsar.

DAW

JO CLAYTON

DAW

Mercedes Lackey

These are the novels of Valdemar and of the kingdoms which surround it, tales of the Heralds—men and women gifted with extraordinary mental powers and paired with wondrous Companions—horselike beings whose aid they draw upon to face the many perils and possibilities of magic

THE LAST HERALD-MAGE

☐ **MAGIC'S PAWN: Book 1**	UE2352—$4.99
☐ **MAGIC'S PROMISE: Book 2**	UE2401—$4.99
☐ **MAGIC'S PRICE: Book 3**	UE2426—$4.99

VOWS AND HONOR

| ☐ **THE OATHBOUND: Book 1** | UE2285—$4.99 |
| ☐ **OATHBREAKERS: Book 2** | UE2319—$4.99 |

KEROWYN'S TALE

| ☐ **BY THE SWORD** | UE2463—$5.99 |

THE HERALDS OF VALDEMAR

☐ **ARROWS OF THE QUEEN: Book 1**	UE2378—$4.99
☐ **ARROW'S FLIGHT: Book 2**	UE2377—$4.99
☐ **ARROW'S FALL: Book 3**	UE2400—$4.99

THE MAGE WINDS

| ☐ **WINDS OF FATE: Book 1 (hardcover)** | UE2489—$18.95 |

Buy them at your local bookstore or use this convenient coupon for ordering.

PENGUIN USA   P.O. Box 999, Bergenfield, New Jersey 07621

Please send me the DAW BOOKS I have checked above, for which I am enclosing
$_____ (please add $2.00 per order to cover postage and handling. Send check
or money order (no cash or C.O.D.'s) or charge by Mastercard or Visa (with a
$15.00 minimum.) Prices and numbers are subject to change without notice.

Card #_____ Exp. Date _____
Signature_____
Name_____
Address_____
City _____ State _____ Zip _____

For faster service when ordering by credit card call **1-800-253-6476**

Please allow a minimum of 4 to 6 weeks for delivery.